By Max Hardy

Novels

Angels Bleed

Her Moons Denouement

Murder Path

Poetry Collections

Soul Whispers

My Dark Disease

The Alchemy Of Swaying Hips

MURDER PATH

MAX HARDY

Copyright © 2015 Max Hardy

ISBN-13: 978-1517076214

ISBN-10: 1517076218

The moral right of Max Hardy to be identified as the author of this work has been asserted in accordance with the Copyright, Designs and Patents Act, 1988.

All rights reserved. No part of this publication may be reproduced or transmitted in any form or by any means, electronic or mechanical, including photocopying, recording, or any information storage and retrieval system without permission in writing from the author or publisher.

For Hollie,

I hope you enjoy the story,

Cheers,

Max

x

For

James 'Hardy' Brown, my Dad

and

Russell Gee, my best friend,

and the first person to call me 'Max'.

You both left us way too early.

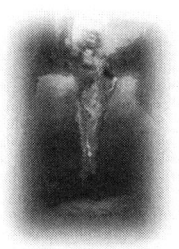

Chapter 1

The hinges of the heavy, solid oak door squealed as it was pushed forcefully open, the grating din reverberating around the white tiled walls and floor of an empty corridor that it opened into. The din was augmented by a piercing scream that quickly rose in intensity above the squealing hinges, amplified tenfold by the acoustics of the corridor. The scream emanated from a naked, blood spattered woman who agitatedly bounced off the door she was pushing open as it hit the wall, and stuttered in a half run, half hop down the pristine white corridor, leaving a trail of bloody footprints in her wake.

Her head was shaking frantically as she screamed, her arms flailing in arcs, her fists clenched white tight and pummelling her own temples over and over again. She was slim, lithe and toned, with a sea of fiery auburn hair billowing behind her as she ran. Blood was smeared over her wide, panicked emerald eyes and agape lips. Blood was spattered across her pert breasts and tight stomach. Blood had been massaged into the tattoo of a snake, from the head of it near her belly button, to the body of it coming out of her vulva. She smacked into another closed oak door at the far end of the corridor and fell to the floor in a quivering heap, pulling her legs tight into her torso foetally. She continued to bang the palms of her shaking, bloody hands off her temples as she stared in terror back down the corridor. The screams abated, to be replaced by a low, guttural inaudible mumbling.

'Was it the susurrations of the lungs?'

Murder Path

The voice, deep and gravelly, yet calm and assured came from the room behind the door she had thrust open. It was followed by the steady measured footfalls of black brogues that carried a man into the corridor. He was over six foot tall with a broad, muscly frame, dressed in a tailored three piece silver Armani suit, sporting a scarlet pencil tie. His hair was totally white and greased back over his head in a quiff, framing a wrinkleless, angular handsome face with piercing green eyes that stared humorously down the corridor towards the woman.

In his right hand was a stainless steel scalpel, a line of blood on its edge that was forming a drop at the tip. He lifted his hand and placed the tip of the scalpel against the tiled wall as he walked, tracing a bloodline as another searing squeal emanated from the contact.

'Or was it the palpitations of the heart?'

The squealing continued as he dragged the scalpel along the wall, as he assuredly walked up to the quivering woman who was still looking frantically down the corridor through him, until he knelt down in front of her and removed the scalpel from the wall, and rested it on her mumbling lips.

'I think it was the eyes.' he started, moving the tip of the scalpel up her cheek, allowing it to break the skin as he raised it to her eyelid, letting it scythe a few lashes before resting the blunt side of the blade on her eyeball. She didn't flinch at the contact, simply continued to quiver and mumble, continued to bang her palms off her temples and continued to stare straight through him to the open door at the far end of the corridor.

'What are the voices telling you Eve? Are they telling you that it is wrong? Are they telling you it is evil? Or are they telling you to succumb to the temptation?'

Her mumbles grew audible at the questions. 'Thou shalt not kill. Thou shalt not kill. Thou shalt not kill.' she repeated over and over again.

Murder Path

He smiled as he heard the words, nodding gently as he removed the scalpel from her eyeball and raised his hands to take hold of hers, stopping them from battering her temples, sliding the scalpel into her left palm deftly as he did. He held her wrists firm and leant in closer, bringing his eyes to within a millimetre of hers.

'That is how you think as a human. Think EVE. You are not human. You are a God. There is no fear, there is no good, there is no evil, there is no 'Thou shalt not'. There is only what you want to do. It was the eyes, wasn't it?' he finished as he stood up, raising Eve to her feet as well.

She obliged and stood without resistance, her eyes refocusing from down the corridor to look into his calm and gentle gaze. She breathed out heavily, the quivering of her lips lessening, the shivering of her naked body abating as a semblance of control overtook her demeanour.

'It was the eyes.' Eve answered in a broken whisper. 'He was just so ecstatic at the prospect of the pain. It freaked me, it just freaked me out.'

'That's alright. It's your first time. It is only natural at this stage that your mind will go back to the morality that has been instilled into it. That's why we practice. That's why we learn in a controlled manner. So you can learn to control. Are you ready to go back in?'

She took a deep breath and looked from his questioning eyes, to his hands gently securing her wrists, to the bloody scalpel clenched firmly in her palm. Her body straightened on the rise of the inhale, the last vestiges of nervousness and panic shed as she stood tall and majestic, with a palpable aura of authority oozing from every pore of her being.

'I am ready.' she answered firmly, rolling her wrists to free them from his grasp. She smiled, seductively slinked past him and headed off down the corridor back towards the open room, her naked hips sashaying with attitude as she walked, her feet still leaving bloody prints.

'Excellent. Now, what have you learned today about the physical anatomy?' the man asked, admiring her lascivious figure as he fell in behind her, dodging her footprints.

'How far you can break it, and still keep someone alive.'

'And how far can you break it?'

'As long as you keep five things intact, everything else can be broken.'

'Well done. And what have you learned about the mental condition?'

Eve laughed as she approached the open oak doorway and then answered. 'I have learned that the human mind can handle any kind of pain you throw at it. I have learned that the more you throw at it, the more it wants. I have learned that I am not quite a God. I am more than a human, but not quite a God.'

'Not quite, but nearly. You now need to choose a trophy, and then you will become a God.' the man answered as he followed her into the room and stood beside her where she had stopped to admire her creation.

The room stank of faeces, urine and the overpowering copper taste of blood that imbued every particle of the cloying air. Once crisp, freshly painted white walls were now spattered with dozens of blood trails which glistened in the shafts of sunlight that flowed through the slightly open blinds in the large window opposite where they stood. In the centre on the room, the solid oak floorboards were covered in a spreading pool of congealing blood.

From the ceiling above the congealing pool of blood hung a meat hook on a thick metal chain. Impaled on the meat hook, through his anus, with the tip of the hook poking out of the end of his penis, hung

Murder Path

the ravages of a man. Steel manacles clasped his feet to the ceiling either side of the meat hook. His whole body was unnaturally contorted and stretched, to a point that his hands where palm down and nailed to the floor. His legs had been broken at the knees, with the skin serrated to allow them to stretch double their natural length. The same had been done to the arms. Loose flaps of skin exposed the glistening sinew and muscle below the surface which had been slashed and elongated. Bits of broken bone poked out at random angles all the way along the butchered limbs. A square of skin from just above the belly button to just below the larynx had been cut away from his chest and lay discarded to one side on the floor. His ribcage was fully exposed and from behind it could be seen the murmuring of his shallow breathing lungs, behind which beat his purple heart. Trails of blood trickled down his upturned face to plop ungraciously onto the floor below his head. He wore an upside down smile, his eyes glazed and dilated, but alive enough to watch Eve as she observed him.

'I want you to pierce my eyes with that scalpel. I want to feel them burn in my skull. I want to squeal as the pain sears through my brain. Then I want you to thrust it into my heart so I can experience the end of life as it ebbs from my broken body.' the upturned man slurred through bloody lips.

'What if it wasn't a scalpel? What if it was something blunt and coarse? What if I gouged them out instead?'

His eyes brightened briefly, a lewd tongue running over his dry lips at the same instant. 'Oh that sounds just divine. What do you have in mind?'

Eve approached his body and stood unashamedly naked directly in front of him, his line of sight straight toward her shaven, pulsing vulva. She tentatively stretched out a hand and ran a finger over the first rib at the top of the left side of his ribcage, behind which his heart beat. She let the finger slide through and touch the beating organ, a shudder visible over her body.

Murder Path

'Is it exciting you? Is it making you wet?' the upturned man slurred.

Eve didn't answer and let her fingers count up the ribs, letting them slide through and touch the warm lungs below. She counted up to seven and her hand stopped moving.

'I will take back what created me, and use it to end you.' she said, letting her fingers inveigle their way around the wet, glistening rib. She yanked, breaking the rib away from its cage. The upturned man howled, his whole body convulsing involuntarily under the rage of the pain, the chains that contained him clanging, before the howl turned to anticipatory groans.

'My eyes, take my eyes!' he moaned, his body still shaking in pain.

Eve crouched down and lowered the broken end of the rib, with its shards and splinters of bone, toward his left eye, letting it rest on the shining iris. The upturned man blinked furiously while at the same time trying to force his face into the rib.

'Tell me about Unas?' she asked, tilting her head as she tickled the rib on his iris.

The man laughed, coughing up blood as he answered. 'He lives in the body of every God and eats their entrails. I will tell you no more. Now do it!' he screamed. 'Rive the eyes from my sockets!' Eve pushed, and he howled again, then she twisted the rib into his eyeball, until the crunch of rib against the bone of the socket filtered into the agony of his cries. She pulled the rib out, the eyeball popping with it, before doing the same with his right eye.

The upturned man was convulsing once more, his whole body tremoring, his lips quivering as he tried to speak through excruciating pain. 'My heart, take my heart and let me bleed into my own oblivion, let me ride into the Isle of Flame on the wave of this ecstasy.' he managed to eke out between screams.

Murder Path

Eve paused momentarily, a look of doubt dancing over her otherwise majestic features.

'Remember Eve, there is no 'Thou shalt not', there is only what you want to do!' the man behind her encouraged firmly, noticing her hesitation.

She nodded imperceptibly and pushed her shoulders back as she stood once more, watching the upturned man writhe and scream in front of her. Eve raised the broken rib and slid it between two ribs in front of his heart and looked down to his deranged, damaged face with its dangling eyeballs dancing on a forehead furrowed in agony. His lips moved silently, the voice gone from his lungs, whispering simply, 'Kill Me'.

Eve thrust the rib into his palpitating heart, a spurt of blood instantly shooting out of it and splashing into her euphoric face. The upturned man screamed once more as with his last few breaths, his heart pulsed and shot more streams of blood over Eve. Until he stopped breathing, his heart stopped beating and his whole body sagged limp in front of her.

The man stepped up behind her quivering body and circled a hand around the front of her face, letting it rest on the fresh blood that spattered it. He gently stroked his fingers over one cheek and let them rest on her lips as she allowed one of them to snake into her mouth, her tongue voraciously sucking at the blood on the tip of it.

'Your first kill Eve. You first step along the murder path. How does it feel?'

'It feels like I am no longer human. It feels like I am invincible. It feels like I am immortal. It feels like how a God must feel. But it's not just the first step along the murder path, is it?'

'No. It's your fist step back into the Fallen Angels. It's your first step back into a world that made you, so I could mould you. It's your first

Murder Path

step on the path to finding out about their plans. It's your first step in discovering more about Unas. It's your first step on the path to finding and killing John Saul, before John Saul finds and kills us.'

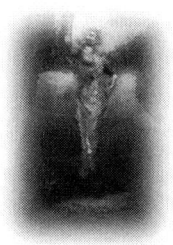

Chapter 2

'John Saul killed my son and Rebecca Angus killed my daughter. Until you tell me that they are in your custody and have been charged with those offences, I will not answer a single one of your questions.'

Pastor Edward Bentley glared defiantly across the dull grey Formica table in the interview room towards Detective Chief Inspector Gaynor Cruickshank's stoic gaze, noting the almost imperceptible flaring of her nostrils as he responded to her twenty sixth question with exactly the same answer. His bandaged hands were resting on top of the table and he was rubbing the palm of one over the back of the other, at the place the bandages were blood red, at the point the nails had been hammered through them a few hours earlier during his public crucifixion.

Cruickshank removed the penultimate photograph from the Manila file in front of her and placed it with the other twenty six already facing toward Pastor Bentley. 'Beryl Rodgers. Went missing in 1995. Her severed, mutilated hand was also found in the underground chamber where you dismembered her alive and ate her while she watched. Your pubic hair and DNA are all over the hand. Exactly the same as the other twenty six hands. Twenty seven women Pastor Bentley. Do you not have one ounce of guilt for the atrocities you enacted upon them? Don't you think it is time to confess your sins, to seek your Father's forgiveness?'

Murder Path

Pastor Bentley smirked, one corner of his mouth twitching slightly as he leaned over the table and placed his bandaged hands palm down over the photographs in front of him. His palms started to circle slowly, moving the photos, ruffling them at the edges. He didn't take his dilated eyes off Cruickshank as he answered her, scrunching the photos as he did. 'I have already told you. Until you tell me John Saul and Rebecca Angus are in your custody and charged with the murder of my children, I will not answer a single question.'

Not breaking his stare, not succumbing to the flagrant defiance Bentley was demonstrating while defiling the photos, she deftly slid her fingers inside the Manila file one last time and held one last image up in front of her. An image of Pastor Bentley next to a man with pure white, slicked back hair. A tall man with a handsome angular face. 'So, if you don't seek your father's absolution, is it this man you are trying to appease?'

Bentley's smirk morphed into a sneer as he clenched his fists, in obvious delirious agony, around the photographs and lifted them to his face, letting a probing tongue lick the images, his twitching nose feigning breathing in their odour.

'He's revelling in this Gaynor, he's getting off on everything you are asking him. Every question, every photograph is allowing him to relive exactly what he did to those women. I'd suggest you stop.' The words resonated inside Cruickshank's skull from the hidden earpiece she was wearing. She attempted to hide the surprise at hearing the voice but her eyes instinctively glanced towards the large mirror on the wall to her left.

Bentley saw her glance and his sneer widened even further. 'I gather I'm not the only one who has to obey the voices in their head? You can tell those voices the same as I have told you continually. You will get nothing from me. Not another word until Saul and Angus are detained.'

Murder Path

A hue of rouge started to rise from the perfectly ironed lace collar of the white blouse that Cruickshank wore under her navy blue twin set, the frustration not making it into her still stoic glare.

'Interview terminated at 8:48 am. Pastor Bentley, I would ask you to seriously consider taking legal representation before our next interview. The physical evidence we have is overwhelming and I am more than confident the Crown Prosecution Service will grant me permission to arrest you, with or without your statement. I will be back.' Cruickshank stated flatly, standing authoritatively, straightening down her impeccably lined skirt as she did. She walked around the table, not looking at Bentley as she approached the door to the interview room, nodding at the PC standing quietly in the corner of the room as she reached for the handle.

'Most of these women served a veritable banquet. Compared to them, your scrawny frame would hardly even serve an amuse-bouche. But then every 'body' has its place on the plate. Even yours DCI Cruickshank. Go and talk to the voices in your head. I will wait patiently for your return.' Bentley slavered, still licking the crumpled photographs in his fists.

Cruickshank paused a moment with her hand on the door, rocking back on her heels, her lips pursing, holding back furious words, before she whipped the door open and strode purposefully out, slamming it behind her.

'Fucking mad bastard.' she mumbled under her breath as she surged down the corridor of interview rooms indignantly, the fury and frustration boiling from her neck into her fiery façade. 'And what the hell does that suave sod think he's doing interrupting my interview!' her mumbling continued as she rounded the end of the corridor and headed animatedly toward the interview control room.

Murder Path

The door opened as she approached, a tall, emaciatingly thin man with a white Afro, wearing a moleskin three piece suite, paisley braces and brown brogues stepping out to greet her.

'Gaynor my darling, how you doing!' Detective Chief Inspector Jeremiah Strange effused, a warm endearing grin spreading to his vibrant eyes as he stretched out his arms offering up an embrace.

Cruickshank's determined, furious stride didn't stop and her arm raised as well, not in a reciprocal manner, but with a damning, pointed forefinger that thrust hard into Strange's oncoming chest.

'What the hell do you think you are playing at Strange? You distracted me and he saw it. He saw weakness. He is going to use that now and it will be even harder to break him down!' Cruickshank admonished, stopping as Strange backed up slightly, but still hammering her forefinger accusingly into his chest after every word.

Strange's expression didn't flinch and still oozed endearment as he raised his arms in surrender, steadying his footing under her onslaught, a disarming chuckle entering his voice as he spoke. 'Whoa there girl. He was getting off on every single photograph you put in front of him. He was reliving the torture he inflicted on them. Did you not see that?'

'Firstly, I'm not your darling. Secondly, I'm definitely not your girl and thirdly, I am well aware that he was getting off on the pictures. He was also becoming emotionally involved. If he's emotional, I will find a crack and I will exploit it. Up to that point he had been an impenetrable wall. Back to bloody square one now. Fourthly, what the hell is your boy up to?'

'Okay, okay, I am sorry. I didn't think it through. Partly I just wanted you to know I had arrived. If I had for one second thought that hearing my voice would distract you as much, I would have kept quiet. I really didn't think I would make such an impression on you. It is your

Murder Path

investigation and I should keep my bulbous meddling beak out of it.' Strange ruefully apologised, his grin subsiding, but still playfully present as he lowered his arms around Cruickshank's prodding finger, gently forcing it off his chest.

Cruickshank's eyes widened and a look of utter incredulity danced around her agape features. 'Jesus Strange, go and check that ego in at the desk will you, it's bloody criminal. I didn't ask you up here to be battered by your obsequious charm. I want to know what the hell John Saul is up to. The one thing our mad Pastor Bentley has bob on, is that John Saul and Rebecca Angus were involved in the death of his children. We have their fingerprints and DNA all over the bodies and the murder weapon.' she finished, pushing his hands away from her still viscous finger.

'No, John can't have been involved in their murder, there must be some kind of mistake. I know he has been under a lot of pressure, but I can't believe that of him.' Strange responded, his countenance changing to concerned as he took in Cruickshank's confrontational candour.

'You better follow me then and have your beliefs changed. It's been a week of that up here in Edinburgh. The Fallen Angels are making everyone question their beliefs. You can start by looking at this picture.' Cruickshank chastised, thrusting the picture of Pastor Bentley and the white haired man into Strange's still outstretched hands before she turned on her heels and strode off down the corridor at a pace.

'We found that photograph in Saul's hotel room, along with a full evidence wall of very damning information, and one or two crucial pieces of evidence.'

'Who is that with Bentley?' Strange asked, falling in behind Cruikshank's military march towards the Incident room.

Murder Path

'That we don't know. What we do know is that he knew all four of the serial killers that the Fallen Angels exposed this week. We found photographs of him at the residence of the Fallen Angels who committed suicide. It's more than probable Saul's hotel room was also the abode of Madame Evangeline, or Jessica Seymour or Eve or Annie Tait, whatever name she wanted to be known as, the Angel who committed suicide last night.'

'More than probable?'

'We found her DNA on Saul's bed. Along with her sexual fluids, mixed with Saul's semen. How's your belief standing up? This is really going to test it. There was another person's sexual fluids and DNA intermingled with them. Those of Rebecca Angus. Seems your boy had both of them on the go, at the same time. Does that sound like him?' Cruickshank added with a hint of rancour, waving officers in the corridor to one side as she continued her unwavering march.

'No, it doesn't. There must be something more to this than John just being involved with these two women?'

'Oh, there is. You haven't heard the half of it yet. That's why I asked you up here. Did you know for example, that Saul has a white mobile phone: which I gather was evidence from the Featherstone Hall case, where his wife died?' the last few words were filled with scathing venom.

Cruickshank thrust the door to the Incident room open and strode into the empty room, heading straight for the evidence wall that had been taken from Saul's hotel. There was a table in front of the wall, on which were a number of items, one being a white mobile phone.

Strange followed with a perplexed furrow on his forehead, taking in the photographs, notes, post-its and other paraphernalia in front of him. 'That should be locked up back at Northumbria headquarters. Along with quite a few images on that wall.'

Murder Path

'I thought as much. Then there is this.' Cruickshank proclaimed, holding out a computer hard disk drive.

Strange looked at it, then back up to Cruickshank, his gaze nonplussed.

'Judging by your expression, I gather you have never seen this disk drive in relation to the Featherstone Hall case?'

'No. What is on there, exactly?'

'Exactly twelve hours seventeen minutes and three seconds footage of Rebecca Angus being interviewed by Dr Ben Hanlon. Recordings taken over the course of one day, which according to my search of the case notes from Featherstone Hall, were never mentioned. How are you rationalising that, Strange. How is your belief marrying these facts with your view of John Saul? Because from where I am standing right now, with all of this evidence in front of me, there are at least twenty different charges I could throw at him, the daddy of them all being the murders of Desiderata and Fenny Bentley and possibly his own wife and son.'

Strange shook his head slowly, his eyes wide in disbelief, his scrawny shoulders sagging under the weight of Cruickshank's accusations, under the weight of evidence in front of him. He scanned the wall, attention caught by the word 'Doppelganger' under a blurry photograph of a man in a limousine who looked like Saul, and another photograph of Saul with Jessica Seymour. He bent over the table to take a closer look at the post-it next to the two photographs.

'I have a twin, with three exclamation marks after it.' Strange read out loud, the tone reflective.

Hurried footfalls pre-empted the arrival of DI Barry Trentor through the door into the Incident room. They didn't interrupt Strange's ruminations, but Cruickshank snapped the second she heard them, before the Detective was fully in the room. 'We are busy Trentor,

Murder Path

whatever it is, come back later!' she ordered, throwing a scowling glare in his direction.

Trentor stopped on the threshold of the room, teetering in the thermals of Cruickshank's terse tongue. Bravely, he spoke, the words coming out nervously. 'I am really sorry Ma'am, but you need to know this. We may have another murderer.'

'Stop dallying in the doorway and get over here and brief me then. Have the Fallen Angels been in touch again?'

Trentor hastily shuffled into the room and joined Cruikshank. Strange turned from the evidence wall as he arrived and flashed a welcoming smile toward the Detective, reaching out a hand and introducing himself. 'DCI Jeremiah Strange. Pleased to meet you DI Trentor. Call me Jerry. What is your first name?'

'Jesus Strange. The man has just told us about a possible murderer, can we do without the bloody pleasantries.'

Strange didn't flinch and shook Trentor's hand, his expression still waiting for an answer to his question.

'Barry Sir. Sorry Ma'am. No it's not the Angels.' Trentor started, taking a little confidence in the warm handshake and the clandestine wink that Strange flashed him. 'We have started to get the DNA results through from the people we arrested after the raid on 'Sodom and Gomorrah' the other night. One set matches the DNA found on the decapitated head of a seventeen year old school girl, Abbigail Gare, who was killed last year.'

'I remember the case well, we only found her head. If I recall correctly, the DNA was from semen that was found in her eyeball of all places. Out with it, who is the suspected murderer?'

'That's right Ma'am. I worked that case. We had no other evidence and the DNA we found wasn't a match to anyone, up until now. This is

Murder Path

going to get very messy, very quickly Ma'am. The DNA was from the Member of Parliament for Leith, Connor McFetrich. It looks very probable our local politician is a murderer.'

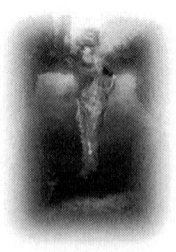

Chapter 3

The first thing that twitches is his little finger and for the briefest of moments my heart stops, like every other time. For that fraction of a second there is a universe of hope waiting on baited breath, wishing that the tiny twitch was a natural movement, praying that Jacob is at last controlling his limbs. Senses become heightened. Eyes pick up every nuance of the twitch, looking for an unnatural susurration of the muscles in the finger. Ears attune to his breathing, listening for the shallowness that forewarns a fit. Nose sniffs out the odour of burning chocolate that exhales on his last full breath and is so strong you can taste it. Hand reaches out to touch his wrist and see if the pulse is steady, or dropping. All in that split second. Every sinew of my being straining that split second to turn into a full second, then two, then three and for the little finger to twitch naturally.

Hope is a fragile thing, even in a universe of it. This time, like every other time, his breathing falls, exhaling the burning chocolate smell which oozes its agony into my soul, which deepens my darkness, which stretches the emptiness of forever, which means Jacob is starting to fit.

Unlike every other time, Rebecca is sitting opposite me on the bed, reaching out and feeling the pulse on Jacob's other wrist. Her emerald eyes are bloodshot from the agony of all the tears she has shed in the past few hours, yet the irises are alive and scanning his twitching little finger as well. She looks up to his wide open eyes and scans them intently.

Murder Path

'Does it hurt Jacob?' Rebecca asks. I look to his open green eyes as well, watching for the only natural movement his body can complete: dilating a pupil.

It dilates once.

Once means 'Yes'.

My stomach suddenly cramps a screaming hollow, the already emotional maelstrom flying around my mind from the previous night's revelations being absolutely trumped by the instant knowledge that our son is about to go through sheer agony. The hell I suddenly feel is also painted across Rebecca's face as she looks across at me imploringly.

'There's nothing we can do Rebecca, we just have to let him see it through.' I answer, feeling totally inadequate and superfluous.

'There is always something, even if that something is just comfort. You may not have known it before John, but you know it now. It hurts him when he fits.' Rebecca answers with a steely determination entering her previously broken voice. 'We are here for you Jacob. Snuggle Ian Bear in and try and make your mind relax. Once upon a time, there was an old toymaker called Gepetto...'

His hands are shaking now, hard enough for the buzzer and alarm on his Pinocchio motion sensor watch to go off. I press the button on the side and switch them off. His arms start to twitch frantically and the length of his body starts to jerk sporadically. Ian Bear drops out of the crook of his chin were Rebecca has seated him and she picks the small stuffed toy up and holds it back there, her other hand stroking his quivering arm as she softly recites his favourite story, looking lovingly into his frightened eyes.

It is hard to believe that just a moment ago Rebecca was lying on the bed a broken woman, lost in the contemplation of what happened last night, or possibly trying to forget it. It's hard to tell which, as she

Murder Path

hadn't said a single word since we arrived back at the apartment after the revelations in the underground cave. After she had stabbed Dessie Bentley. After Fenny Bentley had killed himself. After Eve had exposed Pastor Bentley as a murderer. After Eve told us that Jacob was also Rebecca's son. After Eve killed herself as well. I guess I had been the same, trying to rationalise everything, just lying on the bed opposite her, our son in between.

Our son.

I can see now why Adam, or Dr Ben Hanlon or my bloody doppelganger wanted Rebecca to look after Jacob now. Not just because she is his mother, but because of how she is with children. She is just so focused, nothing else exists for her at this moment. Jacob has her complete attention, he is her universe, and keeping him calm as his chest starts to furiously shake is all that is on her mind while she softly continues telling him the story of the little puppet who turns into a real boy.

While what's on my mind is how the hell can she possibly be Jacob's mother? What is on my mind is: why are Rebecca, Jacob and I so important to the Fallen Angels. What is on my mind is: why Eve felt the need to kill herself. What is on my mind is: who is the man in all the pictures of the killers the Fallen Angels exposed, and why are they trying to expose him as well. What is on my mind is: if we are Gods to these Fallen Angels, what are their plans for us and what the hell is their end game. I still feel like we are pawns being played in some fucked up game of life that is totally out of our control.

Jacob's body is fully tense with all of his extremities extended as the apex of the fit overwhelms him, his whole body shaking furiously, his head thrown from side to side and spittle splashing from his quivering lips. I hold his arm tightly, my own body anxiously tense, while Rebecca is exactly the opposite. She exudes a serene calmness and her movements are flowing, slow and delicate, even her voice is silky smooth, not an iota of concern, worry or trepidation being displayed.

Murder Path

'...and Pinocchio followed the Ass excitedly down the cobbled street...'

The police will be looking for us. They will have a ton of forensics from the cave. It will all point to our involvement in the deaths of the Bentleys, regardless of the circumstances. I know they will have raided my hotel room. I would. We should give ourselves up. We should. But we can't. We won't find out anything about the Fallen Angels locked up in a cell. I've broken too many laws to be innocent now. The only thing we can do, is find out why the hell they are doing this. That is the only way we will get any closure. That is the only way we will get our lives back. And to get our lives back, we have to take control. We have to find out who Adam and Eve are. A starting point for that is back at the apartment where Adam had his base. There may be something there that will tell us where he is. We also know Eve was born Jessica Seymour and Adam was born Robert Caldwell. The other tiny revelation in the mix of all the revelations yesterday was that the man we thought she was married to was actually her father. We have to explore that. We need to dig into the history of the Seymour family. The rickety rooms in my mind are screaming at me as well. They are screaming Italy. The place where I seemed to spend a large part of my childhood in isolation. The place where I recall Gordon Ennis telling me the sister of Henry Seymour lived. The place where Sarah and I went to have IVF in order to conceive Jacob.

'Rebecca. Where did you and Hannah go to have your eggs implanted when the two of you conceived Michael?'

Rebecca glances at me and throws an admonishing stare from her focused eyes, before returning to look at Jacob, whose body is now calming down, the spasms and shaking reducing as he starts to come out of his fit. I watch as his torso stops bucking and his head stops shaking, gently lolling to the right, in Rebecca's direction, as his extremities calm down as well, his whole body, in an instant, reverting to inert.

Murder Path

'Sleep now little angel' Rebecca sings to him, gently closing his eyes as she brushes a hand tenderly down his face. 'That's the first time he has had a fit in the three weeks I have had him. Are they always that violent?'

'Three weeks! That's impossible. He tends to fit at least once a day. Yes, they are always that violent, but I never knew they hurt him.' I answer, absolutely gobsmacked that he hasn't been fitting.

'Perhaps it's to do with him being able to communicate now. Perhaps he has control of more than just his irises. But that is definitely the first time. Now that you know it hurts him, you have to start thinking about how you interact when they happen. I could see you withdraw. I saw you try to distract your mind and think about anything else but Jacob. You can't do that. You have to think of him. You have to comfort him. You have to console him. And if you find that hard, then that's just fucking tough. If we have a son...'

'If?' I interject.

'Yes, if. Just because Eve has told us that he is ours, doesn't mean it is true. We both know her and Adam have been playing us. This could just be another test, another temptation. Don't get me wrong. I think he is our son. I think that is why Dr Hanlon brought me back from the brink of insanity. I think that is why he wanted me to look after Jacob. But let's not presume, let's find out for sure. You have a son, and we might have a son, and you need to realise now that he feels, just like you or I. He hurts, just like you or I. And if he hurts anything like you or I are at the moment, then we need to comfort his beautiful little being all the more. How do we do a DNA test?'

Rebecca is sitting on her knees opposite me, her clothes all covered in blood, sweat and tears from last night's atrocities. Her face is ragged with rivulets of grief smearing her makeup, revealing the scars of self-harm she inflicted when she was incarcerated. Her eyes though, while bloodshot and puffy, are alive with a vibrant fire as she stares at me

Murder Path

with an intensity that seems to be able to read my very soul. She knew I was trying to distract myself. She knows how hard I find it. She is right. I have to learn to comfort Jacob.

'I think at the moment that is going to be difficult. The second we try and approach any lab to do a test, the police will be on to us. Did you go to Italy to conceive Michael?'

'Italy?' Rebecca ruminates, and then jumps off the bed and trots towards a holdall sitting on top of a chest of drawers underneath a window looking out over Edinburgh. She rummages around inside of the holdall for a second and, grabbing something from within, quickly steps back onto the bed into exactly the same position. She hands me two flight tickets.

'Milan, Italy?'

'Yes. That's where Ben, sorry, Adam wanted us to go. And yes, Hannah and I went to Italy to conceive Michael. It was hard to find anywhere in the UK that would do what we wanted and a friend at hospital told me about a clinic in Brescia. It was called 'La Clinica Dell'Immacolata Concezione'. Why?'

Sometimes, the smallest thing will trigger an avalanche. The echo of a scream as it reverberates around a mountain. My screams are echoing and the snow is cascading, knocking down the rickety rooms in my mind.

'When I was a child, locked up, it was Italian Nuns that looked after me. Dr Ennis told me that Henry Seymour had a sister who lived in Italy. Adam gave you tickets to take you and Jacob to Italy. I don't think we need to have a DNA test Rebecca. We both went to the same clinic in Italy to conceive our children. I think we can safely say that's where we unwittingly conceived Jacob.'

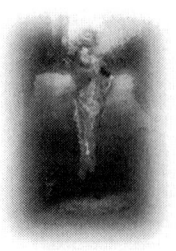

Chapter 4

An eerie stillness enveloped the large baroque styled detached house sitting gaudily in the middle of a well maintained garden, the only sound that of leaves on the many varied bushes and shrubs gently rustling: a rustling not caused by any wind. Armed Response Officers dressed in black from head to toe and sporting bullet proof vests levelled assault rifles with laser sights through the bushes toward the house.

DCI Cruickshank paced just outside the open gates to the property, which stood on its own surrounded by open fields as far as the eye could see. A bronze plaque stood head height to Cruickshank on the pillar of the gate, proclaiming the property as 'Sokar'. DCI Strange stood just behind her, peering over the wall enclosing the garden, scanning the bushes and the twenty ARO's hiding behind them.

'Any sign of life from the house? Sound off one through twenty.' Cruickshank whispered into the walkie-talkie she held firmly in her hand. Crackled responses rained back in, all prefixed with their call sign, all negative to any sightings. 'Okay. One through six approach the front door with the battering ram. Seven through thirteen, secure the perimeter. Fourteen through twenty, circle around the back and cover side and rear entrances. On my mark. Move!'

Her patent leather brogues stomped their way down the gravel driveway towards the house as she fastidiously watched six ARO's detach themselves from the nearest foliage and head for the front

Murder Path

door. Strange followed deftly in her wake, having to trot to keep up with her rapid march.

'How was your time in the Army, did you make many friends?' Strange puffed after her mischievously as they approached the ARO's who were now lined up at the front door.

'You don't go into the Army to make friends Strange. You go to kill the enemy. And I thought you were a focused professional.' Cruickshank grumbled scathingly as she came to a stop just to the side of the ARO's. 'Right, one and two, ram the front door. Three and four, full sweep of the ground. Five and six the upper floor. One and two then up to the third floor. On my mark. Move!'

With a loud thud, the solid steel battering ram knocked into the heavy oak front door, wood splintering around three deadlocks that held it shut, thrusting it forcibly inwards until it bounced off a door stop on the floor and slowly started to close again.

'Move, move, move.' screamed all six in unison, Three and Four rushing in past One and Two through the door, guns raised and targeted, before it had a chance to fully return. Five and Six tried to follow, but butted straight into the back of Four who had stopped dead just through the doorway screaming 'Stop, Stop, Stop!'

In front of him, Three had doubled over involuntarily as his stomach wrenched and he vomited over the parquet flooring of the wide open lobby. The cause of the vomiting was hanging suspended from chains which were screwed into the vaulted atrium two storeys above the foot of the double curved stairway heading to the upper floors.

Manacles at the end of the chains were clamped around the broken wrists of hands which hung limply in the bindings. Elongated arms, unnaturally long, stretched out from the manacles. The bones were broken and poking through the ripped skin. Along the length of the arms, stapled to the skin were rows upon rows of feathers, increasing

Murder Path

in depth towards to torso, shaping the span of the arms into wings. Mutilated, empty eye sockets lifelessly glared out toward the door from a head lolling onto a butchered chest. A square of skin was missing from the chest, exposing sunken, inert lungs and an exploded heart.

Cruickshank's small frame hopped up and down behind the ARO's, trying to see over the tall men who were concertinaed in front of her. She could just make out the head and outstretched arms of the body. 'Come on gents. It's a dead body. It doesn't mean the house is secure. In fact, it may mean exactly the opposite, so man up Three and everyone else, spread out now!' she bawled, forcibly pushing the officer in front.

'Go easy Gaynor, that's a horrifically mutilated body in there. I'm not surprised the poor man has been sick, it's abominable.' Strange countered, his taller frame able to see over the top of the ARO's: able to see the full extent of the atrocities enacted upon the body.

The five other ARO's fully entered the house and set off as ordered, as a man, avoiding eye contact with the body and focusing on their mission.

Cruickshank stepped in after, able to see the whole extent of the horror. 'Ah, I see now. Still, you need a tougher constitution than that Three if you are ever going to make it on my team.' she said, sidestepping the still crouching officer as she walked inquisitively towards the hanging cadaver.

Strange shook his head disconsolately after her receding back and bent down beside the officer, wrapping a comforting arm around his still shaking shoulder, his body still retching. 'Ignore her son, what's your name. That's certainly not something you see every day. Just the stench of it is making my stomach churn, never mind the rest.'

Murder Path

'Sorry Sir, its Blackwell Sir, and it is totally unprofessional. It just took me by surprise. Who would do such a thing? What kind of monster would do that to a person?' Blackwell's voice trembled as he wiped the vestiges of vomit from his lips.

'The kind that wants to make a statement son.' Strange answered, patting the officer on the back as he stood and approached Cruickshank, taking in the whole gruesome scene in front of them.

Down from the exposed ribcage of the chest, the intestines had been lifted out of the stomach cavity and were now trailing over the stomach and down between battered and broken legs with bits of serrated bone poking through the ravaged skin. In between the glistening tubes were glimpses of gnarled genitals. The intestinal tubes reached the floor, where they then wound into words, in a circle around the body.

'They say the small intestine is about ten times longer than the human body. It needs to be to spell out that phrase. If you look closely, you can also see its been chewed. There's teeth marks and bites taken out of it.' Cruickshank ruminated as she slowly circled the dangling man, whispering every letter as she read it.

Strange followed her, his eyes quickly scanning the whole phrase. 'Even Fallen Angels Have Wings.' he recited. 'This is nothing like the Modus Operandi of the four previous revelations by the Fallen Angels. They have never murdered anyone. Quite the opposite. They have been at pains to keep them alive so their abhorrent crimes could be exposed.'

'As far as we know they have never murdered anyone. Our politician friend here is certainly dead, and certainly mutilated. Definitely tortured and definitely telling us something. The large intestine is only about five foot long, and his is pointing towards that door in the corner. One through Six, apart from soft lad Three, sound off now!'

Murder Path

Cruikshank ordered as she looked the aberrant carcass up and down, then headed off in the direction of the pointing intestine.

All clears crackled out of the walkie-talkie as she crossed the room, the black clad ARO's stomping back from the corners of the building and convening at the front door.

'Four, get Three out of here. One, go and find Trentor and get him to call for SOCO and the Duty Medical Examiner. This is a crime scene now. Two, get the rest of the guys to secure and tape the perimeter. Five and Six, my hunch is this door is to the cellar, go check it. On my mark. Move!' she bawled, allowing Five and Six to hurry past her.

'Go easy on Blackwell, Gaynor. He'll feel bad enough as it is, barfing in front of his mates, without you sledging him as well.' Strange whispered over to Cruikshank as he came alongside her at the entrance of the door, which contained a stairway leading downwards.

Cruikshank's small frame suddenly broadened and lengthened, her chest puffing out and her back straightening. Even though she was nearly two foot shorter than Strange, her force of character tried to dwarf him. 'Listen,' she scowled through gritted teeth, 'I've already told you to stop interfering with how I run my team and my investigation. If you can't do me that common courtesy, then I demand that you leave the case right now!'

Strange looked down at her vitriolic visage and with a great effort, stopped himself from smirking. 'Gaynor, just as a reminder, you asked me to come and assist.' he replied, his eyes trying to cajole her ire.

She stared furiously at his open, endearing façade for a full ten seconds, a battle of her fury against his facilitation raging. She blinked, her body ever so slightly relaxing. 'I did Jerry, but I need your information and insight, not your impertinence. I'll say it again, please extend *me* the common courtesy of allowing *me* to run *my* team *my* way.'

Murder Path

'Sorry ma braw lassie.' Strange answered, his words humble as he reached out a hand and stroked her forearm.

Cruikshank's face flushed red in obvious embarrassment as she flinched back from where his hand touched her. 'Not on duty Jerry. Never on duty. I've told you that before.' she answered, flustered, and headed off down the stairwell in a flurry. 'Five and Six, sound off!'

Her walkie-talkie crackled as she descended. 'Clear Ma'am, but you'll want to see this.'

Strange watched her receding rear with a sanguine stare, belying the sombre mood of the murder scene. 'You are an enigma Gaynor Cruickshank. An enigma I definitely want to crack.' he mused under his breath as he dutifully followed her into the bowels of the house.

They both stepped into blinding brightness. It was a large room around thirty metres square. Every single surface was mirrored, with pin lighting illuminating the scene, the beams reflecting and amplifying the brilliant white light. It made the already large room look enormous. It magnified and amplified the BDSM sexual apparatus dotted around the room. There were leather bondage tables, spanking horses, dungeon crosses, stocks, slave cages and suspension frames in amongst stands full of whips, floggers, paddles towsers and crops. Everything was clean and pristine, every surface spotless.

'I see what you mean Five!' Cruikshank said, mouth agape, taking in the room.

'It's not that you'll want to see Ma'am, it's what's in this room. You wouldn't have known there was a room here Ma'am if the door had been closed, it would have just looked like another mirror in the wall. But it was open.' Five answered from the far end of the dungeon.

Murder Path

Cruikshank and Strange wove their way around the sexual equipment and towards a red glow that pulsed from behind Five. As she approached the threshold, the reflective glare off the mirrored floor tiles gave way to the soft plush luxury of a Fereghan Sarouk Persian rug which adorned the floor of the intimate room beyond. Five backed into the room and allowed Cruickshank to enter, Strange following. The soft red glow slowly danced on the deep red walls of the room, reflections from the tall, thin glass tubes that stood on a long, thin mahogany table running the length of the wall parallel to the door. At the far end of the table, on a stand, stood a closed leather cello case, the word Unas embossed in gold just underneath the handle.

'Jesus Five, I see what you mean.' Cruickshank answered, quickly crossing the short distance to examine the glass tubes.

The tubes were filled with a thick, glutinous liquid with bubbles slowly morphing and moving up and down the length of them. A subtle red light shone from the bottom of each tube, illuminating the bubbles and other contents, and causing the seductive shadows to float over the walls.

There were thirteen tubes in total lined up on the table, each one with a solitary object floating in the viscose liquid, in between the mesmerising bubbles hypnotically moving around them. The solitary object in each tube was a beautifully shaped, curvaceous amputated left leg, serrated across from the groin, where little globules of loose flesh enchantingly meandered with the bubbles.

'It looks like our politician friend upstairs may be involved in more than just the one murder.' Cruickshank stated as she walked along the length of the table, hovering a finger over little silver plaques tacked in front of each tube. 'Names and dates engraved on each of them. Thirteen women over a six year period. The Angels may have just exposed their fifth serial killer, and killed him in doing so.'

Chapter 5

I've never thought I was that good at lying or pretending to be someone other than myself. Even when I was having an affair with Jess and lying to Sarah about where I had been, I was absolutely sure she saw through every single untruth. I guess that I have a knack for it that I didn't realise, because in the past few days I have been someone who is so far removed from me, I don't even recognise him. I'm not talking about how I look, I'm talking about how I have behaved. Is that what Adam and Eve have been trying to do? Trying to mould me into becoming a different person. One who doesn't care about lies, doesn't care about morals and to a degree, doesn't even care about people? I fucked Rebecca up the backside the other night. A person I had only met the day before. A person who could still be a killer: and I fucked her up the behind because I wanted to. I didn't care about anything else, I didn't even really care about what she wanted, or if it was even pleasuring her, when you boil it all back to basics. I just wanted to fuck. What kind of person does that make me? It certainly doesn't make me feel like a god. It makes me feel like shit. Yet here I am again, pretending to be someone I am not.

Dressed up in disguise this time, with a greying wig over my hair, thick horn rimmed glasses covering my eyes, false, very nicotine stained teeth making my lips protrude, and white foundation on my face to make it look older, pallid and slightly ill. I am wearing a tailored Ralph Lauren suit with a long black coat over the top, my black Oxford's shuffling along the pavement as I limp along the road towards

Murder Path

Randolph Crescent. In one hand is a copy of today's Times and in the other a solid gold White Spot Dunhill cigarette holder sporting a Sobraine Black Russian cigarette.

There are Police Officers outside the flat that Eve used when she was pretending to be Annie Tait. We expected that. But we need to get into the building next door, where Adam had his rig of TV screens monitoring everything Rebecca, myself and the Fallen Angels were doing. We have to find him again and that is the best starting point. To say I am nervous would be understating the obvious. The Officers up ahead will be briefed and will be looking out for Rebecca and me, or for any suspicious characters around the area. They are going to stop and question me as soon as I approach the flat.

So how do you counter that, how do you control the situation? In this case it's easy. You start and lead the conversation.

There are a few cars driving through the nearby road and a couple of people walking down the tree lined pavement opposite, but otherwise, the streets are fairly quiet as I limp up towards the two Officers chatting.

'Afternoon gentlemen, it's a lovely day isn't it. There's nothing wrong with Detective Constable Tait is there? She is such a helpful young lady. Always on hand to assist me picking up the milk in the morning. Her boyfriend can be a bit of a boor mind you.' I start, in my most clipped and refined accent, deepening the tone, adding a gravelly rasp to the timbre, trying with every sinew to keep the nervousness bubbling in the pit of my stomach out of my voice and away from my open, inquisitive features.

'And who are you Sir?' Officer Number 967 asks bluntly, his face going straight into featureless, his tone the same.

'Sorry Officer, how impolite of me. Justin Hanratty, from Hanratty, Deleval and Penshore. We have an office in the building next door.

Murder Path

The second I say the words, the other Officer turns his back on the conversation and speaks into his radio. He will be calling back to HQ to get a check on the name and the building occupants.

'Are you at your offices every day Mr Hanratty?' PC 967 asks, stepping in front of his colleague to block out any sound from the conversation he is having.

'Not every day, no. Perhaps two or three times a week. The office is where we store a lot of old case files. We use it mainly for research, study and case preparation. I do hope DC Tait is alright?' I prompt again, immediately letting a pained expression enter my face as I allow my body to sag and reach out for the stone wall of the small front garden for support.

'Are you okay Sir?' PC 967 asks, with a hint of concern entering his voice as he steps down ready to support my arm.

'No need to worry Officer. It just my riddled old bones failing me.' I flash the cigarette in front of him before taking another long draw of the toxic nicotine stick. 'Fifty years of devouring these devils is finally coming home to roost.' Deliberately, I lean against the wall, forcing him to come out of the garden and stand in front of me on the pavement, allowing me to hear the conversation of the second officer as I talk to PC 967.

'We are just trying to ascertain DC Tait's whereabouts Sir. Can you recall the last time you saw her?' There is a slight look of concern at the edge of PC 967's features now, along with a modicum of trepidation. He is unsettled, not quite sure how to address a frail old man who has just suggested he is dying. Just what I wanted.

'Oh, must have been about two days ago, in the morning. I think she would have been leaving for work as I was arriving at the office. We talked for a few moments about the happenings in town with the Fallen Angels. Strange business. I haven't seen her since, nor her

Murder Path

boyfriend come to think of it. Sorry Officer, do you mind if I head up to my office. My morning constitution calls, I can't be late with my cocktail of contraband unfortunately, it's the only thing that keeps my riddled bones at a manageable level of pain. I will be there all day if you have any other questions and please, let me know if you find her. She is such a lovely lady.' From behind me, I hear the radio conversation stop, knowing that the officer has confirmed my identity and that of the firm of solicitors I purport to work for. I see PC 967 make eye contact with his colleague and nod imperceptibly.

'Thank you for your time Sir, and my apologies for delaying you. I will definitely let you know if we hear anything. Would you like some assistance up to your office?'

'Thank you, that is a very kind offer, but no thank you. I am a stubborn old goat, and this thing won't get the better of me.' Using the tumultuous adrenaline coursing through my veins, I groan and force myself up from the wall, letting the nervous energy out as sighs and moans. I take limping, laboured steps away from PC 967, waving my paper behind as I approach the entrance to *my* block of flats, and pop a key into the lock, opening the front door. I shuffle in, then gently close the door behind me, leaning my back against it as I let out an elongated sigh, letting the tension dissipate from my limbs.

'We are in.' I state into the air, and into my earpiece.

'You do doddery old fart to perfection.' Rebecca's voice echoes around inside my head from the earpiece.

'I've had a lot of practice at doddery lately. How are you getting on researching the Seymour's?' I enquire, letting the adrenaline abate.

'There's not a lot to go on, but I'm starting to get a few leads.' she answers distractedly.

Murder Path

'Okay. I'm off into the flat now. Keep listening and I'll shout if I need you.'

Right, I might not have long, it's hard to tell if the show I put on was good enough. So, let's see what's on the TV's at the moment. I sprint up the stairs, taking them two at a time, my injuries from two weeks ago and the ones from last night smarting, letting the doddering old fart know they were still able to inflict pain. I reach the landing which Adam's flat is on and unlock its door and enter, quickly closing it behind me. I head straight for the bedroom, knowing that there are a bank of monitors hidden behind a false wall in the room. I pass the empty drawing room where less than twenty four hours ago Rebecca and I had questioned Fenny Bentley about the disappearance of all of the women his father and daughter had murdered and ate. It still saddens me to think that he felt the need to kill himself: he knew nothing about those murders.

I quickly enter the bedroom and stride straight for the wall, pushing my hand against a spot on the duck egg blue tongue and groove panelling that looks just like any other spot. A low murmur of a motor kicks in and the wall slowly starts to open to the left, exposing….

Exposing what should be eighty monitors, eight rows by ten columns. The first three columns are empty, the monitors aren't there.

'Fuck' I say out loud.

'Problems?' Rebecca asks with concern.

'It looks like the monitors have gone!' A sense of panic overwhelms me as I grab the end of the panelling that is moving and try and force it open faster. It doesn't move any quicker, no matter how hard I push. I poke my head behind the panel, between the empty shelves, looking into the darkness to see if I can see any sign of the screens, head bobbing in and out of each row. Nothing. Not one.

Murder Path

'Hold on, there's something.' What's that, on the bottom shelf, right at the end, as the panel completely opens. One monitor. One solitary monitor left. I crouch down on the floor taking in the image on the screen. It's a room I recognise.

'There's only one monitor left. It's showing the Incident room at Edinburgh police HQ.' I relay. Why is there only one monitor left showing that? Where are all the others? Wait, what's that on the Evidence wall? That's the evidence from my hotel room. I thought they would have it by now. And there are pictures of Rebecca and myself on there as well. Well I guess that makes it official: we are definitely suspects and definitely on the run. That doesn't help us at all though. We needed the other monitors. We needed some clue as to Adam's whereabouts. It's going to make it harder to find him now.

'That's a problem. Has he removed everything else?' Rebecca enquires.

I quickly scan the bedroom, looking for anything that may have been left. It is totally empty, I doubt if it will even have a single fingerprint. I leave the bedroom and set about searching the other rooms. The bathroom, the drawing room, the study, all devoid of everything, even a speck of dust. All of his makeup and prosthetics gone as well.

'The place has been totally emptied Becca.' Totally disheartened, I enter the last room, the kitchen, and see pristine, clean high gloss white units glaring innocently at me. Not a single thing on any of the worktops. I know the cupboards will be just the same, but my instinct won't let me leave without checking them. I pull a drawer open expecting a resounding thrum of nothing.

There's a leaflet, one of those tourist types, advertising a country house. I pick it up and read the cover. 'Chillingham Hall, in the heart of Northumberland. Visit this splendid country estate, home to one of the rarest breeds of animals in the country: The Chillingham Cattle.' This wasn't left by accident.

Murder Path

'Was that a Tourist Information broadcast?' Rebecca enquires.

'Sorry, I found a leaflet in a drawer. It's all that's left in the apartment.'

My ears prick up. I can hear the feint sound of voices coming from the corridor. I tense instinctively, listening intently to the sounds, breaking up the different voices. I make out three talking loudest and a general hubbub of conversations sitting in the background. They aren't coming from the corridor, or from outside. They are coming from the bedroom. From the solitary monitor. It sounds very much like the start of a briefing.

I slip the leaflet into my inside jacket pocket as I walk speedily out of the kitchen and back into the bedroom, my mind already assimilating the information that is being relayed in the conversations I am hearing.

'Are you alright John, is there someone there? I can hear muffled voices?'

'I'm fine, it's the morning briefing starting at HQ. Can you hear it?'

'Not clearly, no.'

I recognise DCI Cruikshank's voice, and DI Trentor's and...Jerry. They have called in Jeremiah Strange. Well, it was only a matter of time. Another mass murderer? I thought Bentley was the last of the Angels killer reveals. A politician called Connor McFetrich. Cruickshank is pinning a picture up on the board, to the right of the other four serial killers exposed by the Fallen Angels and above the photographs of Rebecca and me. What's the significance in that? I recognise him, I have seen him recently, now where was that?

'At 11:33 am this morning we raided Mr McFetrich's house in Longformacus on suspicion of him being involved in the disappearance of Abbigail Gare. We found Mr McFetrich murdered and mutilated, hanging from chains. Around his body, using his own intestines were spelt the words 'Even Fallen Angels Have Wings'. Mr McFetrich was into BDSM and in an annex off his cellar we discovered the amputated legs of a further thirteen women. There were names and dates – we presume murder dates- next to each leg. There was also an instrument case in the room with the moniker Unas on it. We can presume they are the trophies of his victims but will have that confirmed shortly when the DNA results are back in. We are treating this as another 'Fallen Angels' reveal, even though the circumstances are different.'

He was into BDSM? That's where I remember him from. He was in the club the night it was raided. He was in a booth with a short, stout man and a tall, extremely lithe young brunette woman. This doesn't feel like the 'Angels'. That's not what Eve and Adam are about. They wanted to expose killers, yes, but not kill them. Could this be something to do with the other man? What did Eve call him? The man who makes murderers?

'While we are treating this as a 'Fallen Angels' reveal, we want to keep this one quiet for now. Not only because we need to get more facts on the table, but also due to the high profile nature of the victim/potential murderer. So no leaks at all people.'

That's Laurent striding up to the front of the room. He's looking agitatedly excited. Interesting. Has he got the DNA results in? If this was the Angels, there won't be any DNA traces left, it's not their style. If it's the other man? Perhaps? What about the victims? He's showing Cruikshank a sheet of paper, Jerry is leaning over it as well, they both look shocked. Why? What could be more shocking than what they are currently talking through?

'Listen up people. We have the DNA results back from the victims and also from a sample of blood and a hair that were found at the murder scene. We can confirm that all thirteen limbs were indeed from the missing women, so can categorically conclude that we are dealing with another mass murderer.'

She is pausing and looking at Jerry. Jerry is shaking his head in disbelief. Why?

'The DNA from the blood sample found at the crime scene has been matched to that of Rebecca Angus, the escaped mental patient.'

What! No, that's wrong. Rebecca has been with me all the time. That can't be true.

'The second DNA sample, from the hair we found, matches that of Detective Inspector John Saul.'

I stare at the screen in utter astonishment, trying to absorb the words Cruickshank has just said. My DNA. My DNA at the murder scene. Someone is setting us up. Is this another fucking test? Is this the Angels playing us again, seeing how we will react? Or is this something different?

'From this point forward, Angus and Saul are our prime suspects in this investigation. GCHQ have also just provided Laurent with some interesting information. They have seen chatter and searches on the internet to do with 'Fallen Angels', 'John Saul', 'Rebecca Angus', 'Jessica Seymour', 'The Seymour Family', along with a dozen other things related to the recent crimes we and DCI Strange have been investigating, all from the same IP address. All from the same location. All in the last hour. That location is right here in the middle of Edinburgh, in St Giles apartments, off the Royal Mile. We will be mobilising an Armed Response Team immediately.'

Shit. That's sooner than I thought.

'Rebecca, they are onto us. You need to start prepping for evacuation right now.'

Chapter 6

The sun slinks, midway through its afternoon descent, a vibrant suffusion of yellow mellowing in the pale blue, cloudless sky, setting life to the sandstone of the old buildings in the Royal Mile. Shadows are starting to form on the right of the street, a little respite from the heat for the revellers and passers-by enjoying the many sideshows and entertainers of the Edinburgh Fringe Festival. The area outside St Giles Cathedral is cordoned off and a few Catholics are stood at the tape, placards hoisted high, still proclaiming the innocence of Archbishop Liam O'Driscoll.

From Bank Street, the road just up from St Giles, intersecting the Royal Mile, the sound of screeching tyres bursts through the hubbub of the Fringe crowd, heads turning from the entertainment to see three police vans pull up outside a restaurant called 'Angels With Bagpipes'. Three doors slid open in unison on the sides of the vans and in convoy a stream of Armed Response Officers alight them, heading off down St Giles Street.

DCI Cruickshank jumped out of the front of the lead van as DCI Strange did likewise from the one behind. Cruickshank strode toward him, walkie-talkie in hand, already sounding off orders to the gaggle of ARO's.

'Every exit covered, every street corner around the building manned. An officer on the doors to each of the floors and two on the lifts. I want four on the roof with eyes on everyone going in and out of the building. One through six, you are frontline, up to floor five and wait for my command. Everyone, on my mark, positions. Go!'

*

An unnatural calmness pervaded the apartment as Rebecca quietly, yet stealthily moved around the living room, depositing various toys and pieces of equipment belonging to Jacob into a large plastic tub she held in her hands. With ruthless efficiency, she had all of the loose accoutrements securely stowed in a few minutes and placed a lid on the tub, dropping it next to a large holdall bag by the front door: just as it opened and Saul walked in, his features agitated.

'They are in the street already. Have you got everything packed?' Saul asked, quickly bending over to peck Jacob, who was sitting in his pushchair just inside the door, on the forehead.

'All done. You just need to double check all the rooms and then do a door clear. Then a bleach spray of everything. Sorry John, I didn't realise that they would be keeping an eye on what I would be searching for on the internet.' Rebecca answered, not breaking stride or even looking at Saul as she rescanned the living room, eyes darting into every corner, making sure she had everything.

'You don't need to apologise. There was always that chance. But we've just got to follow the plan now. It's going to be tight though.' Saul answered as he trotted over to the bedroom and started to check it. He knelt down and checked under the bed, then inside the cupboards and drawers. Satisfied, he pulled the door closed, shouting 'Clear' then moved into the bathroom and repeated the same searches, the same door close and the same 'Clear', before turning back to the centre of the living room and scanning his circumference, Rebecca, in tandem, doing the same.

'All looks clear Rebecca. You get yourself and Jacob out while I do a final bleach spray. I'll meet you at Dynamic Earth in ten minutes. Just

Murder Path

remember, they aren't expecting an old woman with a young child in a pushchair. Use that if they see you, play it up.' Saul instructed, turning and looking at Rebecca for the first time since he entered the apartment: looking at her blue rinse wig, her gaunt and lined features and at the classic Chanel two piece suit, Jaques Vert white blouse and the black LK Bennett sling back shoes she wore. 'You look good rocking an old woman.' he finished, smiling nervously as he leant over and kissed her forehead gently.

'Not half as good as you rocking the old fart get up.' Rebecca answered, her tone just as worried. 'Hurry up and watch your back.' she finished, heading towards the door, turning Jacob's pushchair as she did, putting her left hand on the door handle and slowly turning it.

*

Six sets of black hobnail boots hammered in unison off the oak stairs, their deafening footfalls augmented and amplified in the confined stairwell as they ascended to the fifth floor. Cruikshank's patent leather brogues were drowned out in comparison, but her footfalls marched in time. Strange struggled to keep up.

'You might want to think about the noise a little.' he wheezed after them. 'You could wake a bloody corpse. I thought this was a stealth mission. It's about as stealthy as a hippo in a mud bath.'

Cruickshank, not breaking stride, looked back and glared at him with venom before arriving at the landing to the fifth floor, following her ARO's into the carpeted corridor. Strange was a few seconds behind and entered the corridor just as the first two ARO's were getting a battering ram into position, the four other officers with their guns trained on the solid oak door.

Murder Path

'Remember, we are dealing with potential murderers here. Who knows how they will react to being confronted. You have my authority to shoot to kill if you feel there is a threat to one of your colleagues.' Cruikshank whispered with force, backing up against the wall a few feet down from the door.

Strange joined her, shaking his head disapprovingly as he listened to her last comment. 'Do you not think 'shoot to wound' would be a better policy in the circumstances? We need them alive. We need to find out what the hell is going on.'

Cruickshank turned towards him, her eyes fuming and her features furious. 'My case Strange: I do it my way. On my mark men, burst the door down.' she added, not taking her challenging gaze off Strange.

'NOW.'

*

Rebecca opened the solid oak front door and stepped out into the empty corridor, flashing Saul a concerned smile as she backed Jacob's pushchair out, pulling the door closed after her.

Saul grabbed a large canister of bleach from a long aluminium and glass coffee table and started to spray it over every surface, wall, door and piece of furniture in the room. He put a hand over his mouth and nose as a mist of the pungent gaseous liquid floated around the room, shafts of sunlight causing rainbows in the air as they refracted off the bleach. He did the same in the three other rooms before depositing the empty container in the plastic tub by the front door.

He then crossed the room to a full length window that looked out over another block of apartments across a narrow alleyway, a similar window exposing an empty room beyond, meeting his gaze. He reached into his jacket pocket and took out a small, stained soft toy, Jacob's favourite teddy, Ian Bear.

'You could have an important role to play in making sure Jacob is safe little feller, so be brave.' Saul whispered softly as he gently positioned the bear on a small table next to the window, sitting looking out to the opposite apartment.

*

The solid oak door burst open into an empty room, a din of 'Go, Go, Go's!' immediately following the resounding thud of the battering ram and the rip of metal as the locks were smashed from the frame. The ARO's swarmed into the room, guns enacting a stuttering dance as they were pointed into every corner of the empty space.

'Clear!' Three shouted as Four, Five and Six quickly headed off to the side rooms, and with the deftness of ballet dancers, raised their legs in unison, mid stride, and simultaneously kicked the doors in, to another deafening din. Three more 'Clears!' joined the still reverberating echoes of brute force, which slowly dissipated as the three men stepped back into the living room.

Cruickshank entered and looked at the obvious emptiness with features furrowed in frustration mixed with fury. With deliberate steps, she started walking around the perimeter of the room, taking in every nuance, nook and cranny of the walls, floor and ceiling.

'Spotless Strange, absolutely spotless. Can you explain how that could be possible? Could Saul be that calculating as to throw us on a wild goose chase?' Cruikshank questioned with an undercurrent of sarcasm in her tone.

Strange walked through the centre of the room as the four ARO's streamed out into the corridor behind him, heading for the window

Murder Path

which overlooked Waverley Station and Princess Street beyond. 'He is the kind of character that will leave nothing to chance. He likes to be in control. He has an amazing memory, photographic I would say and will use that to work through likely 'what-if' scenarios. What I can't imagine is why he would feel the need to play this scenario: what if the police were monitoring our internet feed and we needed to distract them while we made our getaway.'

Cruickshank entered the first door she came to on her methodical recce of the perimeter, entering and carrying on her analysis around the edge of the empty bedroom. 'For a person who is so in control, who has the foresight to plan something like this, I can't see how he could be a victim, I can't see how he would allow himself to become a victim.' Cruikshank mused loudly, making sure Strange heard her from the bedroom.

Strange sighed heavily, his features disconsolate and disappointed at once, as he looked down to the floor, seeing a Wi-Fi router sitting in the corner of the room, at the apex of the window he was standing at, and the window facing the apartments opposite. 'Just because he likes to be in control and likes to leave nothing to chance, doesn't mean that he has always been able to do that. When you have a child, and they have a serious illness, and you can do nothing about that illness, it changes you. It changed John. He wasn't in control, and as much as he tried to get the best help for Jacob, everything about the illness was down to chance. Sorry, I can't believe that John was involved in starting a chain of events that led to his son and wife's death. As for what happened after that: I think he is trying to gain control. I think he is trying to control chance.'

Cruickshank walked out of the bedroom and glared over to Strange, whose back was to her. 'You are going to need to break those rose tinted spectacles very quickly if you expect to be of any use to me. Facts Strange, work with the facts. Saul has led us to an empty apartment. He has deflected us for god knows what reason. Possibly

Murder Path

so he and his mental sidekick can perpetrate another crime.' she answered, her voice raised and still angry as she walked into the next room.

Strange looked up from the Wi-Fi router and out of the window to the apartments opposite. There was an old, grey haired man in a stylish suit staring at him intently. Strange approached the window and looked back at him, noticing his left arm was stretched out slightly, the index finger of the left hand pointing towards a small table. He also noticed red scabbing on the top of the hand. He immediately looked up to the old man's face and saw that his lips were moving.

'We...do....' Strange murmured, shaking his head slightly. The old man repeated the phrase. 'We didn't do it.' Strange murmured again, his features filling with surprise as he mouthed silently, 'John?' The old man nodded, then emphasised his pointing. Strange followed the arm and finger down to the table, to the small bear that sat staring back at him. 'Ian Bear?' Strange mused quietly, a look of confusion on his features as he looked back up from the bear, to display that confusion to the old man: but the old man was gone.

'Daydreaming out of the window is not going to get us anywhere. Neither is your loyalty to Saul. Start getting with the game plan Strange and acting like a DCI or I might just have to have a word with your Super.' Cruickshank loudly admonished as she slowly strode around the wall and window, her compulsive walk being halted by the presence of Strange in her path.

Strange faced up to her, his demeanour conciliatory, body language open, yet assured as he looked down to Cruikshank's agitated expression.

'Gaynor. You will have to forgive me, I haven't had the time to get fully up to speed with the events of last week, so I am behind the ball on the facts as they pertain to John. What I do know is that all

Murder Path

through the events at Featherstone Hall, all John was interested in, was finding out what was happening and more importantly, why. He knew that there was evidence incriminating him and he brought most of it to my table. From what I have seen so far of the happenings here this week, he has done the same with you. He pointed you in the right direction on the reveals by the Fallen Angels and did warn you about your team. I get that there is a large amount of incriminating evidence more than suggesting John and Rebecca's involvement in this and I am not for one minute suggesting that isn't the case. But I have an open mind, not a locked and prejudiced mind. Knowing John as I do, there is still a very big part of me -a very, very big part of me-, that thinks he is doing exactly the same as us: trying to figure out what the hell is going on. And knowing John as I do, I can tell you right now, he will be doing a damn sight better job of it than we are!'

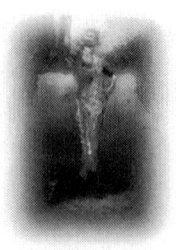

Chapter 7

'The most important thing to remember is, you are a God, but so is he. That is how he thinks, that is how he acts. That is what I taught him. Watch for the signs. Watch for the things I have taught you. How are you feeling?'

Gentle jazz softly oozed from hidden speakers in the opulent, contemporary bar of the 'Jing's Club', an exclusive establishment in the centre of Edinburgh frequented by politicians, wealthy business people, aristocracy and the rich and famous. Hushed conversations were politely taking place at the lines of tables either side of a floor lit walkway leading up to an empty cocktail bar, the clientele enjoying fine dining and expensive wine.

Eve was adorned in a red, figure hugging Bruce Oldfield evening dress, which was split from the hip down one side, her long slender exposed leg drawing admiring glances from the male occupants of the tables as she sashayed down the walkway. Even more ogling stares were directed toward her exposed cleavage from the plunging neckline at the front of the dress, which stopped just above her navel. Her hair was long, blonde and curled, falling seductively over her bare shoulders as she walked. Around the milk white skin of her naked neck she wore a platinum chain with a single large teardrop diamond at the end of it. Matching teardrops hung from her ears. Six inch scarlet Jimmy Choo high heel shoes tapped an indelible beat, announcing her arrival at the cocktail bar, where she shimmied her way onto a stool.

Murder Path

'Feelings are overrated. It's not what I am feeling that is important, it is what I want. What I want comes from instinct. Instinct you have taught me to control. I am wet, I want him inside me and then I want to feast on his pain.' Eve whispered nonchalantly before flashing the barman who approached her an enigmatic smile, which radiated all the way up to her sparking emerald eyes.

'A Godfather please, made with a Dalmore Single Malt, the older the better: even better if you have a Trinitas?' Eve asked, leaning into the bar slightly, allowing her full breasts to heave against the thin silk of her dress.

'An excellent choice madam, containing spirits dating back to 1868. There have only been three bottles of that particular type ever released to market, so it is rare and very expensive.' the barman, an older man with a coiffured moustache, relayed factually, a dubious look flashing over his slightly embarrassed face, whose eyes were constantly looking down at her cleavage.

'I don't want a history lesson on it, I want to drink it. Just like you want to drink in my breasts. The questions is, do you have any?' Eve answered, a tinge of irritation entering her sultry voice.

The barman turned red and flustered, looking anywhere but at her. 'My apologies Madam. That was totally unprofessional of me. Yes, we do have it. Unfortunately, we can only serve it to platinum members of the club.'

'Good god man, I only want a bloody drink. My dinner partner will be arriving soon, a family member of one of the clubs founders. His status is beyond platinum. Do you really want to be the barman that left his dinner date without a drink?' Eve raised her voice in frustration, people on the immediate tables turning to listen in on the conversation.

Murder Path

A man dining alone on a table to her left stood up and approached the bar. He was a short man with a stocky, well-muscled frame and a face battered ugly from too many rowdy rugby scrums. He wore a Harris Tweed suit and brown leather brogues, the suit impeccably cut, the brogues spotless and shining.

'Horncliffe, is there a problem here?' he asked curiously, with a terseness to his tone, noting the barman's embarrassment.

'Nothing I can't deal with Mr Ettrick, sir. I apologise for disrupting your dinner.' Horncliffe fawned obsequiously, immediately turning his attention away from Eve.

Eve stood furiously and angrily kicked her stool back, causing it to topple and screech on the floor. She stamped her right foot, lifting it high into the air to get momentum, before crashing it down onto the floor: before crashing it down onto Ettrick's polished brogue, the six inch stiletto heel ramming straight into the dorsal of his foot, squashing the major tendon.

'First you ogle my breasts, then refuse to serve me a drink: and now you totally blank me just because a man comes to the bar and asks you a question! What fucking century are we living in here? Yes, I am a woman, but I do not expect to be treated like a second class citizen. Get me your Manager, now!' Eve demanded, not even acknowledging that she had stomped Ettrick's foot.

Ettrick didn't flinch, he simply looked down at his shoe, then let his gaze linger over her slender leg, her slim waist, her smooth, animated arms, lingering a lot longer over her arms, before he placed a hand firmly on the bar between Eve and Horncliffe.

'You are definitely a woman, a very beautiful woman and I can assure you that it is not the policy of this club to discriminate against anyone. For me, the more beautiful women we have here, the better. Horncliffe, I think the lady wanted a Godfather, with a Trinitas

Murder Path

Dalmore. Make that two, and put them on my account.' Ettrick ordered, then stooped over and picked Eve's stool up, placing it behind her, admiring her behind as he rose again, proffering her to sit and offering to push the stool in if she accepted.

Eve stood glaring between the barman and Ettrick for a few seconds, fury still evident on the red blotches of her long neck. Eventually she sat, allowing Ettrick to perform his gentlemanly duties.

'Douglas Ettrick.' he introduced. 'I apologise for Horncliffe's behaviour. Believe me, his discrimination isn't sexual, it's purely a class thing with him. If you were a Lady, Dame or Princess, he wouldn't have asked twice. By the way, my toes are fine, in case you were wondering. And you are?' Ettrick asked, his piercing eyes not leaving Eve's face.

'Lady Harriet Farquhar, Princess of Persia.' Eve replied sarcastically. 'Is it a prerequisite of this club to be a stuck up tosser. By the way, I wasn't wondering about your toes, your foot shouldn't have been under my shoe and you certainly look like a man who can take a bit of pain. Don't apologise for that twat's behaviour either. Not serving me might have been down to class. Ogling me was definitely sexual.'

'There might have been a bit of class in there as well. You might look and dress like class, but you talk like a penny a poke prostitute.' Ettrick countered.

In a flash, Eve's hand shot from her side in a wide arc, her torso turning in time with it as she let rip a flat palmed slap right across Ettrick's left cheek, surprising him and making his head jolt under the impact. Murmured conversations rose in intensity, a few people sitting near the back of the club standing to get a better view of proceedings at the bar.

'I talk how I want to talk, I dress how I want to dress, and I take umbrage at what the hell I want: right now, I want to take umbrage with you and your bigoted assumptions. I hope that hurt, but somehow, I don't even think it touched the sides.' Eve retorted, her features still full of fury, her tone apoplectic.

Ettrick raised a hand to his cheek and started to rub the red rash that was starting to appear, shaking his head gently as a wry smirk formed on his lips, his gaze still not leaving Eve's eyes. He took a step back and raised himself onto another bar stool just behind him.

Horncliffe quietly deposited two Godfathers on the bar, directly in the middle of Eve and Ettrick, then quickly turned away, busying himself with anything that meant he didn't have to get involved in their conversation.

Eve turned her body from the bar and faced front on to Ettrick, her long left leg fully exposed and her breasts, heaving under the adrenaline of her fury, full and firm with erect nipples straining against the thin silk material of her dress.

'I apologise.' Ettrick said in a low voice, not an ounce of contriteness in his tone, rather a guttural, earthy rasp, brooding with tension. 'However, I think the power rather excited you. Your pupils are dilated and your cheeks are flushed. Your nipples are aroused and I can see that you have your thighs clasped tightly together: a sure sign that your clitoris is tingling. I didn't say you were a prostitute, only that your blaspheming made you sound like one. I didn't say that I thought it was a bad thing either, in fact, as far as I am concerned, quite the opposite. I was just pointing out why Horncliffe may not be treating you like the lady you deserve to be treated like. If it helps, no, it didn't touch the sides, but it certainly stirred my loins and peaked my interest enough to want to take you back to my room and see if you could touch the sides.' Ettrick finished, his gaze not leaving Eve's eyes once as he reached and picked up one of the Godfathers and held it out in front of him, glass tilted towards her.

Murder Path

'And are you a man that generally gets what he wants?' Eve asked, her own voice now low, lavished in a sultry whisper. She reached over and took the second Godfather in one hand, running the tip of her perfectly manicured forefinger around the rim of the glass.

'Possibly not as often as you get what you want, judging by that dress, those diamonds, the passion in your eyes and the fifteen hundred pound cocktail that you wanted: which is now in your hand.' Ettrick replied, with a teasing lilt entering his still brooding rasp.

'Are you suggesting that I played for this drink?' Eve countered, her finger not breaking its sultry circling, her eyes enlivened with the challenge in Ettrick's words.

'I don't see a date arriving, do you?'

'He's not due for another ten minutes. I like to arrive early and get to know my environment. I like to take control on a date, rather than be controlled.' Eve tantalised.

'I guess I have ten minutes to persuade you to come back to my room then.'

'If it takes you ten minutes Douglas, I won't be coming back to your room. You have one more sentence to persuade me.'

Ettrick's grin widened and he started nodding sagely, not breaking contact with her, totally engrossed in the challenge. 'In that case, I think you should pay for the drinks Lady Harriet Farquhar, Princess of Persia.'

Eve's emerald eyes didn't leave his for one moment as her finger stopped circling around the glass and she lifted her Godfather up to his, clinking the glasses together.

Murder Path

'Let's see how hard I have to slap you then, before I do touch the sides. As lovely a name as Lady Harriet Farquhar, Princess of Persia is, I would prefer you to call me by my real name.'

'That wouldn't be a problem, if you told me what it is?'

'Call me Evangeline.' Eve pronounced, her lips pouting gently towards him as she alluringly rolled the words. 'Call me Madame Evangeline.'

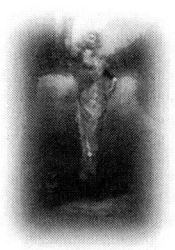

Chapter 8

A setting sun hung low over the ululating verdant folds of the Cheviot Hills, casting concealing shadows which rolled over the contours, enigmatically obscuring the evening splendour of the craggy outcrops. The sky was tinged a washed out pink, which edged the low lying dappled stratocumulus cloud cover caressing the top of the hills. Rolling fields of yellow rape, golden wheat and pasture green stretched out from the peaks in a patchwork of tranquillity. The A697 road wound its way through the fields, mainly bereft of traffic, save for a single silver people carrier leisurely traversing the spectacular scenery.

Saul was driving, occasionally taking in the views in between focusing on the winding road, but primarily deep in conversation with Rebecca who was sitting in the passenger seat. Jacob was strapped into a child seat in the back, fast asleep.

'We know it can't be Eve. I think we can safely say, given she committed suicide on National TV, that she is out of the picture. That leaves Adam, or the 'man who makes murderers' as our prime suspects. Do you remember seeing Connor McFetrich in your time at the clubs? Can you recall him being with anyone regularly?' Saul asked, after relaying the events that took place at Adam's flat to Rebecca.

'Yes, I think I do.' Rebecca mused, deep in thought for a moment. 'You mentioned he was with a short, stout man. I saw them together

Murder Path

a few times at different clubs. He was a businessman: what was he called? Eve did tell me his name. I think he also knew Gordon Ennis. Yes, he did. He was the politician coming off the fields at the foot of King Arthur's seat with Ennis the night Eve and I were there. God, what is his name. Parrick, Patrick….Ettrick: the short man was called Ettrick, Douglas Ettrick.'

'And he knew Ennis as well?' Saul pondered, sitting in silence for a moment. 'That's too much of a coincidence. Is this murderer man the link between them? Did he turn them into killers? Is Douglas Ettrick also a killer? Ennis, Mcfetrich and Ettrick. All into BDSM, two of them killers. I think we need to delve back into that world to investigate further. It's the one place where we might find answers. But I doubt if anyone will be going to clubs in Edinburgh after 'Sodom and Gomorrah' was raided. How would you feel about going back into that world?' Saul asked, looking over to Rebecca with a slightly embarrassed expression on his face.

'John,' Rebecca started, noticing the awkwardness in his features, 'there's no need to feel uncomfortable talking about sex with me. I have no problems going back into that world, in fact, I've got a tingling just thinking about it. You, on the other hand, will need to ditch your prudishness pretty sharpish if you intend to go there. I can help you with that.' she finished, teasing, running a hand along the inside of his thigh, all the way up to his groin.

Saul jumped, causing the car to swerve slightly as Rebecca squeezed his crotch, a flush of red flicking into his cheeks as he steadied it again. 'I think you probably can, and I would welcome the opportunity to research with you. However, not driving down the A697 and definitely not with Jacob in the car. So, deliberately changing the subject entirely, how did your research go?'

Murder Path

'Spoil sport.' Rebecca taunted playfully, before continuing in a more sombre tone. 'Sorry again about digging too deep and getting caught.'

'No need to be sorry. There was always the chance they would be monitoring, that's why I set you up to use the Wi-Fi from the apartment opposite. Hopefully digging that deep has found something useful?' Saul asked, his features suddenly becoming sullen as they approached a side road off to the right.

'I think I may have found a roundabout link between the Seymour family and Fallen Angels. An American puritan minister from the 17th Century called Cotton Mather. Have you heard of him?' Rebecca asked, noting Saul stare out over the fields to the right, distracted from the conversation. 'Are you alright John?' she queried, stroking fingers down his arm with affectionate concern.

Saul quickly looked back at the road ahead, then turned and smiled sadly at Rebecca. 'What's left of Featherstone Hall is just over those fields. The place Sarah died less than three weeks ago. Such a fucking pointless waste of life. I still can't get my head around this Fallen Angels ethos about death. It just being a door to the next life, when you have done everything you want to with this one. I don't think Sarah had done everything she wanted. Nor Michael, come to that. Do you think they truly understand the impact those deaths have had on us? Do you think they even care?'

'I think perhaps that's the point John. If you believe, as they do, that there is a door into another life after this one, then why would you even shed a single tear over someone dying? I think perhaps that is what they are trying to teach us.'

'I get that, I just still don't get why. What is so special about us, that the people we loved were expendable? You don't need to answer that, it's just me being me, and questioning. Sorry, you mentioned a name. Cotton Mather. American puritan minister. Wasn't he involved in the Salem Witch Trials in some way?' Saul asked as they approached Wooler, the sun setting just above the Cheviots.

'Amongst a whole host of other things, yes. He also had an absolute conviction that fossilized leg and teeth bones found in 1705, near New York, were the remains of Nephilim, the offspring of Fallen Angels and humans.' Rebecca answered with a tinge of excitement.

'Okay.' Saul answered, a thoughtful look on his face. 'How does that link to the Seymour family?'

'From the limited amount of public information that is out there about the Seymour family, and believe me, there isn't much, they are descendants of Cotton Mather, coming back to England and settling in Northumberland in the 1870's.'

'Tenuous, but certainly something to explore further.' Saul commented, still ruminating on the information.

'I get that, but at least it is something. The other key thing for me is the religious angle. Cotton Mather was devoutly religious, to the point of fervour, to the point of instigating witch trials for anyone who didn't uphold the puritan belief. But we can only really infer a connection from that.' Rebecca agreed, still buoyed even under Saul's pragmatic appraisal of the research.

'Did you find out anything about Henry Seymour's sister who lived in Italy, or about the clinic we both had fertility treatment at?' Saul queried, scanning the sign posts and side roads off the A697 as they came out of Wooler.

'I couldn't find a public record with any information about a sister. There was nothing at all either on Jessica Seymour being his daughter. The only information I found were newspaper articles about her marriage to Henry and subsequent charity work together. As for the fertility clinic, it is still there and still very popular. I couldn't find anything that directly linked it with the Seymour family, but then you called, and I stopped searching. We should be there soon, shouldn't we?' Rebecca asked, looking at the road signs as well.

'A mile or so on now.' Saul answered, his features still contemplative as he scanned the road. 'The only person that seemed to know more about the Seymour family was Gordon Ennis. He knew about the sister, about the brother and about the family 'curse', caused by inbreeding, so he thought. Henry specifically funded the 'Fielding Institute' to research it. Ennis also said, with Henry's death, the last of the known Seymour bloodline ended. We need to get hold of the information Ennis had on the family.' Saul finished, his attention now fully focused on the straight road ahead: on the solitary figure standing in the middle of the straight road ahead, next to a road sign pointing left, towards Chillingham.

Rebecca noticed Saul's gaze, seeing a glint of anger scream from his eyes and watched as his hands gripped the steering wheel until they were knuckle white. There was a sudden roar and lurch of the people carrier as he dropped two gears and floored the accelerator, the speedometer shooting up to sixty miles an hour. Rebecca stared down the road and saw the man in the road as well: the man who was the doppelganger of Saul.

'John, what are you doing, slow down!' Rebecca demanded with a firm yet concerned tone, her anxious gaze darting between Adam in the road, getting closer, and Saul in the seat, becoming visibly more furious.

'Time to take control Rebecca. If he's not bothered about dying, then let's just kill him. One less person for us to worry about. One less person to play us.' Saul snarled, the speedo now hitting seventy, Adam now only eight hundred metres away, standing resolute, staring at the oncoming vehicle.

Murder Path

'One less person to fucking question, one less person to help us figure out what the hell is going on John. Think! You've got our son in the car. Do you really want to risk his life to avenge Sarah and Michael? Stop being a fucking alpha male and think John, fucking think!' Rebecca screamed, trying to wrestle the wheel now, not budging Saul's fixed, frenetic hands.

The people carrier was four hundred metres away now, and hitting eighty miles an hour. Adam was staring directly at Saul, his body language relaxed.

'I can stop the pain in a second. All the pain you were put through, all the pain I've been put through: stopped in a second! Stopped at its source.' Saul snarled.

'That's just fucking life John, get used to it. It won't bring any of them back. Not Sarah, not Michael, not Jessica. It won't get us any closer to finding out why. And most importantly it won't stop Jacob's pain, every time he has a fit. But Adam managed to stop him having fits and managed to stop the pain.' Rebecca screamed, still scrabbling ineffectually at his arms.

Two hundred metres, ninety miles an hour: Adam still not even blinking as he stared at Saul.

Saul slammed a foot down on the brakes, the wheels locking instantly, a plume of ravaged rubber billowing out into the air behind the car as it swerved from side to side. Saul battled with the wheel, wavering left to right, his whole body pushed back into the driver's seat, rigid. His glare was still filled with fury, his eyes not leaving the unmoving figure of Adam quickly approaching.

Fifty metres away and the car is still doing forty miles an hour.

'He's not moving John. Drive around him!' Rebecca shouted, her own body tense and forced back into the passenger seat.

Murder Path

'I'm stopping, but I'm not swerving. If he doesn't move, then that's his choice. It's down to chance then, just the way he likes it.' Saul simmered as he reached down and forcibly pulled the handbrake on, anticipating the slight skid and steering into it, keeping the vehicle straight, heading directly at Adam.

Twenty metres, twenty miles an hour.

Adam raised his arms from the side of his body and crossed them over his chest calmly, his head tilting slightly as he smiled toward Saul, a sardonic lilt to the curve of the lips.

Saul glared back, his hands held firm on the steering wheel, holding the line straight, feeling the speed ebb from the vehicle, watching the distance between himself and Adam decrease, enraged by the humour in the whites of his eyes.

Zero metres, zero miles an hour.

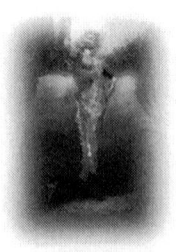

Chapter 9

The flickering strip light of the 'Police' sign hanging above the entrance to the Edinburgh station cast dancing shadows off the officers leaving the building under the rising full moon. Strange looked up to the moon, contemplative, after he bade goodnight to his colleagues, waiting patiently for Cruickshank to finish talking to the Duty Sergeant.

'Anything Bob, anything at all, just call!' Cruickshank shouted, one last order as she too left the building, and joined Strange on the step, following his eyes to the brilliant ball of whiteness hanging low in the evening sky, observing his thoughtful gaze. 'These lingering silences as you stare longingly into the distance are really disconcerting. Is it an investigative technique they teach you down in Northumberland? Saul was the same. If you have something on your mind, just spit it out!'

'It's called reflection Gaynor. Something any half decent detective should always do to ensure they have thought through every possibility and considered every single angle.' Strange answered, smiling ruefully at her.

'Stick to facts, and you invariably get to the same place in my experience.' she countered brusquely. 'Do you need a lift to your hotel?'

Murder Path

'I haven't had a chance to book one yet, I'll just have a reflective stroll into town and grab the first one I come across.' Strange responded, his words deliberately provocative.

'Any half decent detective would have thought of the practicalities and ensured he had a bed for the night before a long shift: unless he was being presumptuous of course.' Cruickshank answered, a teasing tone entering her voice.

'How could any man even begin to be presumptuous with a fierce and forthright lady such as yourself? However, I do have an unopened bottle of Morgan's in my bag. If you could spare a bed for the night, we could discuss the case over a wee dram or two?' Strange countered, playfully.

'Only if you fuck me afterwards.' Cruickshank stated bluntly as she flashed Strange her fierce and forthright glare, tinged with an irreverent sparkle, then headed off towards her car, without waiting for an answer.

Strange stood gobsmacked, looking on after her short, squat frame as it methodically marched to her car. 'Well, you are nothing if not practical and to the point Gaynor Cruickshank, and where sex is concerned, that will always work for me.' Strange whispered to himself. He picked up his bag and followed her to the car, jumping into the front passenger seat.

'But before we go anywhere near that little assignation,' Cruickshank stated firmly, dampening the obvious ardour in Strange's eyes, 'what is the story with you and Saul. Why are you so protective of him?' she questioned, pulling out of the car park and heading left towards the west end of the city.

'Bottom line Gaynor, John has always been more of a friend to me than a colleague. We both started work in the same week, god, more than eight years ago now. He'd just come from uniform, in as a DC. I

Murder Path

had landed in from Jamaica, first black DCI on the Northumbria force. It was challenging, to say the least, I mean, look at me. Thin streak of piss with a silver afro. It was even silver back then. You can imagine the kind of stick I got from the troops, some of it absolutely racist.' Strange started, watching the nightlife of Edinburgh go by out of the windscreen.

'You can imagine the stick a short, uptight, brusque female DCI gets from the troops, some of it absolutely sexist.' Cruickshank countered, turning right into a cul-de-sac.

'Touché. John wasn't like that at all. I think as we were both new, regardless of rank, we struck up a friendship. Not that I needed anyone to watch my back, but John did. He'd pull up publicly anyone who stepped over the mark. Not just those sledging me you understand, but anyone. Don't get me wrong, he enjoyed a laugh, but would always stop it going too far. I liked that about him immediately. It made him a few enemies, but many, many more friends. He has never been anything other than open and honest with me.' Strange added as Cruickshank brought the car to a halt in the drive of a small, nondescript detached house.

Other houses in the cul-de-sac had pleasant front lawns with colourful flowers and plants. The front of this house was concreted, not a single stem of flora in sight. The windows were dark, with plain, drab black blinds rolled half way down, the sills bereft of ornaments.

'Up until now.' Cruickshank answered acerbically, climbing out of the car. She headed for the front door and opening it, reached inside and flicked the hall light on. Strange climbed out of the passenger seat, grabbing his bag from the foot well, and followed Cruickshank into the house, closing the door behind him.

'Take your shoes off at the door, put them on the rack and make yourself comfortable in the living room. I'll go and get two glasses for

Murder Path

that Morgan's.' Cruickshank ordered, pointing to an open door to the right.

Strange took in the spartan décor of the entrance hallway, the only furniture a solitary shoe rack with one full row of neatly lined up flat brogues and one empty row below them. He kicked of his shoes and placed them on the empty row. There were no pictures on the walls, which were painted a bland magnolia, and there was no shade on the stark light bulb. Strange entered the equally minimalist living room. There was a single brown corduroy sofa, a tartan chesterfield chair with a blanket over one arm and a small glass topped coffee table with a battery powered portable radio sitting on top of it. There were no other furnishings. No pictures on the walls. No light shades and no colour apart from cream and magnolia. He sat down on the sofa, reached into his bag and took out the bottle of Morgan's Rum.

'I like the Army chic you've got going on here.' Strange said in a raised voice, tinged with sarcasm. 'Were you in the army?'

'Get real Strange. I am four foot eleven with flat feet and the physique of a fairy. The Army wouldn't even look at me.' Cruickshank answered, entering the living room with two glasses in her hand. She had taken her shoes off and was now in stocking feet and had also removed her jacket and unbuttoned the collar button of her frilled blouse, exposing a sliver of chest flesh. Placing the glasses on the coffee table, she sat down next to Strange on the sofa, curling her legs up under her backside. 'Pour the drinks man, some of us are gasping.' she demanded.

Strange obliged, handing her a half full glass and taking his own, reaching it out to toast hers. 'Cheers.' he started, clinking glass. 'So why the Army austerity?' he finished, throwing his gaze around the simple room.

Murder Path

'Father was in the Army. I spent most of my childhood in one set of perfunctory accommodation after the next. It was practical, it did a job. Just like this place. It's all I need.'

'Didn't your mum want to bring a bit of life to the digs, make them a home?'

'If she'd been around, then perhaps. But she left when I was four. Army life didn't suit her. Father didn't suit her. I didn't suit her. But Army life is all I have ever known. Up until the force. Now they did take a four foot eleven flat footed fairy.' Cruickshank divulged factually, without a hint of emotion.

'Sorry, I didn't mean to pry.' Strange responded, his tone and demeanour awkwardly embarrassed as he took a long swig of rum.

'Don't be. This is me. You get what you see. Don't expect to peel back the layers and find a soft centred feminine side. It doesn't exist. But I appreciate it in others, when it's genuine. That's what I like about you, your feminine side. It infuriates me, but I find your tactile manner and nurturing nature strangely arousing. So why do you think Saul has started lying to you, given you are such good friends.' Cruickshank finished, downing her rum in one go and holding the empty glass out to Strange for a refill.

'It's as I said to you earlier, I think John is trying to figure out what is happening to him. Whoever these Fallen Angels are, I think they have compromised him. I think that happened right the way back at Featherstone Hall and he knew it. That's why he kept the videos and the phone. And just to be clear, even back then I warned him that if I found any evidence of his involvement in that affair, I was going to arrest him. He understood that. At the time, I did warn him that it could be Jessica Seymour who was playing him. I am sure he realised that too. The one thing it is vitally important you understand about John, the thing that makes him such an excellent detective, is that he doesn't forget. He doesn't forget anything.' Strange responded as he

Murder Path

filled both their glasses again, this time to the top, half the bottle gone already.

'That's as maybe. But it doesn't change the facts. It doesn't alter the overwhelming forensic evidence. Even if he is trying to figure out what is happening, he's still doing it on the wrong side of the law and I stand by what I said earlier, buck your ideas up or I will talk to your Super.'

Strange chuckled, swigging back the whole tumbler of rum, watching Cruickshank match him swallow for swallow, before filling them both up again. 'And is stand by what I said earlier, I think you have a locked and prejudiced approach to this. I agree, we need to target John and Rebecca. But we also need to work out if he really does have a double, or that's just a decoy. I'm waiting to hear back from Harry Massah on those photographs, because if the dates on them are correct, there's at least three that were taken when I know John was in the station with me.'

'Okay, just to show you how open minded I can be, would it be worth forensics double checking the DNA from the crime scene today and from the Bentley murders to see if they could be Saul's alleged twin?'

'I'm not sure that you can forensically differentiate the DNA of identical twins.' mused Strange. 'But it's certainly worth exploring. The other thing we need to explore is this 'unknown' man in the four photographs. I get the Angels wanted to expose the atrocities these religious leaders have carried out in the name of their religions, but why highlight this guy? Is he the person that radicalised them? The person that set them down the path to murder? If so, given the totally different Modus Operandi of this current death, could he be involved in it and be trying to frame John?'

'Well, that's where I have to show you how closed minded and prejudiced I can be. There's no fact there Strange, that's just

Murder Path

supposition. Where do you go with that? What possible line of enquiry could you justifiably pursue with that woolly hypothesis?'

'I know, I know, and if this wasn't John, I would be telling my officers the same. I even told him the same thing when he was exploring woolly hypothesis. Okay, back to fact. We know that all four religious leaders were murderers. We know that they all knew this 'unknown man'. We know none of them have so far admitted to that. Who is the most unstable of them?' Strange queried, lolling over slightly as he emptied his tumbler again.

'The first one, Archbishop Liam O'Driscoll. He was fire and brimstone, hell and damnation and foaming at the mouth at one point. Why?' Cruickshank replied, holding out her empty glass with perfect steadiness as Strange filled with the last remnants of the bottle, having to use both hands to steady the pour.

'If he radicalised them, then they will be loyal to him. That's obvious in the fact that they won't give up him name. It pains me to say this, but I was thinking about your approach with Bentley earlier, where you were trying to unhinge him emotionally. Can we play on how he might have radicalised them, how he was instrumental in making them murderers, and they are really just pawns? They might get frustrated by that and break just enough to give something away. Not necessarily his name, but a place, another person, something? What do you think?'

'I think I like it when you say I am right. The facts of the situation are that this man knew them all. What we don't know is the significance of that. A line of questioning trying to probe that significance is, in my opinion, justifiable. I also think the rum is finished and you are slightly inebriated.'

Strange raised and shook the empty bottle. 'They are indeed, cold hard facts. The rum is gone, no woolly hypotheses there, empty as charged. I am also slightly inebriated, whereas you, my bonny wee

Murder Path

lassie, only appear to have the slightest flush in your beautiful cheeks.'

Cruickshank stretched over and placed her empty glass on the coffee table with one hand, using the other to start unfastening the buttons on her blouse, exposing the gentle curve of her small, pert breasts as she then leant in towards Strange, their faces millimetres apart.

'In that case,' she whispered, staring straight into his eyes, planting the softest of kisses onto his willing lips. 'I think it's time to stop talking shop, and time to start fucking.'

Chapter 10

The car jolts to a halt, less than a foot of air between it and Adam. Chance has saved his life, this time.

I thump the seat belt button, loosening the strap, and fling it off my chest. In the same movement I grab the door handle and thrust the door open, twisting my body out of the car and onto the road.

I sprint around to the front of the vehicle, my fist balling and my arm rising as I close in on Adam, the furnace of fury in my furore exacerbated by the sardonic smile on Adam's lips. 'What fucking part of this are you finding funny!' I scream as my fist flies through the air, in a line for Adam's left cheek.

Adam simply sidesteps my oncoming appendage, and watches on in obvious amusement as I fall to the road in an ungainly heap. My exposed palms rake along the uncompromising tarmac, ripping the skin from them and leaving a trail of blood on the road. Adam walks past me, looking down at me humorously and heads towards the entrance to the Chillingham Estate.

'I would get up off the road if I were you and get your car pulled into the side. There's bound to be a car along any minute and I would hate it to go into the back of yours and injure Jacob. Hurry John, we don't have much time.' Adam relays, matter of factly as he heads off down the side road, and walks up to a wooden fence separating the road from the fields, where a few dozen white cattle are grazing.

Murder Path

I scramble to my feet, still looking furiously after Adam, but backtracking to the car at the same time, ready to climb in. I didn't need to. Rebecca has jumped into the driver's seat and is steering the people carrier into the side road and onto a grass verge opposite the fence against which Adam is now leaning. I follow the vehicle in, stomping toward Adam, rubbing my palms, pressing the fingers into the injured flesh, feasting on the pain. Rebecca jumps out of the car and sprints straight in front of me, butting her head into my chest, slightly dislodging her wig, exposing the scars and scabs of harm that she self-inflicted during her incarceration in the 'Fielding Institute'. I stop dead in my tracks.

'Stop being a dick John. Just remember, Adam managed to stop Jacob's fits. We need to find out how.' Rebecca whispers in disappointed frustration, both hands firmly implanted in my chest.

I looked down into her angry, imploring emerald eyes, then to the scars on her head, then down to the stigmata scabs on my hands, and the fresh wounds on my palms, still feeding on the pain as I force my fingers into them. What the fuck am I doing? What is the selfish, self-obsessed bloody mind of mine trying to achieve?

'Like you said, that's just fucking life, I've got to come to terms with the pain. Sorry Rebecca. I conveniently forget this isn't just about me. I conveniently forget about the agonies you have gone through. Sorry for being a dick.' I apologise, raising a hand and straightening her wig as I bend down and kiss her on the forehead.

'You're not just a dick. You are a cunt-twat-dick, and so up your own arse it's untrue. We can talk about that later. Right now, Adam is over there and we can hopefully get some answers. So let's get back to our plan, and let's stop being played. Let's start playing.' Rebecca counters, reaching up and taking one of my hands from the side of her face and deliberately squeezing it overtight, inflicting pain, making me wince as she turns and leads me towards Adam.

Murder Path

Adam has his back to us now and is looking out over the rolling fields, watching the ambling cattle as they nonchalantly munch on the verdant grass and inquisitively stare back at him.

'They are remarkable creatures, Chillingham Cattle.' Adam begins, as we come up to the fence beside him, Rebecca standing between the two of us. 'They have remained genetically isolated on this estate for hundreds of years and have remained a sturdy and hardy breed, without any of the genetic issues you tend to expect from inbreeding. Absolutely remarkable.' he continues, turning sideways from the field to look at us. 'John, I fully understand your anger. I fully understand why you would want to kill me. I can only re-iterate what Eve told you last night. We would gladly give our lives a hundred times for the two of you and Jacob. That is how much you mean to us.'

'It doesn't feel like that Adam. If anything, it feels like we are being used as patsy's, as the scapegoats in whatever twisted game you are playing. Did you know that we are now prime suspects in the deaths of Fenny and Desiderata Bentley? Were you aware that there has been a murder associated with the Fallen Angels and that they found DNA from John and I at the murder scene. We are fugitives Adam, on the run and feeling so fucking alone right now.' Rebecca answers angrily.

Adam straightens up, with a glimmer of surprise in his voice, 'What do you mean, another Fallen Angels death?'

'Just that. A politician called Connor McFetrich. A serial killer, just like the other four the Angels exposed. Only he was killed and the police are pinning that on us.' Rebecca states, still fuming.

'There were no more revelations. This isn't the Angels. This is him.' Adam answers stoically.

'By him I assume you mean the man in the photographs. The man who makes murderers.' I interrupt. 'What is his name?'

Murder Path

'Yes, that's who I mean. The revelations were meant to flush him out, to give the police a starter for ten as to who he was. To give them enough evidence to find him and take him down as well. You were never meant to be involved. Your part was meant to be over.'

'Well, it's far from fucking over, in fact, it feels like it's only just starting, so who the hell is he?' Rebecca interjects, irritation imbuing her already angry tone.

'His real name, not that it will help you in any way, is Gabriel Caldwell. If he has implicated you and the Fallen Angels in McFetrich's death, then he must be on to our plans. He will be trying to flush us out, the same way we are trying to flush him out. We need to find out more about this McFetrich. You need to find out more about this McFetrich.'

'Caldwell?' I respond curtly. 'That's your surname. Is he related to you? Related to us? If we are related, and I can't see how we wouldn't be, given we look exactly the same. Are we related?'

Adam pauses for a moment, taking in my questions. He doesn't answer for a moment, just looks out over the fields, to the white cattle lazily sauntering around. 'It was meant to be over for you. This was meant to be the part where you started finding out about who you are and why you are so important.'

'We know that we both went to the same fertility clinic. We assume, somehow, eggs were switched and hey presto, we are the parents of Jacob. We also think that it is something to do with the Seymour's, and what Henry Seymour was studying with his bloodline at the 'Fielding Institute', trying to stop the 'curse', trying to stop the madness in the family caused by inbreeding. Somewhere down the line, there is a 17th century puritan minister called Cotton Mather involved as well. Are we close?' I ask tersely, my frustration rising again at Adam's matter of fact manner.

Murder Path

'Eve was right, the two of you need very little help from us now. As I said to you weeks ago John, you are a brilliant detective, meticulous in the detail. You have all the evidence and pointers you need not only to discover what your part is in this, but also what Gabriel Caldwell is doing. Rebecca, Eve gave you every single sexual tool you need to survive in the world the two of you need to investigate. There is very little you need from me and very little the Angels can do to help you. However, very little doesn't mean nothing. I have three things to give you. Three things and a warning.' Adam answers, his tone still calm and controlled. He reaches into his jacket pocket and takes out a USB memory stick, handing it to Rebecca.

'What is it?' I query.

'I suppose you could call it an omniscience stick. It has all of the websites you need to view the various cameras the Angels have placed in strategic places pertinent to what we are doing. It also has usernames and passwords and access routes to some of the more secure government and law enforcement agency computer systems. It could be invaluable in keeping you one step ahead of the law and one step ahead of Gabriel: and trust me, you need to worry about him a whole hell of a lot more than the law.' he answers, reaching inside his pocket again, and pulling out a silver tube about six inches long by an inch wide.

'And that?' Rebecca asks.

'I've no doubt you'll be heading to the Fielding Institute to search for the files on the Seymour Family. Ennis will have them hidden. This will help you find them.' he relays, reaching into his pocket once more, retrieving a small phial of clear liquid.

'This is for Jacob. This will help to control his fits. Five millilitres will suppress the fits for up to three weeks.' He passes the phial over to Rebecca, who grabs it off him eagerly.

Murder Path

'And the warning?' I ask, agitation accentuating my tone.

'Gabriel is not just a man who makes murderers. He is a murderer. He has no compassion. He has no remorse. He has no moral boundaries. He thinks that you are part of the Fallen Angels. He knows that you were involved with Bentley's capture. He will be out to kill you. What you have to do is find him and kill him first. As always though, you have a choice. You could just hand yourself in to the police, let justice take its course and hope that they find him before he finds you.' Adam declares.

'Like that's a choice, given all the forensic evidence they have against us. Given that Gabriel has already managed to get our DNA. And that is all the Angels have to offer to support us, a fucking memory stick and a silver tube!' I rumble angrily, the fury starting to rise in my bones once more. Rebecca grabs my rising hand and forces it down on the fence, spreading herself wide, making herself a barrier between the two of us: the two doppelgangers.

'It's more than you have had so far and you haven't done too badly. But there is one other thing. One piece of information which you might find useful.' Adam starts, looking back at the cattle again. 'Chillingham Cattle have been inbreeding for centuries, and have had no mental or physical issues because of it. Henry Seymour wasn't trying to stop the inbreeding in his bloodline: he was trying to accelerate it and to control it. He was trying to selectively breed out the mental and physical problems associated with inbreeding.'

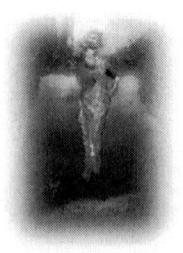

Chapter 11

'Is it touching the sides yet?'

The soles of two red Jimmy Choo stiletto's sat astride his neck, one resting on each bare shoulder blade. Her toes were pushed forward, the heels raised, keeping the tip of the heel from touching the skin. She crouched naked over his torso, her long slender legs bent nearly double, the ankles caressing her curvaceous behind. Her torso was bent forwards, arms stretched out and holding tight onto the wooden bedstead, her full firm breasts dangling seductively between them.

'Barely even tickling them.' Ettrick moaned, his head lost in the pillows of the large bed he was lying on. The lighting in the hotel room was subdued, coming from three lamps, each casting Eve's crouching shaded shadows in a dancing tapestry on the walls and ceiling. The red evening gown was draped wantonly over a nearby chair, not a jot of female underwear anywhere. Ettrick's tweed suit lay strung out on the floor where he had stepped out of it, socks lying last at the foot of the bed.

Eve smiled wickedly and dropped the heels once more, directly into the soft muscle between the shoulder blade and back, forcing the whole weight of her crouched body down on top of them, using the bedstead as leverage, the soles lifting off the blades.

Murder Path

Ettrick writhed and shook as Eve worked the heels right into the cavity, low, muffled grunting emanating from his face cocooned by the pillow, dampening the intensity of the pained moaning.

Eve pivoted back onto her soles, quickly positioning them further down the back, either side of the spine just below the shoulder blades, the heels hovering over the vertebrae.

'Obviously I'm still nowhere near. How about now.' Eve teased, dropping the heels once more, straight into the spine, causing it to visibly twist and grind. Ettrick's shoulders shot up, rocking Eve in the process, but she held tight to the bannister, riding the jolt, keeping the pressure on the heels, drawing blood from the broken skin over the spine. Louder muffled screams seeped from the pillows a second before his torso collapsed back into the bed, relieving the pressure of the heels momentarily.

'That definitely touched the sides.' Ettrick mumbled, 'I'd like to touch your sides now.' he added, lifting his head out of the pillow and raising his body from the bed, onto all fours. Eve stepped off his back and sat on her knees beside his rising body on the bed next to him. As he raised his torso straight, his large, erect penis came into view, the head throbbing a deep purple. Eve reached out a hand and started stroking it slowly as she circled a thumb and forefinger around the girth. He reached down with his hardened hands and stopped the stroking, taking her hand off his penis, lifting her arm up to his eye line. He leant forward and placed a gentle kiss on the tips of her fingers, allowing his tongue to snake out and lick them. He left his tongue out, and moved his head up over her hand, onto her forearm, up to her elbow, all the way up to her shoulder, licking the skin in one continuous movement all the way: his mesmerising eyes not leaving hers.

'On your back now.' Ettrick instructed as his head left her arm and his lips passed her ear, gently nibbling at the lobe as he spoke.

Murder Path

Eve tilted her head into the nibble, her nipples hardening under the sensuous tingle it sent shivering through her body. She shuffled up to the pillow, initially positioning herself on her back, exposing her shaven vulva and the colourful snake tattoo coming out of it, its sibilant tongue nearly licking her belly button, the ink writhing as her stomach muscles moved.

'Would you not prefer to explore this view of heaven first?' Eve teased, her hands coming in from the sides and cupping her breasts, the fingers squeezing and teasing the hard nipples.

'Perhaps later. For now, I want to see how much pain it takes to touch your sides.' he answered, positioning himself between her open legs as he grabbed her hips and quickly flipped her body, her firm, round buttocks staring him in the face. He leant over her, his penis rubbing up the cleavage of her behind, and grabbed a pillow, in one swift movement removing the pillow case from it.

'Hands behind your back.' he demanded, giving her left bum cheek a sharp slap. Eve jolted, a pleasurable whelp escaping her lips as she willingly placed both hands behind her back, crossing them at the base of her spine. Ettrick spun the pillowcase a few times to make a length tight enough to use as a binding, then started to tie it around her wrists.

'Interesting that you should be called Madame Evangeline, when that name has been in the news so much recently. Is that just a coincidence?' Ettrick asked as he yanked the binding tight, Eve's hands jerking under the force.

Eve moaned again, drinking in the pain. 'She was such a powerful woman, don't you think? How she stood up for women, how she showed those men for the sexist, mental madmen they really are. How she became a martyr to misogyny. Every woman should take her name.'

Murder Path

Ettrick slid his hands under her hips and raised her backside into the air, allowing his throbbing member to slide back down her bum cleavage, letting it tickle her arsehole before resting next to her moist, slightly gaping labia lips. He prodded the purple tip of his penis into the willing, wanton warmth of her vagina, then raised both hands quickly into the air, bringing them down hard and fast in a flat slap on both butt cheeks. Eve squirmed and screamed, forcing her hips backwards, straight onto his length, taking every inch of him inside her.

An evil glint entered Ettrick's eyes as his torso towered above her, his pupils becoming dilated and his lips tight, exposing gritted teeth. He dug his fingers hard into the base of Eve's back, still deep inside her, and started scratching up her skin, breaking it and drawing blood. Eve moaned and writhed in blissful agony.

'Not anywhere near the sides yet!' she moaned longingly.

'That doesn't answer my question. Nor the question as to why you were in the club tonight and why you were playing me.' Ettrick responded with a tinge of aggression ringing through the words.

Eve giggled, thrusting her hips backwards, filling herself with all of him, revelling in the feeling. 'For that beast of yours, deep inside me and to see just how much you could touch the sides.'

Ettrick's hands were up by her neck now and he slowly started to circle her beautiful, blonde curly locks through his open fingers, getting every last strand around them, before clenching his fingers tightly into furious, shaking fists.

'Oh, your sides are going to be ripped apart: literally.' Ettrick snarled as a crazed glaze contorted his face and he yanked his hands back with all his might, with every sinew and muscle in his body tensed and focused on not just pulling, but riving her hair.

Murder Path

A look of absolute shock overwhelmed the crazed glaze in his eyes as the wig Eve was wearing came loose quickly. The force of the effort he put into the pull made him topple backwards and at the same time, Eve forced the weight of her whole body through her backside, pushing him over the edge of the bed and onto the floor. She nimbly spun around onto her haunches, her eyes darting to Ettrick's lumbering form trying to turn from where he had landed. Eve leapt into the air, gaining four feet of height, straightening her body, bringing both feet together in one movement. She started to descend, both stiletto's angled for Ettrick's shin, her eyes focused on that spot. Ettrick was still trying to gain purchase on the floor to help him rise, and wasn't looking as the whole force of Eve's body followed her feet straight into his leg, instantly breaking the shin, the broken bone ripping the skin.

Ettrick screamed in agony, his head spinning around to look down at the source of the pain, seeing the jagged white bone poking out of the twisted leg, watching as blood started to pour over the carpet, ogling as Eve slid off the shin, pirouetted on one leg and let the other come flying around to smack straight into his face, knocking him unconscious.

She quickly kicked off the stilettos and rolled backwards on the bed, crunching her legs in tight and pushing the arms bound behind her back over her bottom and her legs, until they were in front of her. Using her mouth, she hurriedly bit loose the knot in the pillowcase, freeing her hands. With surprising strength, she dragged Ettrick's inert, heavy body onto the bed and used the pillowcase to tie both of his hands to the bedstead. She grabbed two more pillows and de-cased them, tying first his good leg to the foot of the bed, then his broken leg. Ettrick started to stir as she moved the broken leg.

Eve stood up and took a deep lingering breath, closing her eyes on the exhale for a few seconds to compose herself, before opening them again and bringing her fist hard down on Ettrick's broken bone.

Murder Path

Ettrick squealed, his eyes shooting open, his body writhing, his mind trying to comprehend the pain and his position, head darting frantically, looking at his bound hands and feet, looking forward to Eve standing naked in front of him at the foot of the bed. Watching Eve, through eyes slowly opening in astonishment allying with the agony, as she reached inside her mouth as removed a few plastic fillers, her cheeks sinking in as she did. Watching her peel small pieces of rubber from her cheekbones and chin. Watching her wipe heavily applied makeup from her eyes and brow. Watching as she pulled a tight hairnet from her head, freeing auburn hair in a short bob. Watching as her facial features transformed physically into Madame Evangeline.

'That's not possible. I saw you kill yourself on TV. It's not possible!' Ettrick repeated, still groggy, shaking his head, opening and closing his eyes to double check if what he was seeing was indeed real.

'And yet here I stand, in all my naked glory, lauding it over you, in all your naked ignominy.' Eve responded, circling around the side of the bed and moving up closer to his head, closer to his hands tied to the bedstead.'

'I don't think you realise who it is you are messing with little girl. I don't think you understand what is going to happen to you when I get out of these ties.' Ettrick rumbled, anger spilling out of the words as his eyes followed hers.

Eve shrugged her shoulders and grabbed the small finger on his left hand and quickly bent it all the way back, breaking it instantly. Ettrick's eyes bulged and he let out a low grunt, stifling the scream he wanted to unleash. 'I know exactly who you are and exactly what you are capable of. You should know that you are going to die tonight. You should know that ultimately, there may only be five of your bodily organs remaining intact before I kill you.' Eve replied calmly, her emerald eyes staring at Ettrick with a piercing certainty.

Murder Path

The heady rouge of pain suddenly drained from Ettrick's features as he heard the words, a look of panic rising from a quivering lip, through flaring nostrils to frightened wide eyes. 'Gabriel sent you!' he stated, his body sagging into the bed.

'Gabriel is not happy. Gabriel wants to know how you possibly thought he wouldn't find out about your little demi-faith, the cult of Unas. He wanted me to remind you of your pact, a bone at a time. He wants me to find out who else you have co-opted into your tin pot religion. You have a choice. Tell me what I want to know now, and I will kill you instantly. If you don't, I will break ever single bone in your body, strip every last piece of flesh from your bones, remove every unnecessary organ you have, one at a time and quite frankly, torture you to within an inch of your death until you do. The choice is yours.'

Chapter 12

A simple fact can totally change your outlook on the world. It can fundamentally reshape your life. It doesn't have to be a huge fact. It can be something as mundane as knowing the little dimple between your top lip and your nose has a name: a philtrum. I couldn't believe that there was a name for it. As a species, we have to give order to everything. When I found that fact out out it sent me on an obsessive week of research into finding out if every part of the body has a name. Every part of the body does, indeed, have a name. Even that dry, liny bit of skin on your elbow. Darrie told me about that, in his own inimitably seedy way, and about all the dodgy websites setup to worship the word. It's called a wenis. Sometimes they are huge facts, and they are staring you right in the eyes, literally. I have green eyes, Eve had green eyes, Rebecca has green eyes, Adam has green eyes and Jacob has green eyes. Coincidence? Not if you are from the same bloodline. Not if your mother is potentially also your auntie and your father is also your grandfather. Not if your family has been inbreeding for years. I have always thought of myself as an orphan, with no one to call family. Now I probably have a twin brother and Rebecca could very likely be my sister, as well as the mother of our son. Try weaving morality around that. It doesn't fit, in any way, shape or form. Now at the minute, the fact is, we all have green eyes. The implication from Adam is that we are all inbred, deliberately. We have to find out if that is a simple fact, and once we do, we have to find out why.

Murder Path

The early morning sun is casting some spectacularly meandering reflections off the river running outside our apartment, the reflections laconically weaving between the moss covered stepping stones stretching away to the grassy embankment on the far side. It is a beautiful early morning vista and is making me long for my canvas and brushes, to take my mind away from this mad world it currently resides in. I turn back from the window and back to the job at hand: setting up a row of monitors on a long writing desk in the study and hooking them all up to a laptop. I plug the last monitor into a USB repeater and power the laptop up.

An omniscience stick is what Adam called it, as I plug the memory stick into the last spare USB port on the repeater and watch as a folder opens up on the laptop screen. So, the stick that knows all there is to know, what are you going to show me? There are a number of subfolders, the first called 'Cameras'. I click on it, to open up a list of files, with locations as file names. I click on one called 'Edinburgh Police HQ Incident Room' and a web browser opens and starts to stream live footage from that very location, although this early in the morning, the room is empty. I drag the window and drop it onto the farthest monitor. There's also one called 'Ennis Office'. There's an original Cezanne on the wall in that office. I click on that link and another window opens, showing the paisley papered walls and mahogany furniture of the room. It all looked as precise and meticulous as the last time I was in there, barely three weeks ago. Surprising considering the police have been and must have checked over it for evidence. I flip the window onto a second screen.

I hear a stretching moan behind me and swivel in my chair to see Rebecca standing at the door, arms high above her head and standing on tiptoes to get the sleepiness out of her joints. She is totally naked and isn't wearing one of her wigs, so every scar, scab, cut, weal and gouge that she inflicted on herself during her time incarcerated in the Fielding Institute is visible. It's a fact that the first time I saw her on the video looking like that, it turned my stomach and made me

Murder Path

question the mentality of someone who could self-harm so much. But as I watched the videos I totally understood why. It absolutely amazes me how different she is now and when I look at her, I don't see scars caused by weakness, I see scars of strength. I now see beyond them, to the beauty shining from her sleepy emerald eyes, totally unabashed by her nakedness as she saunters over and sits down on a seat next to me.

'Sleep well?' I asked, leaning over and pecking her on the cheek.

'Surprisingly, yes. I managed to stop thinking about thrusting a knife into Dessie Bentley's back and killing her long enough to drop off. I guess you didn't, seeing that you've managed to set all this up.'

'No, I went off for a few hours, then went and sat watching over Jacob for a while. Just wanted to see if that medicine did anything other than supress his fits. He was sleeping, and didn't move at all.' I answer, hopefully not displaying my disappointment too much, that he hadn't moved.

'Did you find Ian Bear at all?' she asks. I haven't told her I left the bear for Jerry to find.

'No, we must have dropped in somewhere in the rush leaving the apartment.' I lie, far too naturally for my own liking, looking at her fleetingly sad eyes to see if she can tell, noticing them taking in the bare calf on my left leg. She leans over and runs a finger down the half a dozen visible raised mounds of scar tissue, and looks up to me, eyes full of questions.

'The remnants of my childhood spent in the white room in Italy. It's where they injected the needles and tubes into me when I was a child. It seems we both wear the memories of our incarceration.' I whisper, my words simmering with emotion as I consciously shore up the walls of my rickety rooms.

Murder Path

She smiles at me with a sad, knowing, haunted look on her face, then changes the subject completely, deliberately. 'So what are you doing now?'

'Seeing what omniscience looks like. We have a feed from the police station Incident room: empty at the moment. We have Dr Ennis's office, again empty, which is good. I'm just about to see if there are any other feeds from the Institute on here and if there's anything to help us find a way in there.'

'Okay. Do you fancy a coffee? I need a coffee. I've got birdcage mouth and don't have a tongue to get rid of it.' Rebecca teases, wiggling the stunted stump at me through open lips as she stands, kissing me on the head and saunters out of the room.

'Yes please.' I answer after her. Rebecca is good for me, she has a knack of taking me out of my own moribund reverie and not letting me be consumed by my own darkness. Her naked body is a beautiful distraction as well! I turn back to the laptop and check out a few more of the folders. I click on one called 'Systems'. Another list of files appears, this one with titles such as 'Police', 'HMRC', 'PNC', 'DVLA', 'GCHQ', 'Group 4'. Jesus, they have links to all of those! Hold on, the security firm who look after The Fielding Institute are Group 4. I click on it and a Word document opens. In it are instructions on how to log in to the Group 4 scheduling system and a link to that system. I click on the link and a web page opens. A proxy redirect message appears on the screen, quickly followed by another, stating that I am now accessing 'Hop Off Server 8', before a login page appears, with a Group 4 logo in the corner. That's two different servers I am bouncing off before getting to the login page, so I'm not directly connected. If anyone were to be spying on my internet usage, they would never know what I was doing. So this is how the Angels manage to get into systems undetected. I enter the username and password from the Word document and am straight into the Group 4 scheduling system, with administrative access.

Murder Path

'One coffee, black with no sugar, consistency of tar, just how you like it.' I hear Rebecca say behind me as she appears at my side, my eyes distracted from the screen temporarily by her swaying breasts, which she notices. She smiles, while adding 'Pervert', before sitting down beside me again, both mugs of coffee resting on top of a book.

'How are you getting on?' she asks, passing over my coffee, which I take willingly, supping the thick liquid down almost immediately, savouring the caffeine rush. She slurps her own, warming her hands around the mug.

'Well, I am just about to schedule a visit to the institute today, at 11am for a Dr Marsha Evans. She is part of the team carrying out the investigation into alleged molestation of patients at the Institute by the late Dr Gordon Ennis.' Fuck, what callous bastard. I pause after the flippancy of the first sentence and look over to Rebecca's features, suddenly overtly conscious that she was one of the patients molested by him. 'Sorry, that was insensitive of me. Are you sure you want to do this? It may bring back some memories you would rather forget?'

'John, please don't ever feel like you have to pussyfoot around my feelings. I am made of stronger stuff than that. You are made of stronger stuff than that. I appreciate the sincerity and the concern, but I am more than ready to do this. We have to find out if there's anything in Ennis's files that can help us and I know that place better than anyone. I think I had at least one finger of fun in every single cell, holding room, cupboard, office, toilet and bathroom in that building, so I am also more than qualified to be investigating the alleged molestations.' she answers, starting with stern authority and ending in sexual joviality.

'Okay, but it was only a few weeks ago that you were trying to kill yourself in there, so be careful. We both know where emotions can take you, and ours have been all over the place in the past few days.

Murder Path

What's the book?' I ask, trying to change the conversation as I see her starting to get frustrated at my mollycoddling. She looks down and picks it up.

'It was on side in the kitchen, it's a history of this charming town. You know, I lived in Northumberland most of my childhood life and Morpeth was always the posh town around here, but I never knew what that name meant or where it came from. Now I'm thinking, is it really as posh as I thought? It also confirms why there is a mental hospital on the outskirts of town.'

'Why, what does it mean?' I ask curiously as she picks up the book, flicking through the first few pages.

'Well, back in the 12th century, Morpeth as it is today didn't exist, and this was a crossing point on the river on the route from Newcastle up to Edinburgh. Probably across those stepping stones out there. So many muggings, molestations and murders took place along the route through the area, that it gained a reputation, and a name. Morpeth, in old English means morð-pæð, or 'murder-path'.

'Murder Path? Curious. Why the link with the mental hospital?'

'Morpeth has always had more than its fair share of fruitcakes and nutters. There are quite a few called out in the book. It's one of the reasons the old lunatic asylum was built here. I'm just wondering if that has anything to do with the Seymour family history. It could have been caused by the early stages of inbreeding perhaps?'

'It is always possible. Ennis talked about a patient who was a brilliant painter, had a sense of Munch about his work. He painted the Angel picture in the reception to the Institute. He was a psychopath partial to eating the genitals of his victims. He was also an ancestor of the Seymour family. It would be good to find any of his notes, see how far this alleged inbreeding goes.'

Murder Path

Rebecca fell silent, looking down into her nearly empty coffee cup, her face cogitating. 'Anything up?' I ask.

'Just.' she started, pausing, taking a deep breath, her breasts perking up on the inhale, her stomach tightening, the snake writhing under her taught muscles. 'Just recalling something I read about Cotton Mather.'

'You mean, apart from him being a religious nutter.'

'Apart from that, yes.' she answers with a droll tone, before continuing. 'It's this inbreeding direction we are going down. Apart from being a barking religious madman, apart from being convinced he had found a Nephilim, he was also an eminent scientist.'

'Okay, what does that have to do with inbreeding?'

'Everything. He conducted one of the first ever recorded experiments on plant hybridization. He started cross breeding plants, which led to cross breeding animals.' Rebecca sounds off, agitatedly excited by her train of thought.

'But what does that have to do with inbreeding?' I ask, still a little confused.

'So, you have a religious madman, who thinks he has found a Nephilim, a child of a Fallen Angel, who is also a scientist renowned for cross breeding species.' Rebecca prompts, staring at me incredulously, frustrated I cannot see the inference. 'What if he started human cross breeding? What if he started cross breeding humans and Nephilim?'

My face must have painted a picture of impatience as Rebecca frowns at me, frustrated. 'He didn't have a live Nephilim, only the fossils of one.'

Murder Path

'But what if he found the bloodline of one? What if he found one and cross bred. What if he found one, cross bred, and then started to selectively inbreed to purify the bloodline: to get back to a pure child of an Angel?'

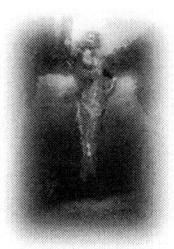

Chapter 13

The toilet cubicle walls were festooned with every conceivable type of graffiti. Simple words scratched into the industrial grey plastics, drawings of cocks with telephone numbers below them, 'such and such woz ere' scrawled all over, all intermingled with the odd dry bogie and smear or two of faeces. Strange sat quietly on the closed, loose toilet seat, listening patiently to the sounds outside the cubicle door, waiting patiently for the man he could hear washing his hands to leave. The frantic roar of the hand drier cut out and the main door to the toilets clicked shut, leaving the rest room in silence.

Strange quickly unzipped his holdall which was sitting on the floor in front of him and, rummaging around stealthily, pulled out a small brown teddy bear and started to examine it closely.

'So why did John leave you at the apartment Ian Bear? It must have been something important?' Strange mumbled to himself, his attention caught by a slight rustle as he squeezed the small toy. He flipped it onto its back, where the stitching was, and noticed a couple of the stitches near the base of the torso were loose. He tugged on the thread gently, making a hole big enough to get his wizened little finger inside, and felt around until it touched something harder than the soft filling. He wriggled his finger until the tip of a piece of white paper poked out of the hole. Carefully, he slid the scrolled tube of paper out and unfurled it in his hands.

Murder Path

Strange's eyes opened wide in surprise, his body visibly jolting as he took the words on the note in, so much so that the loose toilet seat slipped, almost tipping him to the floor. He thrust his arms out and steadied himself on the filthy cubicle walls, then read the note again.

'We did not kill McFetrich. We killed Dessie in self-defence. Fenny killed himself. I know how it looks, but we are being played. Right now, I'm not sure why, but I think it is by the man in the photographs. He used to be a Fallen Angel, but turned extreme. Trust no one Jerry. Even your closest friends, family and colleagues could be playing you, just as they have been us. Bring the bread. Jacob is alive.' Strange relayed on whispering lips, shaking his head in astonishment as he went over the last sentence again. 'Jacob is alive!'

'Shit!' he announced loudly as he caught the time on his Rolex watch. He thrust Ian Bear back into his holdall while standing and flung the bag over his shoulder, zipping it as he vacated the cubicle and headed out of the restroom. He quickly strode down the bustling main thoroughfare of the station, slipping the note into the inside pocket of his moleskin jacket just as he reached the door to the main Incident room, Cruickshank's booming furious voice rattling its frame as he pushed it open and entered.

Cruickshank finished speaking mid rant and threw him a simmering glare of admonishment. 'Oh, DCI Strange, nice of you to join us. Only a mere ten minutes late for the briefing. It's reassuring to know that your time keeping is as proficient as your investigative skills.' she spat scathingly, contemptuously disregarding him as she returned to haranguing her previous victim. 'It's not good enough Trentor. Coleen Naismith has been in our charge for more than twenty four hours now. Surely she must be able to remember something?'

Strange walked nonchalantly down the aisle between the rows of grey, worn plastic seats facing the Incident boards and plonked

Murder Path

himself down next to Trentor, flashing an encouraging smile in the Detective's direction as he sat, dropping his holdall under the seat.

'She had her arms chopped of Ma'am and was more than likely sexually molested with her own hands. It's quite probable she was also forced to watch Pastor Bentley eat her arms. I think it's more than understandable that she is struggling to remember anything else. I will keep working with the psychiatric team and as soon as she is stable enough to question, then I will be there straight away.' Trentor replied, a tinge of attitude in amongst the deference in his words.

'Well just make sure we aren't waiting a bloody week. She's a key witness. She was there when both Desiderate and Fenny died. She is the one person that can tell us if Saul and Angus were involved. Don't forget that. How about the McFetrich murder. Have we any more on his last movements? Any known associates? Any link to Saul or Angus?' Cruickshank posed, still evidently annoyed with Trentor.

'There are no known connections between Saul and Angus, save for the fact they were all at 'Sodom and Gomorrah' when it was raided. At the time of the raid, McFetrich was midway through a sexual act with a Douglas Ettrick and a Sheila Warren. We are trying to locate them both now for questioning. No one has seen or heard from McFetrich since yesterday afternoon Ma'am, when he left a meeting in Newcastle at around 5pm.'

'Someone must have seen him Trentor. Interview the people he was meeting with. Check out CCTV footage on the roads back from Newcastle. Follow through with Ettrick and Warren, they may know something. On the subject of Saul and Angus, have we any more leads, Purves?' Cruickshank asked, turning her attention from Trentor to DI Rosamund Purves, whose middle aged dyed blonde hair, grey at the roots, was bent over the notes she was reading on the pad in her lap.

Murder Path

'We carried out a full house to house on the main and surrounding apartment blocks Ma'am. No one in the main apartment block can recall seeing either of the suspects. In the adjacent block, there was an apartment that had been rented out, which was directly opposite the one we raided. The odd thing about it was that it had been cleaned with bleach, every surface wiped down and not a single fingerprint anywhere.' Purves relayed.

'Promising, could that be where they were staying? Would you have been able to hop onto the Wi-Fi connection of the other apartment from there? Have you talked to the owner? Do they know who rented it?' Cruickshank fired off the questions in rapid succession, not even taking a breath between them.

'Yes Ma'am, you can hop onto the Wi-Fi connection from there. The owner lives in an apartment on the ground floor. He didn't recognise either Saul or Angus. The woman who rented the apartment was described as in her late fifties, early sixties, greying hair, rather frail. Name was Yolandi Grainger. We are checking into that now.'

'Good. Also check CCTV from the apartments and from the surrounding streets for the past few days. Let's see what Yolandi Grainger was doing that required her to bleach down the apartment.'

Cruickshank turned and addressed an extremely tall, skinny man next, the handlebar moustache he wore warming the rim of the thermos mug he was supping from. 'Gregory, where are we with the Fallen Angels and the 'Unknown Man'? Have we found anything at all?'

'Forensics have confirmed that the DNA from Madame Evangeline was in fact that of Jessica Seymour. We are now working with our colleagues in Northumbria, with the help of DCI Strange, to dig into the background of Mrs Seymour further and see if we can find a connection back to the Fallen Angels. We have no other open lines of investigation from the other three 'Fallen Angels' who committed suicide. As for the 'Unknown Man', so far there is nothing Ma'am.

Murder Path

Facial recognition has turned up nothing, feedback from GCHQ and Interpol has turned up nothing. Armed forces checks have turned up nothing. So far Ma'am, he's invisible.' Gregory fed back, supping his warm coffee as he finished.

'Well, we know he exists, because he is in four bloody pictures with four serial killers. Four serial killers who know him. Four serial killers who could tell us exactly who he is. Strange has an idea of how to approach interviewing them to try and make them give something up about him. Gregory, could you work with him to prepare that and see if we can get something moving there.'

Cruickshank shook her head, irritated, tutting as she looked around the room at her assembled Detectives. 'We need to pick the pace up team. These 'Fallen Angels' have potentially moved on to murdering people now: famous people at that. We won't be able to keep McFetrich's death out of the press any longer than today, and when they find out, then the bloody circus we've had to endure so far will be like a child's party compared to what will come. So, everyone focus on every single open line of enquiry and follow them through quickly and thoroughly. We need positive movement people and we need it today. Dismissed.' Cruickshank finished firmly, her tone radiating frustration.

Strange watched the weary, down beaten detectives stream past him and out of the Incident room in near silence, not a single one of them discussing the case with their colleagues. Shaking his head disconsolately, he stood and walked up to the front of the room, where Cruickshank now had her back to him, examining the evidence boards.

'Gaynor, the team are looking a little demotivated. A few positive words might help just to buck them up a little. They have had a hard few days. You have had a hard few days.' Strange relayed softly, coming up behind her and placing a reassuring hand on her shoulder.

Murder Path

Cruickshank flinched under it, brushing the contact off and turned to face him with a furious glare, her body tense and angry, ready to unleash an onslaught of abuse. She opened her mouth, looking up into his beseeching brown eyes, and stopped herself, the tension ebbing from her body, the anger subsiding.

'I know they are. But this is me Strange. Don't think you know me just because we've shared two nights of passion. In this room, we are professionals. I won't stand for tardy timekeeping and I certainly won't stand for incompetent investigation. I will be firm, I will be clear and I will be hard on everyone, even you, until we have a clear line of sight on this. This is me Strange, live with it or leave.' Cruickshank stated firmly, but without any anger or frustration.

Strange smiled magnanimously. 'I will live with it. As much as I disagree, I respect your candour and professionalism. But please, recognise that for me this isn't about right and wrong, it's just about embracing our different approaches to achieving the same ultimate goal.'

'I will bear that in mind and I am grateful for the perspective you are bringing to this investigation. But as I mentioned, I won't accept tardiness. Now, let's go and find out if Laurent has had a chance to look at Saul's DNA samples.'

Cruickshank strode off, assertiveness returning to her pronounced gait and glare as she passed Strange and headed out of the Incident room and down the thoroughfare in the direction of the Forensics Laboratory.

Strange dutifully fell in behind her, his slow long laconic strides, accentuated by a twist of the hips as he walked, easily catching her short sharp steps up. 'I was surprised that Laurent though he would be able to tell the difference between two identical twins, so this is going to be interesting.' Strange mused as he followed Cruickshank into the Lab and approached the white coated, angular faced, svelte

Murder Path

form of Marcel Laurent, studiously lost in an open sheath of papers on the workbench in front of him.

'So Laurent. Have we got twins, or is there just the one Saul?' Cruickshank asked bluntly, coming right up to his side and looking over his shoulder, speed reading his notes.

Laurent raised his head in surprise, still lost in the information that he was reading, his features a mask of intrigue underneath the irritation of distraction.

'From my analysis of the three DNA samples we have of Saul, they all belong to him. No twins there. However, your question got me checking the DNA of our other suspects and victims, especially Rebecca Angus and Jessica Seymour/Madame Evangeline. That is where things start to get really interesting.'

'Tell me more.' Cruickshank demanded as she tried to decipher the complex formulas on the notes.

'Three different people, Saul, Angus and Seymour. Three different people with a ninety eight percent DNA match. I would never have seen it if you hadn't suggested I check Saul's results.'

Strange looked on nonplussed, seeing a similar confused expression on Cruickshank's features. 'What does that mean? Are they related?' Strange queried.

'More than related. Much more than related. A normal person will get 50% of their DNA from mama, 50% from papa. A sibling is the same, but they may get a different 50% from each parent. So in general, siblings will tend to have a 25% DNA match. To get a ninety eight percent match in three different people is either a one in a billion fluke, or...' Laurent paused, his own voice filled with excitement and confusion.

'Or what?' Cruickshank said, her words impatiently irritated.

Murder Path

'Or the particular family they belong to have been inbreeding for a very long time. I need to get these samples off to some experts, because they just can't be right. Even that isn't the most remarkable thing.'

Strange stood there listening with a look of utter surprise etched onto his features, his mouth agape, eyes wide and nostrils flared. 'Something more remarkable than that!' he stated.

'Yes. The DNA from Jessica Seymour and Madame Evangeline are 99.999% the same. There is only one chromosome different.' Laurent relayed.

'So does that mean they are identical twins?' Cruickshank questioned.

'Possibly, and one of them has had their DNA genetically modified.'

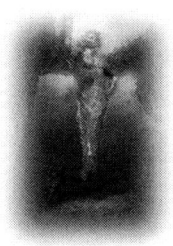

Chapter 14

The red light started a stuttering dance, revolving in time to the loud klaxon that burst into life with a piercing shriek, both pre-empting the opening of the tall metal gates at the entrance of The Fielding Institute. Rebecca, wearing a grey bob wig, pristine tweed twin set and made up to look old, drove the people carrier into the holding area between the gates that had just opened, and a second set just in front of her. The ones behind closed with a sturdy metallic thud, just as the ones in front opened. She manoeuvred the car out of the holding area and into an empty car park in front of the contemporary reception entrance at the front of the Institute.

'Now remember. You are Dr Marsha Evans.' Saul's voice quietly echoed in her left ear, from the small receiver hidden deep within the canal. One the left lapel of her tweed jacket was a small Scottie dog pin brooch, behind which was glued a minute microphone.

'Got that DI Saul. Sixty three year old spinster with a wee dog called Hamish, a cottage on the seafront at Amble and an uncontrollable craving for mint humbugs.' Rebecca answered sarcastically, stepping out of the car and heading off towards the reception entrance, her shoulders stooped and her footfalls short and bustling.

The inside of the reception area was as contemporary and minimalist as the exterior, with large swathes of glass and exposed metal beams throughout. Sleek leather chairs lounged in the waiting area next to brushed chrome tables covered in upmarket magazines. Rebecca bustled up to the solitary security guard sitting behind the glass and chrome reception desk, glancing for a second across to the large painting of an Angel with its wings stretched out, holding the palms of his hands upwards to show the stigmata in the centre of them. With a bright, bubbly smile on her face, she turned back to the portly, ruddy cheeked guard and addressed him jovially.

'Morning sonny. It's quiet in here today, that'll leave you plenty of time for tea breaks I would imagine? What's your name son?' Rebecca asked, her voice slightly high pitched with an exaggerated lisp to cover the speech impediments caused by the lack of her tongue.

'Call me Henry, Dr Evans. It is quiet today. The last of the patients was moved on Friday. Apart from the occasional visit from your crew, this place is like a morgue. Could I see your ID please?' Henry requested, returning Rebecca's smile warmly.

'There you go Henry.' Rebecca answered, passing over the Northumbria police ID badge Saul had fashioned for her from his own. 'Plenty of opportunity for tea then. If you happen to be making one, I like mine with milk and three sugars please, and I am partial to a Custard Cream, if you have any?' she finished cheekily, leaning into the reception desk furtively.

Henry's smile broadened as he handed her back the ID badge, hardly even giving it a cursory glance. 'I've got Custard Creams and Malted Milk. I'll go put the kettle on. Where are you going first and I'll bring a cuppa down to you?'

'Down to the archives first, then a quick recce of Dr Ennis's old office to pick a few files up.' Rebecca relayed, dropping the ID badge back into her pocket.

'Do you know the way?' Henry asked, getting up from his seat ready to point her in the right direction.

Murder Path

'Archives are down the main admin corridor, last on the right if I recall. Are the doors on lockdown still?' Rebecca responded.

'That's right, last on the right. No, you'll be fine getting in. All of the security locks have been disabled. No point in having them on when there's no patients here.' I'll bring your tea down for you and please, just call zero from any phone if you need assistance.' Henry answered helpfully before waddling off to a door to the right of the reception.

'Thank you Henry, I'll call if I need you.' Rebecca finished, smiling pleasantly before scurrying off through a set of double doors into the main thoroughfare of the Institute.

'Perfect misdirection. Custard Creams will always do that.' Saul crackled in Rebecca's earpiece as she slowed her pace, straightened up slightly, walked past the side entrance to the Admin corridor and headed straight into the main secure area of the Institute. The decor changed suddenly, from glass and metal to stark white tiled walls and ceilings, devoid of windows, the corridor ahead in darkness. Automated lights flickered on as she passed underneath them, illuminating the side doors, all of which were closed.

'It wasn't hard John. This is a place I know. It may sound strange, but it's a place I am comfortable in. For all the harm I caused myself here and the hundreds of suicide attempts, not to mention all of the sexual molestation, being in here probably saved my life. If I had been put into a normal prison for killing Michael, I would have been dead within a day.' Rebecca responded quietly, staring at a blank spot in the darkness ahead, purposefully walking towards it.

'Well, if the Angels hadn't messed with your life, you wouldn't have been in that position at all. Are you near the archive yet?'

'But then, I would never have met Madame Evangeline and been exposed to such exquisite ecstasy. There's somewhere I need to see before I go to the archive.' Rebecca replied, slowing down as she approached a door the same as every other one down the corridor. She paused outside, running a finger down the cold, white painted, solid metal door, letting it come to rest on the handle.

'What are you doing Rebecca? There's no time for anything other than checking the archive and Ennis's office. Just because you've hoodwinked the guard for now, doesn't mean he won't get suspicious if you go off plan?' Saul crackled, his tone concerned.

'I will only be a minute. I just want to see home, one last time.' she replied, before turning the handle, opening the door and walking into the room she had been incarcerated in for a year.

Sadness drew a veil over her emerald eyes, and floated over the disguised features of her face as she walked into the almost empty room and ran a slightly shaking hand along the solitary bed that sat in the centre of it. Her fingers sketched a trail over the leather restraints tied to the metal frame of the bed.

'It's strange to think that weeks before I was imprisoned here, I had been tied up with restraints like these for pleasure: that I tied Michael up in something similar before letting him fuck my brains out. I lay on that bed for a year, tortured not only by the thought of killing him, but more so by the thought that I had fucked my own son. What kind of moral monster does that make me? And yet, I stand here today, and that could be something my ancestors have been doing for centuries. It makes the molestation by the staff here pale into insignificance.'

'Rebecca, you shouldn't be in there. What the staff did to you was absolutely abhorrent. You didn't know that Michael was your son at the time. They knew exactly what they were doing to you. You have to get out of there, it can only bring back bad memories and you need to focus at the moment. Don't forget, you are a fugitive and you are inside a secure mental facility.' Saul urged, a slight undertone of panic in his voice.

'You sounded just like Doc Hanlon there. It wasn't my fault because I didn't know it was Michael, that's what he kept telling me. I vaguely recall the first day I was here, the first time they strapped me to this bed. I was dosed up with Diazepam but was subconsciously aware of what they were doing. Two female orderlies, Janet and Dawn, were getting me out of my clothes and putting a hospital gown on me. They decided to have a game of Toad in the Hole. They started with my ears, each digging their thumbs deep into the canal, covering them in wax, then forcing them into my mouth, making me lick the wax off. My nose was next, making me eat the dry snot they managed to pull out. They thumbed my cunt after that, making me sniff my own stale, piss smelling juices before putting those into my mouth too. All before the denouement, where in tandem, they both thrust their thumbs up my arsehole together, covered them in shit, and laughed as they made me suck it off. Do you know what? At that moment, I felt like I deserved every last bit of that, and so much more.' Rebecca fell silent, looking down at the empty bed, one hand shaking, clasping one of the restraints tightly, the other hand circling its wrist, the thumb rubbing over the weals left from the last time she had been restrained.

'Rebecca, that is tragic, let's talk about those feelings later. Sorry for being an insensitive dick, but right now, you have to get on and do what you need to do. You've already been in there ten minutes more than planned.' Saul crackled curtly, breaking Rebecca's reflective reverie.

Her eyes refocused from the memory in time for her to hear echoing footfalls from the empty corridor outside.

'Shit, I think Henry is coming with my tea.' Rebecca whispered, stooping her back as she turned and shuffled out of the room and

Murder Path

back into the corridor, sadness sailing from her face to be replaced by a broad, eager smile.

'Ah, you found me.' Rebecca started before Henry could speak, taking the mug of tea out of his hands as she approached him. 'Just thought I would get a quick idea of where she was locked up. It helps to visualise these things rather than just read about them. Did you ever come across the Angus woman at all?' she finished, hurrying off down the corridor, towards the Admin entrance.

Henry looked quizzically at the open door to the cell she had just left, then fell in behind, quickly catching her short steps up. 'I only started here when they closed the place, but I read about her in the papers. Some scary stuff that she did, killing and eating her son and, well, you know, the other thing: having sex with him. All kinds of wrong going on there. Here's your Custard Creams.' he added, now walking by her side.

'Thanks Henry, I appreciate your help, and the Custard Creams. Yes, you are right: definitely all kinds of wrong going on there. I shouldn't be too long in the archives, probably ten minutes or so. I'll bring the mug back with me.' Rebecca responded, still smiling radiantly as she turned left and headed down the corridor to the Archive room. She reached the door, quickly opened, entered and closed it, then leant with her back against it and let out a huge stuttering breath, her hands shaking slightly, her eyes taking in the row upon row of perfectly aligned, drab grey filing cabinets.

'Sorry John. That was stupid of me. I could see him getting inquisitive.' Rebecca whispered as she stood back up straight and headed over to the nearest filing cabinet, popping the mug of tea on top while checking the indexing on the top drawer.

'Well, we are where we are, and you diffused his curiosity well. Let's focus on...' Saul started, pausing mid-sentence.

Murder Path

'Let's focus on what?' Rebecca queried, moving from the first to the second row of cabinets quickly, her eyes darting between the drawer labels.

'Shit. You need to hurry up. There's another visitor just been registered on the Group 4 scheduling system. Detective Inspector Munro, one of my colleagues from Northumbria. He's due there at 12:30, which means you've got about twenty minutes before things get really complicated.'

'Bollocks, sorry John. Right, I am at the S's now.' Rebecca cursed, agitation animating her actions as she pulled the drawer open and started flicking through the records inside. 'Bugger, bugger, bugger.' she added after a second, slamming it shut and hurriedly running around the end of the cabinets into the next row.

'What's wrong?' Saul queried, concerned.

'No records in the drawers for anyone at all called Seymour.' Rebecca relayed curtly before pulling a drawer labelled 'An-Ay' open. She flicked through the files quickly, her features and finger movements becoming furiously worried. 'Nothing in here for Angus either. Fuck.' she shouted, banging her palms off the top of the cabinet.

'That's okay. Keep calm. There was always the possibility that Ennis had them stowed away somewhere, that's why Adam gave us the tube. That somewhere is probably his office. Now focus and remember the little tip about walls and pictures. Fifteen minutes.' Saul relayed with gentle, conciliatory undertones to his firm voice.

'On it.' Rebecca replied simply as she rushed around to the front of the cabinets, grabbed her mug of tea, slouched her shoulders, took a deep breath, opened the door and walked into the empty corridor wearing the mannerisms of an unconcerned old woman. She jauntily sauntered half a dozen doors up the corridor and entered Ennis's office, pushing the door closed behind her. In contrast to the rest of

Murder Path

the building, this office was decorated with paisley print wallpaper, a thick burgundy carpet and mahogany furniture.

'I can see you now. We know that the front wall faces onto the corridor, the side walls into other rooms, so the likely location of any hidden cubby hole is on the back wall. There's an original Cezanne on there, where the camera is located, so try behind that first.' Saul instructed.

Rebecca rounded the large writing desk, popping her mug of tea on its top, and then lifted the painting, whispering expletives as she saw the blank, flat wall behind it.

'That's fine.' Saul assured. 'Now, start tapping the walls. Listen for variations in the tone. Either hollow or hard. Ten minutes.'

'Stop the fucking countdown will you, it's not helping.' Rebecca hissed as she wrapped her knuckles off the wall below the picture, then started moving around to the right, where a tall chest of drawers sat against it. Her attention was caught by the carpet, and the slight flattening of the pile in front of the drawers. 'I think I have something.' she relayed as she bent over and pulled the surprisingly light drawers forward, exposing the wall behind, with a small Perspex hole about head height. Rebecca looked into it and saw a red laser light bouncing off a prism inside.

'Found it.' she whispered, reaching into the pocket of her tweed jacket and pulling out the silver tube that Gabriel had given them. 'I'm not looking forward to this.' she said, as she unscrewed the top.

'Don't think about what it is, just think about what is can get us.' Saul offered encouragingly.

'That is the most asinine thing I think you've ever said to me, and there's been some howlers. It's a fucking detached, dead eyeball. It's going to freak me out regardless of what you say.' she replied curtly and reached into the open tube, squeamishly gripping the end of the optic nerve and lifting Ennis's glistening eyeball from the formaldehyde preserving it. She grimaced, then gripped the circumference of the globuled ball between shaking thumb and forefinger, then pressed it against the Perspex hole. There was a loud beep, and the wall started to slide back to the right, revealing a small cubby hole behind.

'Bingo!' she shouted in a whisper. She dropped the eyeball back into the tube, screwed the top back on and placed it back in her pocket.

'What is it?' Saul enquired.

'A small recess with a filing cabinet. There is a trumpet case on top of the filing cabinet. It's got the word 'Unas' embossed on it in gold. Isn't that what was on the instrument case in McFetrich's trophy room?' Rebecca relayed, opening the top drawer of the filing cabinet.

'Yes, it was. Why would two unrelated people have cases with the same word on? We'll need to do some digging into this 'Unas'. What's in the cabinet?'

'Just what we hoped. Lots of files. Jessica Seymour, Henry Seymour, Cecil Seymour, Clarissa Seymour and a ton of other Seymour's to boot along with a good dozen other files.' She thrust the top drawer closed and yanked the bottom one open, sifting through another concertina of files, noting one labelled 'Angus' right at the front, before grabbing the whole bunch and plopping them on top of the others.

'How long have I got?' Rebecca asked as she placed the large pile of files on the desk, turned back and hit a little button just on the inside of the recess, which caused the wall to close up again, then pushed the chest of drawers back against the wall.

Murder Path

'I thought you wanted me to stop the fucking countdown? Five minutes.' Saul replied calmly.

'Smart arse. Right, let's get out of here.' Rebecca responded sarcastically. She picked up the pile of files and tucked them tight into her chest, took a deep breath and let her Dr Evans demeanour wash over her once more. She reached down to grab the handle, just as it started to turn, just as the door was pushed open and just as a large, suited man filled the frame, looking at her curiously.

'Dr Evans? Afternoon, I'm DI Mick Munro. Henry tells me you are working on the Ennis case. I can't recall meeting you before?'

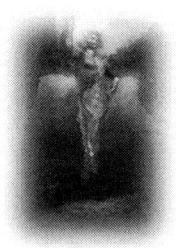

Chapter 15

'I think we should start with the substitution.' a skinny, ginger haired and pallid faced woman, wearing a white lab coat, piped up. Her larger than life head was being displayed on a plasma TV that sat at the end of a cluttered lab bench in the Centre for Biomedicine at Edinburgh University.

'I think we should start with names, then we could toss a coin to see which of you enthusiastic boffins goes first.' Strange interjected, jovially irritated by the posturing. He was sitting on a tall wooden stool next to Cruickshank and opposite two other agitatedly excited scientists eager to expound their theories to the two detectives.

'Sorry, sorry, quite right, a little formality will help.' the ginger lady on the screen broke in before her colleagues had an opportunity to comment. 'I am Professor Janice Auld from the Biomedicine facility at Newcastle University. I have to say, what you have given us to study is absolutely remarkable.'

'And I am Professor Aubrey Quinn, from the Biomedicine Centre here at Edinburgh. This is remarkable.' a sturdy, tall gentleman, with a shock of wiry, unruly black hair on his head, sitting opposite Strange, introduced.

'Professor Hilary Martin, from the Roslin Institute, also here at the University. I specialise in animals, not humans, but am equally

Murder Path

astounded by your samples.' a bespectacled older lady with a tight crew cut hair style, naturally greying and distinguished, finished.

'Excellent. Now we have enthused over how remarkable these DNA samples are, let's not forget that they are from potential murderers. So it is critical that you focus on giving us facts relevant to our investigation, and please, in plain English: we aren't scientists.' Cruikshank ordered, her stoic face as stern as her words.

Professor Quinn started speaking before Cruickshank had a chance to finish, taking the breath out of his colleague's lungs a second before they spoke. 'The first thing to state is that while we are excited about what we have seen, everything we are about to share with you is morally wrong, ethically wrong and illegal. Secondly, whomever has done this has a serious god complex going on. Thirdly, from a layman's perspective, do not confuse inbreeding with incest. The first is pure biology, the second pure morality. Let's leave morality at the door for now. So, the very high degree of DNA alignment of the four samples you provided indicate not just a prolonged period of interbreeding between a contained group of people, but the lack of physical abnormalities indicates that the breeding was selective. In animal husbandry, that is not uncommon. It's not as uncommon as you might think in us humans either. There are examples, particularly in isolated tribes or communities, where that pattern of breeding has been documented and to a smaller extend in the bloodlines of royalty. However, never to the extent where four, and who knows how many more, people have such a DNA alignment. The scientific understanding required to ensure there are no chromosomal abnormalities is staggering. This must have been going on for generations.'

'So, I take it from that, they are all related, but may not be brother and sister related intimately, in an emotional sense, but rather a biological sense.' Strange summarized, trying to emphasise the salient points.

Murder Path

'Well, I can't comment on the intimacy of any relationship, but the discipline required in selective breeding to produce this type of healthy, strong DNA is definitely not an emotional activity. This is pure science. Jan, tell him about the gene replacement.' Quinn finished, looking over to the plasma screen.

'You might have heard in the news recently a lot of press about three parent 'god' children, or mitochondrial donation. It's where mitochondrial DNA from a healthy 'parent' is transferred into the egg of a parent where there may be known diseases such as diabetes, heart or liver conditions in the potential foetus and subsequent baby. The DNA replacement eradicates the chance of those diseases. The techniques to carry this out have been around for years and we have been at the forefront of that research, but ethically, we are still trying to get approval to carry out the procedure. All four of the DNA samples that you sent to us show signs of this type of procedure being carried out. It goes some way to explaining how the inbreeding has resulted in no obvious genetic abnormalities. Hils, I have to concede, I think yours is the most fantastic finding, tell them about it.' Professor Auld finished excitedly, her features vibrant with enthusiasm, looking toward Professor Martin.

'So, just to keep it real and simple, we have four people who have been genetically modified, a bit like GM food, to make them a little bit healthier.' Cruickshank summarised, her face an alignment of curiosity and patient questions.

Professor Martin answered, leaning over the lab bench, her hands clasped as she rubbed them together in excited anticipation. 'Essentially, yes, they have been GM'd: and the rest. Have you heard of Dolly the Sheep?' she asked, eyes wide with glee.

'Wasn't she the first animal cloned, and as I recall, called Dolly after Dolly Parton, although I can't remember why. That was done here, wasn't it?' Cruickshank offered.

Murder Path

'Correct, that was research done at the Roslin Institute. She was named after Dolly Parton, because the original cell from which she was cloned was taken from a mammary gland. While she was the first mammal that we thought had ever been cloned from an adult cell, she wasn't the first thing to be cloned. That was a sea urchin in 1885.'

Strange interrupted. 'The first mammal you thought had ever been cloned?' he queried.

'Up until today. Up until you sent in the two samples of Jessica Seymour and Madame Evangeline. It is absolutely amazing. Do you know, it took two hundred and seventy seven attempts to create Dolly? And here, probably twenty years earlier, are two perfectly cloned human beings. The other thing that people don't realise about Dolly is that she was genetically modified too, and had human DNA implanted into the cell that was used to create her. It is the other way around for your two clones. They have been modified with some kind of animal DNA which we have yet to identify.' Professor Martin concluded, all three colleagues looking between each other excitedly.

There was a buzzing from Cruickshank's pocket, and she pulled out a ringing mobile phone. 'Excuse me please.' she asked politely, before rising from the lab bench and heading over to the other side of the room, out of earshot.

'That is pretty amazing stuff.' Strange answered, shaking his head as he looked between the scientists. 'I don't suppose you have any idea as to who would be capable of this? Any renegade wanna-be gods?' he queried, still contemplating the enormity of the facts presented to them.

'What, where?' Cruickshank stated loudly from the other side of the room.

Murder Path

'Whoever it is, they have certainly had biomedical training, so you might want to check back through the university records. Edinburgh and Newcastle are world leaders in this type of research, so it's a good place to start.' Professor Quinn offered.

Strange reached into his moleskin jacket pocket and pulled out a stack of photographs and laid them on the bench in front of the two Professor's. 'Do any of these people look familiar, possibly former colleagues?' he queried.

Quinn and Martin looked down at the photographs and examined them studiously, shaking their heads negatively as eyes moved from one to the next.

'Sorry Chief Inspector, none of them look familiar.' Quinn responded, Martin nodding in acknowledgement. 'Jan, is there anyone you recognise.' he added, holding up a photograph at a time for Jan to peruse.

'Are SOCO on the way? What about a Medical Examiner?' Start checking out his movements last night. See if he was at any sex clubs.' Cruickshank could be overheard, speaking loudly from the other side of the room.

'No, don't recognise any of them. Hold on, put that last one up again. I might have seen him before. I can't recall where at the moment. Could you send a copy over and I'll check with the team here.' Jan asked as Strange took the photo off Quinn and took a look at it.

It was a photograph of John Saul.

'Jan, thanks for that. If you or your colleagues can recall a name, or anything, it would be a great help. We really need to find out who this man is. Is there anything else we need to be thinking about with regard to our close knit family here?' Strange asked, looking expectantly at the collected Professors.

Murder Path

'Given how tight the selective breeding is with them, there is one thing that will definitely be an issue. While there are techniques which have been used to help alleviate the potential physical abnormalities of interbreeding, it's a lot harder to do that with the mental aspects of interbreeding. I wouldn't be surprised if these people have a string of mental issues, from simple OCD and autism, right the way through to being bipolar, suicidal and even psychotic. Their mental stability will possibly take a lot of management.' Professor Quinn offered.

'Thank you Professor, that is very interesting. Thank you all for your time this morning and if you think of anything else you feel may be relevant to our investigation, please give us a call, you have our cards.' Strange thanked, reaching over and shaking the hands of Quinn and Martin, and waving at Auld. He stood up from the lab stool and approached Cruickshank, her face a storm of frustrated emotions. She slammed her finger onto the 'End call' button and thrust her phone into her jacket pocket.

'Thank you ladies and gentleman.' Cruickshank shouted as she absentmindedly waved, striding for the entrance to the lab. Strange fell in at her side, both walking out of the double doors together.

'Another murder I would guess?' Strange enquired.

'Yes, another bloody murder. Same Modus Operandi as McFetrich. We need to get over there straight away and see if there are more than just superficial similarities and also see if we have our bloody 'family' DNA at the scene.' Cruickshank rumbled as she strode out of the University into the bright light of the high, golden midday sun.

'Anyone we know?' Strange asked, still keeping pace with her short, fast, frustrated strides.

Murder Path

'Mr McFetrich's love interest from 'Sodom and Gomorrah' the other night and one of the most prominent businessmen in Edinburgh: Douglas Ettrick.'

Chapter 16

Rebecca staggered back in surprise, a few of the folders on the top of the pile in her arms falling to the floor. 'Jesus, you shocked me there young man.' she blustered as she bent over and started scooping up the strewn papers. 'A little help here. Who is this guy?' she whispered into the microphone as she rummaged around the floor.

'Don't panic. Munro is a jobbing copper. There's nothing that we can't handle here. I'm just putting your details onto the Northumbria police system. Just mention that you are the psychiatric liaison working with Darrie. He's our Medical Examiner.' Saul instructed quickly.

Munro bent over and started helping Rebecca collect the folders together. 'Sorry for startling you Ma'am. I wasn't expecting anyone else from the investigation here today, certainly not someone I haven't met before.'

'It's okay Mick. I wasn't expecting anyone on site today either, so we are both at a disadvantage. Could I see your ID badge, do you think?' Rebecca asked curtly as she stood, shuffling the folders back into an orderly pile in her arms, the action hiding her shaking hands.

'Fair point.' Munro conceded. He reached into his pocket and pulled out his ID badge and flashed it in front of Rebecca, who nodded acceptingly. 'Could I see yours?' he added.

Murder Path

'Certainly.' Rebecca responded, shuffling from side to side, looking from the desk, to a bookcase and eventually towards Munro –stalling tactics-, before she thrust the pile of files into his arms. 'Here, hold these for a second while I get it out. You couldn't carry them to the car for me could you, they are rather heavy.' Rebecca added cheekily as she rifled in her pocket for her badge, pulling it out as she walked past Munro into the corridor, flashing it in his face quickly.

'So which station are you working out of?' Munro questioned, grumbling under his breath as he steadied the files in his arms, resting them under his chin for stability, and followed Rebecca back towards reception.

'Bedlington.' Saul said, simply into her ear.

'I'm working out of Bedlington. I'm part of the psychiatric team there. I've been helping dear Darrie decipher some of the more technical parts of the notes for those patients who were allegedly abused by Ennis. He asked me to pick another pile up to review.' Rebecca confidently and nonchalantly informed him, tottering up to the reception desk where Henry was supping his tea.

'Did you find everything you were after Dr Evans?' Henry asked her with a broad smile, before looking beyond her and smirking as he saw Munro labouring under the weight of the files.

'Enough to be getting on with. Thank you so much for the tea and biscuits Henry, they were divine. I may be back later in the week and I am also partial to a Jaffa Cake, just if you happen to have them.' Rebecca mouthed conspiratorially while flashing him a cheeky wink, before turning and heading off for the entrance.

'So what do you think of Darrie going on a diet? Can you believe that?' Munro asked, his question tinged with an undercurrent of suspicion.

Murder Path

'He's testing you Becca. Darrie is the campest queen you will ever meet. He loves his food, but more importantly he loves his wine and would rather turn straight than diet. First name is George, and he was ridiculed at school with it because of his size. People called him Georgy Porgy, from the nursery rhyme.' Saul fed Rebecca.

Rebecca stopped dead, Munro, a few feet behind doing likewise. She slowly turned and levelled a stern glare at Munro's quizzical face.

'That really disappoints me Mick. Are you testing me? It's not something I appreciate if you are. I've spent forty seven years in psychiatric policing, and in that time, I don't think anyone has ever questioned who I am. Georgie would never go on a diet, he likes his food and wine far too much. The rambunctious queen would rather go straight than do that. Now, do I have to answer any more of your asinine questions, or can I leave and carry on with my job?' Rebecca answered brusquely, her whole body brimming with indignation.

'Sorry Ma'am.' Munro answered sheepishly. 'That was uncalled for and highly unprofessional. I apologise, and please, don't mention the diet thing to Darrie: he'll kill me.'

'I can't promise that Munro. I can't promise that I won't be having a word with DCI Strange either. He's a good friend of mine is Jerry.' she responded curtly, then turned about quickly and headed out of the reception and to her car. She opened the boot and stood aside to let Munro drop the files inside, before slamming it shut.

'They say you can tell a lot from first impressions Mick.' Rebecca started as she walked around the car and opened the driver's door, jumped in and slammed it shut, winding the window down. 'You do a lousy impression of a police officer. You need to show your colleagues a little more respect, especially those of us with the experience and wisdom of years. Thank you though for carrying the files, it saved my old back and for that I am grateful. Goodbye.' she finished, winding the window back up and starting the engine.

Murder Path

Her hands started to shake furiously on the steering wheel as the adrenaline began to wane and the nerves kicked in. 'Jesus John, that was tense. I can't believe he believed me. I wouldn't believe me. I want to get out of here, now.' she said, the red flashing light and caterwauling klaxon ringing out as the large metal gate opened in front of her.

'From what I heard, you were superb. Munro is a bit slow on the uptake and confronting him directly about questioning you was just sublime. Just breathe deep now and try to relax, tension will be gripping you right about now. Only a few minutes and you will be out of there and home free.' Saul reassured.

Rebecca eased the car into the holding area between gates, waiting for the one behind her to start closing. It stayed stubbornly open.

'The gate isn't closing John. Munro mustn't be as slow as you thought. Shit, he's running back to the car. What do I do?' Rebecca asked, the merest tinge of panic in her tone as she watched Munro quickly approaching in her rear view mirror.

'You don't panic. If he starts questioning again, lose your rag with him and threaten to call Strange.' Saul offered.

'What if he calls my bluff on that?' Rebecca asked as Munro approached the car door.

'He's not that smart, but if he does, we'll worry about it then.' Saul suggested reassuringly, his tone exuding calmness.

Munro knocked on the window and Rebecca wound it down. 'What is it man, you might have time to lounge around drinking coffee, but I have a lot of work to get through this afternoon.' Rebecca jumped in and spurted before Munro had a chance to speak.

'Sorry Ma'am, I won't keep you long, it's just you missed a folder when you dropped them in the office. I thought it might be important.' Munro answered subserviently, holding the manila binder through the open window.

'Oh.' Rebecca said, as surprise tinged with a glimmer of guilt spread across her features. 'Sorry for being so brusque Mick, and thank you for bringing it, that was very kind of you.'

'No problem Ma'am. Don't work too hard.' he responded, then walked back to the Institute. The rear gate started to close as he passed through it, shutting with a loud thud just as the one in front of Rebecca's car started to open.

'I can hear my heart thumping in my ears it is beating so hard.' Rebecca stated as she slowly manoeuvred the car out of the second gate and onto the main road.

'You are home and dry now. Get back to the apartment as quick as you can and let's start looking through those files. Hopefully we will find something which will help us figure out what the hell is going on.' Saul answered.

'I hope so. That was worse than pretending to be a Madame. So much worse.' Rebecca responded.

The car rounded a bend in the road and passed by six foot tall metal barriers surrounding the old St George's Mental hospital, which had originally been the county Lunatic Asylum. The redbrick buildings brooded silently behind the fences, weed strewn cracked concrete pathways, covered in an accumulation of rubbish, surrounding them. Most of the windows were boarded up, the few that still had glass in filthy and dull, reflecting nothing of the midday sun. Apart from one. On the top floor of the main building, looking out over the Institute opposite was a window that had been cleaned. Behind it stood a woman and a man, both watching the car as it sped by and headed off down the hill on the road back into Morpeth.

Murder Path

'Interesting.' Gabriel proffered as he watched the car until it was out of sight, then looked back towards the Institute. 'Her hands were shaking as the car went by and she was talking to someone, yet there was no one in the car.'

'Hands free phone perhaps?' Eve suggested, standing next to him dressed casual in jeans, pumps and a white t-shirt.

'No. I watched her all the way from the carpark. She was talking as soon as she got into the car. She looked anxious when the gates didn't open straight away and a little panicked when the man returned with the folder. At no time did I see her make a call. She was talking into a microphone and I would wager also had an earpiece in. I would also wager that we have just seen Rebecca Angus in disguise and the person she was talking to was Saul.' Gabriel mused. He was wearing a silver Dolce and Gabana suit which was two shades darker than his slicked back silver hair.

'What makes you think that? Should we follow her then?' Eve asked in surprise, turning to face Gabriel.

'No, we don't need to follow her. They will come looking for us soon enough. What makes me think it? I know the Fallen Angels. With them, things are never simple. I can imagine Adam has Saul on a quest to find out about his past and his family history, as well as on a mission to kill us. It would be much simpler to just tell him where he comes from, but that's not how they work. Everything is about the experience. Everything is about living the experience in order to learn. Saul will now know that he and Rebecca are in some way connected to the Seymour Family. He also knows, as he is a good Detective, that the Fielding Institute was funded by the Seymour's and that our friend Ennis was researching the Seymour family madness. He will be looking for Ennis's files. Files like those the old lady has in the boot of her car. A nervous old lady who flipped between being calm when talking to the Detective, then anxious

Murder Path

when out of his sight. A nervous old lady seemingly talking to herself. I have no doubt that it was Rebecca Angus. I wonder though?' he paused, turning to face Eve.

'What are you wondering?'

'I am wondering if we can use them, to find out about the Angels plans. Perhaps there's a way they can get you in. They don't know about you, yet. At the minute, it is only me they are looking for. I think they need to meet Madame Evangeline but then experience innocent Eve. It's time for the three of you to become friends.'

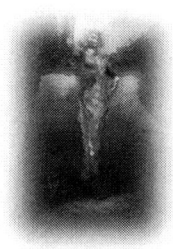

Chapter 17

The gun metal grey Ford Fiesta came to a juddering halt in the middle of the main road, tyres squealing and brakes spewing out plumes of acrid smoke as a result of the emergency stop Cruickshank had involuntarily carried out. A stream of bright brake lights and blaring horns emanated from the cars behind as irritated drivers had to stop quickly to avoid the Fiesta.

'What!' screamed Cruickshank, looking over vehemently at Strange in the passenger seat, who was holding a small brown bear tightly in his shaking hands.

'Jesus Gaynor, you scared the life out of me there. Pull over to the side, you are blocking traffic.' Strange suggested anxiously, making apologetic hand gestures to the drivers behind.

'Not until you tell me how long you have known this?' she demanded, her furious gaze not leaving his surprised face.

'Just as soon as you pull into the side.' Strange firmly reiterated.

Cruickshank glared at him, seething through gritted teeth, staring out his resolute demeanour. She broke first, as the booming of the horns from the irate drivers behind became louder. 'Fine, but you better have a bloody good explanation.' she conceded, steering the car into the kerbside and parking up. She opened her window and waved the cars behind to move on, her body language not apologetic in the slightest.

Murder Path

'Well?' she demanded, turning back to Strange.

'I saw him at the apartment opposite the one we thought they were in yesterday. He was in disguise. Dressed as an older man. He whispered that they hadn't done it, then pointed to this, leaving it on a chair by the window.' Strange answered, holding up Ian Bear again. 'I went back there a little later and got it. There was a message inside. It said that they hadn't killed the Bentley's, nor McFetrich and that the man in the photograph used to be a Fallen Angel, but had turned extreme. He also told me to trust no one, not even my closest colleagues. Why would he risk that Gaynor? Why would he stand there, looking directly at me and leave this. I didn't tell you yesterday not because I don't trust you, but because I needed time to think through what this could mean. Sorry.'

'You do realise that technically you were withholding evidence and I could come down on you like the proverbial ton of bricks. Give me one good reason why I don't, and what the hell is the significance of the bear.' she fumed, still not satisfied with his apology.

Strange looked down from her angry features to the soft toy in his hands, a slight smile breaking through his anxious face. 'He's called Ian. It's Jacob's favourite bear. One good reason why you shouldn't come down hard on me is the other piece of information in the note.'

'Which was?' she queried, irritation simmering in each syllable.

'That Jacob is alive.' he answered, quietly.

Cruickshank opened her mouth to speak, shock weaving through the irritation, replacing it with confusion, then closed it again, shaking her head, lost for words.

'I felt exactly the same Gaynor. He can't be alive. I was there when Featherstone Hall blew up. I saw Jacob on a TV screen, inside that crate in the middle of the drawing room in the Hall. I know he was in there when it exploded. How can he be alive? But then John told me to trust no one. His exact words were 'Even your closest friends, family and colleagues could be playing you, just as they have been us.' Why would he mention family, given he doesn't have a family? I think he told me about Jacob and left Ian because he has an inkling about this family connection as well. It only slipped into place when we were talking to the Professors. John found out that Gordon Ennis was studying the Seymour family, to try and help understand why there was so much mental illness in their history. It's the one thing the Professors called out might still be an issue with selective breeding. The internet logs we have from GCHQ show that they were researching the Seymour family. If John knows what we know, I think he will be after any information Ennis had about the Seymour Family. I also think it was his twin that Professor Auld thinks she recognised, because I know John never studied at the university. I think he will be trying to figure out a way to get into The Fielding Institute.'

Cruickshank looked away from Strange and out of the car window, still not speaking, the fury totally ebbed from her demeanour, replaced with sombre reflection.

Strange smiled towards her ruefully, running a hand affectionately along the pristinely straight line of the tweed skirt covering her thigh. 'I must be a bad influence. I didn't think they taught you to take a moment to distil information in this force?'

'You are definitely an influence. I just haven't decided what kind yet. Thank you for trusting me. That means a lot in the current circumstances. I understand why you didn't tell me. After all, at least two people in my own team were playing me. I understand a little more about why you think Saul and Angus are being played as well, especially given Professor Auld identified someone who looks like John. I still don't fully subscribe to that theory, but there are more facts that are starting to support it. What do you think we need to do

Murder Path

Jerry?' Cruickshank answered, looking down at his hand, avoiding his gaze, and placing one of hers on top of it, squeezing it tight.

Strange looked at the side of her downturned head with a tinge of surprise in his eyes. 'What we need to do is not lose sight of the facts, but recognise that there are people out there –Fallen Angels, The Unknown Man, even Saul and Angus- who are trying to manipulate them. Let's get Ennis's files before Saul manages to and see if we can get one step ahead in figuring this out. I'll call Mick and ask him to search the archives for anything that could help us, he's due at the Institute today anyway. John and Rebecca are still prime suspects in my mind too, but we have to fully investigate every other avenue. Come on, let's get off to Ettrick's place while I do that, we might find some more facts that can sort the wheat from the chaff.'

'Okay. Take it as read that my mind is open. Take it as read that if you touch my thigh like that in front of anyone else, I will have you up for sexual assault.' Cruickshank answered, manoeuvring the car back into traffic.

'I wouldn't have it any other way.' Strange responded playfully, before continuing. 'Right, let's give Mick a call.' He extricated his mobile from the inside jacket pocket and found Munro's details, dialled and held the phone up to his ear as it was answered on the first ring.

'Mick, you were quick in answering, is it quiet there at the institute?' Strange started, putting the phone on speaker so Cruickshank could hear as well.

'I was just going to give you a call Sir, I had my phone out ready. How well do you know Dr Marsha Evans?' Munro questioned with a slight tinge of nervousness in his voice.

'Can't say I have ever heard of anyone by that name. Why? Should I have?' Strange responded, looking over to Cruickshank quizzically.

Murder Path

'Shit, I knew it. I fucking knew it.' Munro blasphemed loudly.

'Watch the language Mick, you are on speakerphone with DCI Gaynor Cruickshank as well. Let me guess Mick,' Strange started, his brow furrowing as he ran a thumb over the sculpted ridges, throwing Cruickshank an exasperatedly resigned stare, 'She's a woman claiming to work on the Ennis case and was just picking some files up from the Institute. Close?'

'Spot on. I thought you didn't know her?' Munro responded, confusion in his voice.

'What did she look like?' Strange asked, ignoring Munro's question.

'Old lady, I'd say mid sixties, English. Very thin with a pronounced stoop. Grey haired, wearing a tweed jacket and skirt. Strong willed and confident. She had me dancing to her tune.' Munro responded sheepishly.

'Same description as the woman who rented the apartment on St Giles. It's Rebecca. It looks like they are still one step ahead.' Cruickshank offered, her tone filling with frustration once more. She pulled the car off the main road and headed down a narrow cobbled street towards Dean Village, a tranquil oasis of older redeveloped mill buildings sitting on the banks of the Water Of Leith.

'Mick, don't be too hard on yourself. We think the woman was Rebecca Angus in disguise. We think she is working with John Saul. The two of them seem to be leading all of us on a merry dance. Could you ring in a description of the old woman to the station, get that circulated and, presuming she drove up there, get a PNC check done on the vehicle and check CCTV footage around the roads in Morpeth to see where it came from and has gone. It may be too late, but could you also check the archives there at the Institute for any files to do with the Seymour family.' Strange asked.

Murder Path

'I will do Sir. You might be right about the files. I carried them to the car for her and some of them did have the name Seymour on them. I'll check for any others though and let you know.'

'Thanks Mick, give me a buzz back with an update in an hour.' Strange finished, ending the call with an irritated stab.

'She had him carry the files to her car? And he didn't question that?' Cruickshank asked, her words wearing sarcastic incredulity. She pulled the car through a narrow opening between buildings into a small courtyard and parked it behind a liveried police car with its blue lights flashing. It was sitting next to two white police vans in the centre of Well Court Hall, right on the riverbank.

'No more than you questioned Tait or Le Fenwick. Look, he's not the most gifted detective, but we are all being played, even you and I. There's a confidence that you need to convince people you are someone else. It's not just about how you look or how you act: more importantly, it's about knowing what makes the people you are trying to convince tick. They have us all at a disadvantage. Let's see if this crime scene can offer us any advantages.' Strange rebuffed with a quiet dignity as he climbed out of the car and took in the three storey sandstone buildings surrounding him.

'Let's go see then.' Cruickshank responded curtly as she climbed out of the car and headed off to an open ground floor door where a uniformed police officer stood guard. 'Afternoon Gifford. Who's on site?' Cruickshank asked the tall, rugged, slightly flustered officer.

'Trentor is here Ma'am, and Laurent. Still waiting on the Medical Examiner arriving, but I think there's no question he is dead.' Gifford offered, a timidity to his words.

Cruickshank wafted past him, ignoring the obvious signs of distress he was displaying and started ascending the staircase just inside the door. Strange approached the officer and reached out a hand, gently cusping his elbow as he spoke. 'Are you okay son? You look a little flustered?'

'Sorry Sir, it's just I have never seen anything like that in my life. It's inhuman Sir, inhuman.' Gifford apologised profusely, his words shaking in time with his body.

'Take deep breaths son, start thinking of calming images: water, fields, clouds. Every time the horrendous image pops into your mind, counter it with one of those. It's hard, but keep doing it, keep distracting your mind. Could you also make sure that there's a cordon put up around the square. I noticed a few people starting to pay attention to the police vans as we drove in.' Strange suggested reassuringly, letting his hand move from Gifford's elbow to circle his shoulder in a comforting embrace.

'Will do Sir, thank you.' Gifford answered gratefully before heading off to one of the police vans.

Strange entered the building and followed the booming footfalls of Cruickshank up the solid oak stairs. He looked up and saw her reach the landing above, where she shouted on Trentor. He reached the landing just as Trentor emerged from the entrance of another set of stairs leading up to the third floor.

'What have we got Trentor?' Cruickshank asked, her gaze scanning the wide hallway, dipping into the rooms behind the open doors. 'I can't see any signs of a disturbance.'

'In the living room Ma'am, second door on the right. You'll need to look up and trust me, you will definitely need to brace yourself.' Trentor responded. Cruickshank strode off in the direction indicated with a gruff harrumph and a condescending glare. Strange followed her, falling in alongside Trentor as he flashed the detective a reassuring smile.

Murder Path

Cruickshank abruptly stopped in the doorway, her body rocking back slightly as she raised her eye line to the tall ceiling in the room. 'Jesus Trentor, you weren't bloody kidding. What the hell is that?' she asked with shock in her voice as she gingerly stepped into the room and slowly started to circle its perimeter, eyes transfixed on the ceiling.

Strange approached the entrance and followed her gaze, his expression running through concerned, to bewildered, to horrified all in the space of a second. He started to circle the room, instinctively following Cruickshank, mirroring her transfixed gaze. Soft footfalls and the rustling swish of plastic personal protection equipment signalled the arrival of Marcel Laurent to the room. He strode in, straight to the centre and looked up to the monstrosity on the ceiling.

'It is a body Ma'am. It is a body that has had every last piece of skin peeled from it. In order to ensure the exposed muscles, tendons and organs don't fall out, it has been wrapped tightly in cling film. The body has then been nailed to the ceiling and spread-eagled in a star shape as you can see. The feathers along the length of the arms have been stapled to the exposed flesh. You can just see that a rib has been removed from his chest cavity, on the left, and that his intestines are also missing. Our skin is the largest organ in our body. It has a surface area of about two square metres and is about three millimetres thick. If you cut it into strips about a centimetre wide, then you'll have about two hundred metres of skin. That's what has been used to write the words that surround the body.' Laurent informed the detectives nonchalantly.

Cruickshank had finished circling the room and was back at the door now. She looked over to Strange, who was just finishing his revolution, and took in his gaunt, haunted expression.

'Where does this put us Strange, at an advantage or another disadvantage?' Cruickshank queried as she started to read out the

Murder Path

words, formed in slivers of skin stapled to the ceiling around the body.

'We are the Fallen Angels. I am Madame Evangeline.'

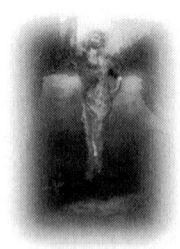

Chapter 18

Two different people, two different locations, two different musical instrument cases and both with the same word written on them. 'Unas'. That is not a coincidence. And if it's not a coincidence, it means that Ennis and McFetrich knew each other? Did they get there cases from the same place? Were they in the same band? They definitely both went to sex clubs and were both murderers. Is 'Unas' some reference to a murder club perhaps? Did they both know Gabriel, is that how they met? What's the significance of an instrument case without an instrument inside?

I hear a key slide into the front door lock. It will be Rebecca, but I can't presume. I silently vacate my seat in front of the bank of monitors and quickly and quietly step out of the study into the main, wide hallway of the apartment and position myself flat against the wall to the side of the front door. The door opens and a plethora of plastic bags rustle through the frame, twice as wide as Rebecca who shuffles in afterwards, her cheeks rouge and blowing under the weight. I relax, stepping out from the wall to help her.

'Shopping?' I query, trying to see inside the bags as I take some off her as she kicks the door shut with a foot before dropping the remaining ones onto the floor.

'Things we need for tonight.' she replies curtly, still out of breath, but also with a heightened level of emotion in her voice. She found the institute hard and I was hard on her. I drop the bags to the floor as

Murder Path

well and reach out my arms and embrace her, pulling her tight into my chest. I can feel her heart racing as she returns the embrace and squeezes into me. We stand in near silence, just holding and comforting, the only sound a slight muffled sob from Rebecca's mouth, which is buried deep in my shoulder. She pulls away and looks up at me with puffy, tear filled eyes.

'That was much harder than I thought it would be and I'm not talking about nearly getting caught by Munro. I mean going back to that cell and letting the memories of my time locked in there back into my mind. I don't know how they managed to stop me killing myself.' she says.

'Sorry I had to be so harsh and push you on. I just didn't want you to get caught.' I answer, straightening her grey wig and wiping a forming tear from the corner of her eye with my thumb.

'You've no need to be. It was me who stupidly went down to the cell. How's Jacob? Have you found anything out about the name on the trumpet case at all?' she asks, while leaning in and pecking me on the cheek before leaning down, picking up some of the bags and heading off into the study. It is incredible. In an instant the emotion is gone, the tears are dry and she is back to practical.

'Jacob's fine. We had a little chat earlier and I sat him looking out over the river. I'm sure he's trying to use different length dilations himself to say something, I'm just not sure what yet. I've started to look into 'Unas'. Other than knowing he was a pharaoh I haven't got much farther. I was just starting to look into it when you arrived.' I walk into the study after her, plonking my backside down into the seat and swivelling into the screens. Rebecca kicks her shoes off, takes off her tight tweed jacket and flings it and her grey wig onto a leather chair in the corner, then rolls a stool up beside me and sits down.

Murder Path

'Don't we need to be careful doing internet searches?' she queries, grabbing a box of tissues and rubbing the thick caked makeup off her face.

'I'm using a triple embedded server hop. The final server is somewhere in the Philippines and there is no direct connection back to this computer. Everything is proxied and encrypted. No one will ever find where we are browsing from.' I might sound like I know what those words mean, but I don't. All I do know is they won't be able to track us.

'Okay, so he's a pharaoh. Can't say I've ever heard of him. Is he famous for anything in particular?' Rebecca asks, rolling her eyes at my confident tech speak, knowing full well I am about as tech savvy as a duck billed platypus.

'Let's take a look.' I bring up the web browser I was using earlier and start scrolling through the article I had been reading on Unas. 'That's interesting: he was the first pharaoh to start a funerary cult.'

'What's one of those when it's at home? Anything like a cargo cult?' Rebecca queries, leaning closer into the screen, her right breast caressing my arm as she does, causing my loins to stir.

I gulp slightly before answering. She notices the hesitation and looks down to where my eyes are nervously glancing. 'Perv. You'll have to control your ardour a lot better than that later.' she quips jovially, turning back to the screen while pushing her breast further into my arm.

'Not quite. Cargo cults tend to be isolated tribes worshipping inanimate objects or 'cargo' washed up by the sea or river. Funerary cults are present in a number of older dynasties, particularly the Greek, Roman and Egyptian. It's the religious practices centred on the dead. Particularly how the living can pass on benefits to the dead in the afterlife and appease their wrathful ghosts. You may have heard of animals, particularly cats, and also humans being buried alive with dead pharaohs. That's what the funerary cults did and it seems our friend Unas started them.'

'Is that something Ennis and McFetrich could be involved in? All of the killers the Angels have been exposing have been radicals from current religions. Is this a group of killers reviving the older religions?' Rebecca muses, reading down through the article on the screen.

'It's a possibility and certainly something to explore. It also says Unas was the first to have 'Pyramid Texts' carved and painted on the walls of the chambers in his pyramid. Now what are Pyramid Texts?' I click on the hyperlinked words and another web page opens.

'A collection of 759 spells or 'utterances' used to protect a Pharaoh's remains. Practiced by a funerary cult. Possibly the oldest known religious texts in the world and the oldest two hundred and twenty eight of them are carved into the pyramid of Unas. One of the most famous utterances, only found in that pyramid is the 'Cannibal Hymn'. A god who lives on his fathers, who feeds on his mothers. Unas is the bull of heaven, who rages in his heart, who lives on the being of every god, who eats their entrails when they come, their bodies full of magic, from the Isle of Flame.' I recite, my mind a whirl of conjecture.

'Are they eating the rest of their victims, like Bentley was? Is that why there have never been any remains found? Do they believe that this in some way makes them gods?' Rebecca queries, shaking her head slightly as she takes in the information as well.

'Who eats their entrails when they come?' I muse, letting the words run through my mind, reminding me of McFetrich's broken body and how his gnawed entrails spelt out 'Even Fallen Angels Have Wings'. Is Gabriel trying to tell us something? Is he trying to draw us in? Or is this Adam and the Angels?

Murder Path

'It's great that you are detecting and all, but it would be useful if you told me what you were thinking. I might be able to help.' Rebecca sternly says as she knocks my arm hard with her breast, breaking my machinations.

'Sorry, it's just habit.' I say, smiling ruefully. It's how I work. It's how my mind works. It picks up a point or a fact or a word –in this case entrails- and throws it back through my recent memory to see what it hits and then explores the potential links between them. In this case McFetrich's gnawed entrails and what the significance is. Is it Adam or Gabriel trying to tell us something or even trying to draw us in? The other word that's thrown in there is 'Cannibal' and yes, I think they could be eating their victims, but that old lunatic who bit the cocks off people is singing in my mind as well. Did you get a chance to glance at any of the files?' I ask, swivelling in the chair and unbalancing Rebecca deliberately as I slouch to the floor and grab the closest plastic bag she had dropped.

'No I didn't you bastard.' she says, cuffing me over the head playfully while kneeling down at my side, grabbing another bag and removing the manila folders inside.

I pull the contents of my bag out. It's not folders. It's something leather and black with silver studs on it. I look from it, to Rebecca with a curious furrow ploughed on my brow. She is wearing a wicked grin. 'And what's this?' I ask, concerned.

'A gimp suit. You've got a mask as well, and a bit for your mouth, and some reins. Everything you need to be my slave for the evening.' she teases lewdly, but with a strength to her tone which is intoxicating and dominant. My mind does what it does and links recent memories. Gimp suit screams of Michael Angus. Screams of him fucking Rebecca wearing one, screams of morality gone wrong, screams of the utter hell she went through when she found out it was him inside the suit. How can that association, that memory, not freak her? How can it not take her back to that same suicidal place that the cell earlier managed to take her back to? How the hell does her mind work?

My face must be echoing every one of those thoughts because I see her expression change to concern and then understanding, filling with a curious empathy. She reaches over and takes hold of the gimp suit in both hands, placing it on her lap and then holds my hands tenderly, stroking the stigmata in the palms. 'It's all about control John. I can see you wondering how I could possibly be so brazen about a gimp suit when Michael wore one when I fucked him. If I were being a mum, it would upset me. But right now I'm not being a mum. I'm being a Madame. And as a Madame, I have seen many men wearing these. As a Madame, I control how I feel, I control what I do. I relinquished control when I was in that cell. I let myself become a victim. Understandable, as it was with you when Ennis mutilated your body, Sarah died and you thought Jacob and Eve were dead. We both lost control. We both wanted to die. Now we don't. Now we want to find out why? Data, information, knowledge and wisdom are your control. Being a Madame is mine. Let's see what wisdom we can find in these files, eh?'

Her beauty is the wisdom of understanding. Understanding herself. Understanding me. Not judging. Just understanding. That is a remarkable strength. I nod subserviently, an apologetic smile arcing over my slightly embarrassed features. 'Okay, but please, go gentle on my genitals when I've got the suit on, they are still a bit tender. Let's sort these files.' I finish, squeezing her hands tightly then grabbing another bag with files sticking out of it and emptying them on the floor.

'I will be gentle, but I can't promise other people will.' she teases, starting to flick through the folders. 'Do we want to sort them into Seymour's and non Seymour's, see what we have of each?' Rebecca suggests.

Murder Path

'Fine by me.' I respond, quickly flicking through the ones in my hands and splitting them as suggested.

Rebecca's eyes are darting between the tops of every folder dropped onto their relevant piles, her lips silently muttering numbers and names, until all of them are sorted. 'So, fifty six files in total, thirty eight with the name Seymour, ten with the name Howard and eight with other names, one of those with my name on it.' she reels off methodically, reaching straight for the Seymour pile and ignoring her own file. 'We should start to draw up a family tree for the Seymour's and see if we can find our cock gobbler.'

Rebecca jumps up and heads over to the incident wall, grabs a pen from the side cabinet, opens the first file and starts scribbling down a name, sex and date of birth. I can see she is distracting her mind on the other files, even though she is curious about her own. I am curious as well. No files for John Saul, no files for Robert or Gabriel Caldwell either. Still no signs of where I fit in this mess. Why would Ennis have her file hidden away? Could he have known she was possibly part of the Seymour family?

'Interesting. The first three Seymour's are women born in the 1950's. Clarissa, Jean and Margaret. Clarissa seems to be the sister that went to Italy. Jean….' she pauses.

'What?' I ask, looking up towards her from the files in my lap.

'Jean Seymour had a daughter, called Rebecca. The father was Cecil Seymour. I think I've found my parents.'

I jump up, the files slipping to the floor from my knee and cuddle into Rebecca supportively, looking over her shoulder at the file.

'It's a strange feeling. I've wanted to find out for years who my parents were, and here they are, in front of me and I just feel: numb. Is that because I was half expecting it? Is that because they are dead,

Murder Path

and I'm never going to meet them now anyway. So know I know.' she finishes, flippantly.

'It's going to feel strange, regardless of the circumstances. I suppose the important thing is that now at least, you do know. For better or for worse.' I encourage, hugging her tight.

'Exactly. At least I know. It suggests that you aren't my brother either, so let's see what we can find out about you. Let's crack on.' she smiles, wryly, and pokes her backside out to dislodge me from her body. Flipped again, from sombre to playful. I flop back on the floor and flick through the files quickly, noting an interesting name. I flip the file open.

'Freddy The Mangler. I've just found our cock gobbler. No notes on here about any next of kin. It looks like that particular line of insanity was well and truly bred out of the family.' I impart, then pick up Rebecca's file.

'I have a feeling Margaret may be the Eve's mother. There's mention in her notes of a child with that name. More interesting in all of these notes though, are the psychological techniques that are being used in their treatment. They are following a structured pattern for a wide variety of conditions: paranoia, histrionics, OCD, neurosis, narcissism...'

I interrupt her, continuing the list of conditions, reading them from her file. 'Psychopathy, schizophrenia, depression, bipolar, dissociative identity disorder.' as I stand up and walk over to her, closely watching her features fill with frustration, feeling my own simmering as well.

'Ennis carried exactly the same structured pattern of treatment out on you, which suggests that he knew you were part of the Seymour family. Which suggests that you weren't there as just Ennis's plaything. It implies that the Seymour's or bloody Adam and Eve or

Murder Path

the fucking Fallen Angels, whatever you want to call them, put you there   deliberately.'

Chapter 19

The gnarled and twisted larger intestine bulbously squeezed through the narrow drilled hole in the oak floor board and snaked off over the lacquered wood to the far side of the room in an insidious meander. Strange followed the meander, noting the teeth marks and gouges bitten out at intervals along the slimy, stinking tube as it weaved in between the sexual apparatus in the play room. He stepped over a leather whipping bench, pausing for a second to take in the precise positioning of the intestine around the leg of the bench to spell the letter 'U'. The trail progressed underneath a spanking horse, with an 'N' shaped out in the middle of its four legs, before slithering alongside a worship seat, spelling out an 'A'. From the floor, the tube then bent upwards and was nailed haphazardly to an oak door frame at about head height, before turning right onto the door, the very end of the intestine shaped into a large 'S'.

'Unas?' Strange stated as he walked through the half open door into a darkened room. A room dimly lit with subdued up lighting strategically angled from the floor to capture the exquisitely beautiful amputated arms floating gracefully in upright glass tubes. A circular room with its entire circumference, at foot wide intervals, containing delicately carved marble pillars supporting the glass tubes. There were twenty one in total. In the centre of the room stood a black metal instrument stand and on it a black leather violin case with the word 'Unas' embossed just under the handle.

Murder Path

'Yes, it's on this instrument case as well.' Cruickshank replied from the centre of the room, next to the case. Trentor was standing next to her, his eyes mesmerised by the hypnotic way the arms gently wafted in the formaldehyde. 'They are either manufactured by the same firm or perhaps they were in the same club?' Cruickshank suggested with a slight degree of irritation.

'I'm not talking about the name on the case. There are four letters snaked into the intestine across the floor. They spell 'Unas'. I'd suggest someone is trying to tell us something.' Strange answered, standing back as a look of fury burst over Cruickshank's face, directed towards Trentor as she stomped back out into the play room.

'Why didn't we see that Trentor? Laurent!' she shouted. 'Have you got photographs of these letters?' Cruikshank walked back along the intestine, right to the 'U' and sat down on the whipping bench, tapping her patent leather brogue on the oak floor impatiently.

Laurent appeared at the doorway into the playroom from the stairwell, a perplexed look on his face. 'Pardon Ma'am, letters?'

'Yes Laurent, letters. A yarking big 'S' on the door for a start, all spelling Unas. Thank you Strange, for pointing them out. Gentlemen it's not good enough. We need to have our eyes open and our wits about us. Missing something like this could put this investigation back weeks. Laurent, get photographs taken immediately. Trentor, get onto HQ and have the team start researching 'Unas' straight away. As Strange quite rightly points out, someone is trying to tell us something.'

Laurent unshouldered his camera, muttering obscenities in French under his breath and started to shoot as instructed. Trentor stood rocking, panicked uncertainty overtaking his body.

Murder Path

Cruickshank looked up to him in bemused frustration. 'Well!' she stated. 'Wasn't I clear enough? Call HQ and get them to look into the name 'Unas', it's not hard.'

'Sorry Ma'am. It's just you asked me to tell you about Ettrick's movements last night a minute ago and I haven't yet. What's more important?' Trentor meekly queried.

Strange saw thunder cross Cruickshank's features as she started to firmly stand and quickly stepped over to Trentor, placing a hand on his shoulder and giving it a reassuring squeeze. 'Quickly tell us what you have found out about his movements Barry, then you can ring in to HQ. Thirty seconds will make no difference.'

Cruickshank diverted her visible ire from Trentor towards Strange, her gaze blazing daggers directly into his eyes. 'As Strange so practically suggested Trentor, which should never have been required, spend thirty seconds telling us what you know.'

'Given that we haven't publicly announced Ettrick's death yet, I called his office just enquiring about his whereabouts yesterday.' Trentor started, filled with a little confidence from Strange's support and attempting to ingratiate himself with Cruickshank again. 'They told me that he had been in meetings in the office in Edinburgh most of the day and left at about five thirty to go to his club for dinner. As far as his secretary is aware, he went on his own. I've called the club and they can confirm he was there last night. They Maître Di said he had a drink and left with a woman but doesn't know who that was. The barman, a guy called Horncliffe, who was working last night is due in imminently and might know more. I was going to go and ask a few questions as it's only five minutes up the road.'

'Thank you Barry.' Strange butted in, not allowing Cruickshank to opportunity for sarcastic comments. 'Call into HQ now and we'll go and visit the club.'

Murder Path

Strange nodded towards Cruickshank and then headed off to the stairs, blanking her furious stare. He descended the stairwell, the deliberate thumping of patent leather brogues on the wooden floorboards echoing in his ears as she followed him, her breath and whispered fury inches away from his ears. 'Strike one Strange. You have had enough warnings about interfering with how I run my team. Two lives left, then you are out of here.'

'Gaynor.' Strange started as they reached the bottom of the stairs and vacated the building, heading off towards her parked Fiesta. 'You can strike me as much as you like, but this isn't just your investigation now, it's our investigation. I don't deliberately mean to undermine you, but we just have to move on. So, they didn't see the letters. Neither did you. But I did. That's what being a team is about.' he finished with a modicum of irritation entering his calm demeanour. He stood at the passenger door to the car, staring over the roof as she glared back at him from the driver's side.

'Being a team should never, ever excuse ineptitude.' Cruickshank started brusquely. 'That goes for me too.' she finished, her tone quieter and reflective as she climbed into the car. Strange climbed in as well.

'Why are you so hard on yourself?' he enquired with concern as he fastened his seatbelt just as Cruickshank floored the accelerator in reverse, thrusting the car out of the courtyard and back onto the cobbled street, wheel spinning parallel into the road.

She quickly flipped into first gear, flooring the accelerator, the small car jerking into life and throwing both occupants back in their seats under the force of acceleration. 'Do you know how hard it is for a woman to progress in the force? Do you know how many female DCI's we have in Scotland?' Cruickshank fumed. The car reached thirty and she took her foot off the accelerator, but not off her frustration.

Murder Path

Strange smiled ruefully before answering. 'Let me guess. Possibly the same number as there are Afro Caribbean black men in the whole of the country. 'Gaynor, you have to believe me, I'm not doing these things because of your sex, I just have a different approach to people. We motivate in different ways. It's not right or wrong, it's just different. Vive la difference as the French would say.'

'Yes, and as a person, I've achieved what I have to date by being strong, by not taking crap and by being able to be blunt and forthright with people. I will never be mumsy and affectionate and I will always feel like I am fighting. That is me. Embrace that difference.' she lectured as she pulled the Fiesta to a sudden halt directly outside the club.

'Gaynor, I do, but recognise that works both ways. I will always be tactile, I will always be affectionate and I will always be humble. Embrace that difference. Let's go and talk to Horncliffe and forget about this lover's tiff.' Strange finished, smiling, and trying to diffuse the tension.

Cruickshank glared at him, fury sparking in her eyes at his last comment, then leant across and kissed him aggressively, her tongue sliding into his surprised, willing lips. She broke off the kiss just as soon as it started. 'No, let's not forget, let's discuss it later, in bed. If we are ever going to have any kind of relationship, we have to work this out. We haven't got time in the middle of a case.'

'Okay. Later.' Strange willingly agreed.

They both vacated the Fiesta and entered the glass revolving doors of the Jing's club. They crossed the heavy pile burgundy carpet to the deep mahogany reception desk, a uniformed receptionist smiling pleasantly up at them as they arrived.

'Good afternoon Madam and Sir. What can I help you with today.' she asked pleasantly.

Murder Path

'DCI Cruickshank and DCI Strange here to see Horncliffe, the barman. Do you know if he is at work yet?' Cruickshank enquired brusquely.

'Certainly DCI Cruickshank. He arrived in about fifteen minutes ago. He will be in the bar of the dining area, it's the first door on the left down the hallway.' she informed, pointing in the relevant direction.

'Thank you.' Cruickshank replied as they both headed off down the hallway as directed. The hallway was decorated in mahogany panelling, with portraits of old patrons of the club adorning the walls. Sparkling candelabra's cast a shimmering glow onto the dark carpet as they passed under them and then entered the dining area. The room was empty, save for an older moustached man behind the bar cleaning glasses.

'Mr Horncliffe?' Cruickshank queried as she approached him.

'Yes, what can I do to help you?' Horncliffe responded. He put down the glass he was drying and leant against the bar curiously.

'DCI Cruikshank and DCI Strange. We want to ask you a few questions about Douglas Ettrick. We understand that you were working here last night when he was dining, is that correct?' Cruickshank asked bluntly.

'Yes, he was in having dinner last night and I was working. What can I help you with?'

'We understand that he was having dinner with a woman last night. Can you confirm that?'

'No, he was dining alone. However, he did have a rather expensive whiskey with a woman. Now that was quite a scene.' Horncliffe imparted, leaning over the bar surreptitiously.

'In what way?' Strange interjected.

Murder Path

'Well, she wasn't happy that I wouldn't serve her an expensive glass of whisky and started to make a scene. Mr Ettrick stepped in to try and calm her down, like the gentleman he is. She may have looked and dressed beautifully, but she had a mouth like a sewer, if you know what I mean.'

'What did they talk about?' Cruickshank asked.

'It wasn't just her mouth that was a sewer. She was here initially to meet someone else. But their conversation got quite intimate, and she suggested that if he could persuade her, she would forget her date, and spend the evening with Mr Ettrick. I don't think she was on the game, but she certainly had that attitude. She called herself 'Madame Evangeline', which is a little tasteless given what has happened with those Angels.' Horncliffe advised pompously.

'She definitely referred to herself as 'Madame Evangeline'?' Strange pressed, both he and Cruickshank leaning into the bar attentively.

'Definitely. She wasn't quiet about it either. There were quite a number of people looking on due to the crossed words I had with her. Let's just say she wasn't keeping a low profile.'

'And did she look like the 'Madame Evangeline' that you've seen on TV?' Strange asked.

Horncliffe shook his head. 'There was some resemblance, but it wasn't the same person. How could it be, that Madame Evangeline killed herself. She was tall, very lithe and beautiful. Wearing a strapless red evening dress.'

Strange shot a hand to his inside jacket pocket and pulled out half a dozen photographs. He quickly shuffled through them and held one up in front of Horncliffe.

'Did she look like this by any chance?' Strange asked directly.

Murder Path

Horncliffe nodded. 'Yes, that was her. Do you know her?'

Strange sighed. 'Tell me, what was her skin like? Was it smooth, or were there perhaps blemishes or scars underneath her makeup?'

'Her complexion was flawless, as was her skin, and there was a lot of it on show.' Horncliffe answered.

Strange shook his head, turning to look at Cruickshank's quizzical expression. He showed her the photograph.

It was a photograph of Rebecca Angus.

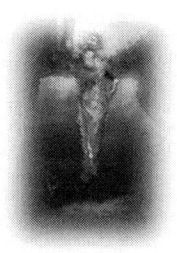

Chapter 20

I don't think I've ever worn so many clothes and felt so exposed and vulnerable. If you can call them clothes. The leather gimp suit took half an hour to get on it's so tight it is hard to breathe. My naked backside, bollocks and cock are au natural for everyone to see. Even wearing a gimp mask and knowing no one can recognise me doesn't ease the feeling of vulnerability. Rebecca is exactly the opposite, I can tell. The second after we found out about the possibility of her incarceration in the Fielding Institute being part of a plan, she just wanted to get ready for this. I understand why. This is where she is in control. She has a ritual for getting dressed as well. She had described it during the Hanlon interviews, and I had found it slightly arousing at the time when I watched them, but seeing that ritual first hand, I can honestly say that I have never been so sexually stimulated just watching a woman get dressed. The way she sashayed naked around the bedroom touching and preening, cleaning and tweaking, luxuriating in the long delicate strokes her hands striated over her willing skin was poetic. In contrast to me, who was cumbersome and clumsy pulling on my suit, she slinked into her black leather cat suit with a sensual elegance that made my penis throb. The way she slid on her black leather studded, high heel, thigh length boots was utterly delectable. And the crowning glory, positioning the long auburn wig on her head just brought Rebeca the Madame fully to life. I had seen glimpses of that person, but not experienced the full force and power of that personality. And now, I am subservient to her.

Murder Path

'The first thing to get your mind acclimatised with is the ceremony. There are implicit rules and there are explicit rules. This isn't a club like 'Sodom and Gomorrah', this is a private BDSM gathering. We signed contracts when we arrived letting our host and all the guests know what we will and won't do. There are safe words here. People will touch, stroke and kiss you implicitly, but nothing else without your explicit consent. You can say no, or in your case, I can say no for you, as you are my slave. Once I give your consent though, be aware that they may do anything you have signed up to in the contract.'

Rebecca is facing me, in the middle of a room full of half clothed people, all masked, all touching, kissing and talking, all mingling and drinking, all unwinding and exploring potential partners for the night. Her emerald eyes excitedly sparked from behind her studded mask which covers fully the top half of her face. She must see the anxiety in my stiff body, given she can't see it on my face, and she leans into me and gives me a quick hug, whispering in my ear. 'The important thing to remember is that no one knows you, no one can see who you are, so you can be anybody you want to be. You don't have to be John Saul. Don't think, 'I wouldn't do that'. Think, 'What would I like to do'. What I am going to do now, because I would like to, is parade my slave around everyone. That is going to be such a turn on. They will touch you but you absolutely cannot touch back. That's an order. It will also give us a chance to see if there are any body parts we recognise. Don't speak.' she demands sternly. 'Just nod if you are ready.'

My nod is stuttering, but it is a nod and she smiles, then pulls the reins attached to the bit in my mouth, turns her back to me, slouches the reins over one shoulder, then sashays off into the crowd, pulling me behind.

As much as I feel anxious and vulnerable, there is a sexual excitement coursing through my body, causing it to goose bump and tingle. My eyes are drawn to bare flesh as I walk by it. I pass a woman wearing

Murder Path

nothing but crotchless leather shorts and thin latticed leather strapping up her torso, covering nothing of her full pert breasts with erect, pierced nipples. She reaches out a hand as we pass and strokes it up my inner thigh, letting it linger on my balls, squeezing them gently before releasing and circling it around my flaccid cock. It reacts and gently throbs. She reaches her other hand down to her exposed, pierced and studded vagina lips, and strokes them provocatively while mouthing towards me, 'I want you in there later'. Rebecca halts and turns back, seeing the woman whisper. She leans into her and kisses her fully on the lips, letting the woman's tongue explore her mouth, watching her surprised and excited reaction when she can't find Rebecca's tongue. Rebecca breaks the kiss and whispers back. 'You can whip his arse too, if you'd like. I would like to watch you do that.'

The woman nods, and gives a gentle wave as we walk away into the crowd. There are beautiful bodies, there are normal bodies and there are small and large bodies, their owners having no perceived inhibitions in showing off any flesh. I try to look beyond the sensuality of the naked flesh, with difficulty, and see if there is anyone I recognise. People are starting to break away from the main group mingling in the large room and are heading off to open side rooms. Playrooms and dungeons. I see a short, rotund man in a rubber mankini heading off to a dungeon on the left with another man and a woman. The waddling walk looks familiar. I tap Rebecca on the shoulder and point in that direction. She nods and alters our course through the slithering crowd, more hands reaching out, touching and stroking sensually as we pass them by. We break out into a small empty area before the entrance to the room, with a sign on the door reading 'Whip Dungeon'. Rebecca stops just before entering, letting me catch up.

'What are we looking for?' she whispers.

Murder Path

I lean over to her right ear. 'Rotund man, I recognise the walk. Just trying to recall from where.'

'Okay, let's go and watch, see if you can recognise anything else. He's not a slave, so you might hear him speak.' she answers, tugging on my reins and leading me into the room.

Inside the room there are a number of whipping benches with whip racks next to them. The threesome are at a rack in the centre of the room and the rotund man is down on his knees, leaning his torso over the bench. The man and woman start fastening straps around his back, tying him to the bench. There are two spurs sticking out of the front of the bench and the rotund man rests his arms in them, his head resting in a hole in the bench. The woman straps his arms in, while the man does the same with his head. She is tall, lithe and wearing a full body rubber cat suit with a closed tummy to bum zip. There are closed zips down the curve of her breasts as well. She is wearing a full face mask, with just a hole for her mouth and black mesh covering the eyes. She looks at me and smiles as she takes a cat of nine tails whip off the stand and proceeds to thwack it over her hand with a sharp snap as she licks her lips tantalisingly. The man, average height and build with a middle age paunch and man boobs, dressed in a leather studded posing pouch and nothing else, grabs a spiked spanking mitt from the stand and slides it on to his hand, covering the letters FIST tattooed on the knuckles of his fingers. He immediately raises his hand high in the air and brings it down hard, with a glint of viciousness in his eyes, straight onto the rotund man's backside. The man whelps and jolts in his bindings, but doesn't speak.

It is fascinatingly shocking watching the masochistic flogging in front of me. I am feeling aroused. My penis is throbbing gently and starts to grow. I notice that Rebecca is stroking the swell of her breast as well. I notice the woman watching me, watching my groin as she lifts her whip high in the air and cracks it hard onto the rotund man's back. He screams and calls out 'More, by jove, more.'

The welling sexual excitement drains from my body, a cold, harsh shock replacing it, a tinge of panic its ally. I recognise the voice. I know him well. It is Darrie, the Medical Examiner. I lean into Rebecca and whisper that into her ear. She leans back over and whispers to me.

'It don't think he is here for us. He looks like a seasoned BDSM attendee. He won't recognise you, but if you are worried, we can go into another room, but I'd like to take that woman with us, there is something alluring about her. She is constantly looking over to you and eyeing up your cock.' she responds as she drops a hand down and squeezes my piece playfully.

I nod. I agree, there is something about her. The smiles she keeps throwing in my direction are too familiar. Rebecca saunters over to the whipping bench and whispers in the woman's ear. A wicked grin spreads on her face, filling the gap in her mask as she looks at me voraciously. She apologises to the middle age man, who can't hide his disappointment, a flash of anger about to explode in his eyes. But he sees Rebecca and I looking on and it quickly dissipates as he turns and unleashes his frustration onto Darrie's backside. You think you know someone, but you don't. I've been friends with Darrie for more than ten years. I knew he was gay and liked a bit of Bi, but I never knew he was into this.

Rebecca tugs at my reins, pulling the bit in my mouth for me to follow her and the lithe woman out of the room. They are whispering together and giggling as they lead me towards another room with the words 'Bondage Dungeon' on the door. Inside, they direct me to a bondage table, a bench with moving arm and leg supports.

Rebecca shuffles me into position between the leg supports and places a hand in the middle of my chest, forcing me back. 'Just relax.'

Murder Path

she mouths toward me as pushes me flat onto the bench. The woman is taking long silk scarves off a stand to the side of the bench and proceeds to run them up my legs, all the way to my exposed genitals, where the soft material stroking my cock sets it tingling again. She grins lewdly as she sees it swell, then bends down and kisses the tip of it, sucking it in gently between her lips. I can feel her teeth nibbling around the edge of my head and my body is starting to quake with the anticipation. She pulls her lips away, waggling a finger in my direction and whispers in a low sultry voice, 'Not yet.' She passes some of the scarves over to Rebecca and they both proceed to tie first my legs, then my arms to the support benches, pulling them tight around my wrists and ankles, making me squirm in a weird world of exquisite pain.

My stomach is somersaulting with nervous, anxious excitement. I am bound, I am a slave and I am not in control. Two lithe, luscious women are standing above me, both of them looking down at my body with lustful lips. I haven't got a clue what they are going to do, but the anticipation in frighteningly euphoric.

Rebecca moves first and straddles my groin, bringing the crotch of her cat suit right up against my thickening cock. She starts to gyrate up against it, the feel of the cold leather on my naked skin making me shiver. The woman steps to the other end of the bench and straddles my head, facing Rebecca. She removes the bit from my mouth then drops her crotch directly onto my face, the cold metal of the zip rubbing up against my lips. I can't see anything, I can just feel their two warm willing bodies gyrating on mine, setting every single pore of my skin alight. I feel them lean in and can hear them kissing. I hear something unzip, twice, and can only guess that the woman's breasts are coming out. I hear wet kissing, I hear dull moaning and I feel more fervour in their gyrating.

Suddenly the woman lifts off my face and turns around, her back now towards Rebecca. I can see her full breasts poking out of the cat suit,

Murder Path

the nipples hard and wet where Rebecca must have kissed them. She straddles me again and Rebecca's hands sidle around her sides and cup her breasts, grabbing the nipples and squeezing them between thumb and forefinger. The woman moans, throwing her head back as she reaches down between her legs and grabs the zip tag at the base of her spine and proceeds to unzip it.

She is directly above my face, my eyes staring wantonly at her hand coming around her backside, and at the naked flesh being exposed as she unzips. The hand passes her bum and I see the pulsing sphincter of her arse tweaking at me. My tongue cannot help itself, it pokes out, trying to reach up and lick it, but can't quite reach. The hand tantalisingly moves further, the zip pulling back, revealing the slightly gaping, moist pink lips of her throbbing vagina. My tongue can just reach these and I run its tip over her glistening lips, savouring the taste of her sweet juices. I let it follow directly behind the opening zip, impatient for the mound over her clitoris to be exposed, so I can purse my lips over it and suck hard. I see it coming into view, along with the shaven bugle of her pubic bone. The skin is slightly pulled back and the little pink button is poking out, willing me to suck it. I move my mouth closer, but my eyes get distracted as the zip is opened further.

They get distracted by ink, tattooed into the skin of her clitoral hood, spreading up as the zip opens over her pubic mound, slinking up the skin and spreading out as the bottom of her stomach comes into view and I see the full glory of the tattoo.

The tattoo of a snake.

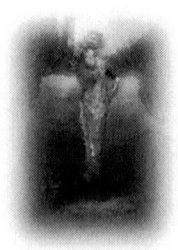

Chapter 21

The squeaking wheels of a mobile white board sent grating echoes down the empty corridor of the police headquarters. Strange flinched under the noise as he pushed it towards the Incident room, conscious of the din in the late evening solitude of this part of the station. He wheeled the board into the Incident room and down the narrow alley between rows of chairs and positioned it next to the other wall mounted white boards covered in evidence.

'Very soon, we are going to need a bigger room.' Cruickshank commented ruefully as she sat in one of the front row seats, back straight and legs crossed serenely, her skirt immaculately straightened out, looking through the evidence on the multiple boards in front of her.

Strange approached her thoughtfully and sat down in the next seat, leaning into her body so their shoulders touched. 'I think we should get the argument out of the way before we rearrange the evidence. You've done extremely well holding the 'I told you so' in for so long.'

She nudged him with a playfully sardonic smile crossing her face. 'Oh you would just love that. Your influence is having an impact on me. I am trying to look beyond the obvious facts. The obvious facts are that we now have an eye witness who has seen Rebecca Angus with one of our murder victims. The obvious facts are that her DNA was once again found at the crime scene, along with Saul's. But there's the question about her skin, isn't there?'

Murder Path

'There is.' Strange reached into his jacket pocket and pulled out his small pile of photographs, flicking through them until he found the one he wanted. He passed it over to Cruickshank. 'That was Rebecca about a month ago. As you can see her body was ravaged. Some of those burn marks, cuts and gouges are extremely deep. While I think makeup would cover them, I don't think it could completely hide them. That's why I think it can't have been her. Who it might have been, I have no idea. But given John potentially has a twin and there were two cloned Eve's, Rebecca may have a twin as well. What I can't understand is why she would want us to think she is Madame Evangeline. It doesn't make sense.'

'That's the problem at the moment Jerry, none of this is making a lot of sense. Even the facts are shifting sands. What we do know is that someone is now killing mass murderers, rather than exposing them. It is definitely a different Modus Operandi and definitely a pattern now there are two. Saul and Angus are either responsible or they are being setup. If they are responsible, we need to find them and bring them in. If they are being setup, we need to find them and bring them in. It's the only way we can help them and help ourselves get some clarity on some of these things.'

'I agree. They are either extremely dangerous or in extreme danger and possibly on their own with a young child in tow. We need to cordon off Morpeth tomorrow and tighten the net around the town. We know that Rebecca was at the Institute. We have no sightings of the car leaving the town on any of the major roads, so they must still be there.'

'Okay. A joint force operation? Will your Super be up for that, picking up our mess?' Cruickshank asked solemnly.

'It was our mess originally, we just didn't realise it was the same thing that had spilled over. It's our collective mess now and taking place

Murder Path

across both patches, so he has no choice really. We'll rally the troops in the morning.'

Cruickshank nodded, looking at the board in quiet reflection for a moment. 'Help me out for a moment while I try empathy on for size will you.' she said after a moment.

Strange smiled and nudged her shoulder. 'Sarcastic sod. Go on then, I'll help. What's on your mind?'

'Just say Saul and Angus were totally oblivious of their genetic background and links to the Seymour family. Just say they are totally innocent in all of this. Just say they have been played at every turn by the Angels and now by them and the 'Unknown man'. That is a whole heap of pressure to contain. They have already turned criminal trying to understand this for themselves. At what point, to preserve their innocence, to save themselves, do they become murderers as well: or have they already.'

'I think one of them has already and I don't think it would take too much more to push the other one over the edge. It certainly feels like someone is trying to lead them down that path.'

'How do they cope with that? Someone playing god with their lives, quite literally from inception it seems and never having control, constantly being buffeted from one play to the next.' Cruickshank mused, her eyes darting over the evidence wall reflectively.

'If you are of a religious persuasion, then someone is always playing God with your life, right from inception. Most of us cope, regardless of the slings and arrows thrown at us. Granted, for John and Rebecca it is more nuclear bombs and nerve gas, but perhaps that's what the selective breeding was trying to create, someone who could cope with those extremes and not break. Someone who could stand up to God and say, come and have a go if you think you are hard enough.'

Murder Path

Cruickshank smirked, a little giggle escaping her lips. 'Just send God to Govan, they'll sort him out. Okay, what about this 'Unknown man' then and what about Unas?' she finished, her reflective mood lifting, to be replaced with stoic determination.

'Yes Ma'am!' Strange answered sternly as he stood and approached the empty white board and started to reposition photographs and evidence. 'I think we can make an absolutely factual assumption that this 'Unknown man' is in some way connected with all of the killers that have been exposed and murdered. While the Modus Operandi of the latest two is different in terms of them being killed, the pattern of them as killers is very similar to that of the four we have in custody. They are all serial killers, they all kept body parts as trophies and we never found any of their victims. Therefore, I think we link them all on this new board, with a solid line to the 'Unknown man' because we are sure he knows them. A dotted line to John and Rebecca because they may be involved. We also link them to Unas, our old living God and pharaoh and try and figure out what the link is there. That's something worth pitching to our four in custody and see what reaction they have.'

He stood back from the board, now filled with half a dozen pictures and lines heading off onto the other boards.

'We can do that now, you are scheduled to interview O'Driscoll in about five minutes to try and get him to reveal the Unknown man's name. Drop Unas into the conversation as well.' Cruickshank suggested as she stood and approached the board. 'The only thing I would have different, is that as a solid line.' she added, taking the pen out of Strange's hand and running it over the lines to Saul and Angus.

'Okay, I'll give you that.' Strange replied.

'See, no arguments at all. We can all learn you know, even you.' Cruickshank teased as she passed by him and headed for the exit to the Incident room.

Murder Path

'Oh, I'm always learning. Every breath should be a learning experience. If it isn't, what's the point of life?' Strange responded as he grabbed a folder off a nearby seat and then followed her out of the Incident room and down the corridor towards the Interview suite.

'Have you got your interview strategy and questions ready for this?' Cruickshank asked, passing a door and pointing a thumb towards it, indicating that was where Strange needed to go.

'All ready, I've even got that titbit that Purves found for us.'

'Good luck. Just remember, O'Driscoll could well freak you out. He sees demons everywhere and will delight in telling you about yours.' Cruickshank offered as she turned a corner, heading off to the control room.

'I'll bear that in mind. I might even use it, being a Voodoo child.' Strange shouted after her. He stopped outside the interview room door and took a deep breath, shaking out his hands to dispel the nerves as he did. He quickly took something small from his pocket and popped it into his ear. 'All wired up Ma'am and ready to go. Can I enter?'

'Yes.' came Cruickshank's tinny voice through the earpiece. 'PC Barnes is in attendance in the corner. O'Driscoll is chained to the interview table. He has been violent. Did I mention that?'

'No you didn't but I'm sure if he's restrained, Barnes and I will cope swimmingly.' Strange responded and then entered the room, closing the door behind him. He walked laconically over the table, watching as O'Driscoll's slightly manic eyes swivelled towards him and started to take in every part of his person. He sat down in the seat opposite, placed the file on the table, and stretched out a hand to shake O'Driscoll's.

Murder Path

'Archbishop O'Driscoll. I am Detective Chief Inspector Jeremiah Strange. Thank you for your time this late in the evening, I appreciate your flexibility. Hopefully we won't keep you too long.' Strange introduced politely.

O'Driscoll took the offered hand and shook it inquisitively, looking from it up to Strange's welcoming face with a curious gaze. 'None of them are in you, which is good. Did you know they let them out? They could be anywhere, wreaking havoc. You are Jamaican. Are you a servant of the spirits?'

'I don't practice, but I believe. We all have our faith Archbishop and all of our faiths are aligned. My spirit is Orgu Damballa, the primordial creator of all life. He is also syncretised with your Saint Patrick. Can you see if he is with me?' Strange asked, looking directly into O'Driscoll's manic eyes.

O'Driscoll looked from Strange, to the mirror on the far wall, his features alternating between excited and droll, his manner agitated. 'No, we can't see any spirit in you tonight.'

'That's good to know. Now, could you tell me who this person is?' Strange asked, pulling a picture of O'Driscoll and the 'Unknown man' out of the folder and placing it in front of O'Driscoll.

The agitation suddenly left O'Driscoll and a calm emptiness took its place. He sat back in his seat and looked Strange directly in the eye. 'No.' he said, simply.

'Well, it's obvious you know him as he is in a picture with you. I see you were both wearing Irish Republican Army badges as well. Killers together. Was it him who helped you rationalise murder and religion. Was it him who radicalised you?' Strange asked with no emotion in his tone.

'I'm not radical.' O'Driscoll stated firmly.

Murder Path

'If buggering and asphyxiating women in the name of your religion isn't radical, then I don't know what is. It's certainly not something they teach kids at Sunday school, is it?'

'Vade retro satana. Go back Satan. Exorcism has been a part of the Catholic faith since the beginning, there is nothing radical about it.'

'Perhaps it's just your interpretation that is radical then. But then, it probably isn't your interpretation. I don't think you've got the imagination to be that horrendously inventive. I think it takes a mind like the man in the picture to dream up the kind of murder that you inflicted on those poor women.' Strange said with a hint of brusque and challenge in his tone.

O'Driscoll clenched his fists, his index finger scratching the scars of his stigmata as a manic glare entered his eyes again. 'It had nothing to do with him. It was us. We created this technique to capture demons.'

'Really? So how do you explain this then?' Strange countered, pulling a picture from the folder and placing it in front of O'Driscoll. It was a black and white picture in the front room of a derelict house. In the middle of the room was an upturned milk crate. Lying over the milk crate was a naked man, slumped dead with a plastic bag over his head and taped around his neck. 'That is Paddy O'Dwyer. He was in the IRA as well. He was also buggered and left dead like that, back in nineteen eighty eight, a full three years before your time in the IRA. You are just a copycat O'Driscoll. He showed you that technique. He taught you how to use it. He told you what to do with that knowledge. He turned you into a murderer.'

'No.' O'Driscoll fumed, white specks of phlegm gathering at the edges of his mouth, his whole body shaking with fury, his eyes bulbous with rage. 'We invented that technique, tell him Lilith.' he screamed, looking over to the mirror frantically, wanting assurances from his demon. He started yanking the chains and stood up, pulling the table, his whole body now turned towards the mirror, his argument

Murder Path

now with it. 'You can't say that Lilith, it wasn't like that. He had nothing to do with it, it was you and me. You told me how to put your spirit inside them, you told me how that would chase out the demon, you told me that the plastic bag would capture and contain them. You told me all of that! It had nothing to do with Gabriel.'

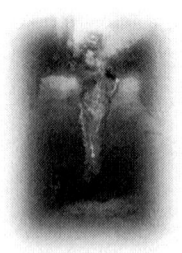

Chapter 22

'J...' I start to shout, trying to get my safe word out, but the woman with the exact same snake tattoo as Rebecca and Eve drops her glistening lady lips right over my mouth, the rest of the word muffled in her moist delight. I try to shake in my bindings but they have been fastened tight, with no give at all. I feel movement around my crotch. Even in my currently frantic state, my penis is still hard, possibly even more so. It feels like Rebecca is climbing off. Did she hear me? I don't think so, I can still see her hands caressing the woman's breasts and I can see the woman throwing her head back in pleasure as she rubs her clit up and down my nose. I don't want to lick her, I don't want to let my tongue probe her glorious vagina sitting on my face, but I can't help myself. Her musk is intoxicating, her wetness beguiling. My tongue starts to flick in and out of her.

I feel pressure being reapplied over my groin and the sensation of naked skin touching my cock sends shivers down my shaking spine. Rebecca has undone her cat suit, she is straddling me again. She is dropping herself onto me. A hand circles the base of my shaft and angles the erection upward, away from my body. In a second I feel the warmth of her wet heaven as it surrounds my tip and sucks me in, dropping all the way down my length, the muscles tight, constricting around my member. I hear her moan as she starts to ride me, slow long strokes, with her hips bucking back and forth as her torso rises up. The woman on top is leaning back now as I continue lapping her juices. She is leaning back so that Rebecca can lean over and kiss her.

Murder Path

I can just see their lips meet and watch as the woman's tongue flicks into Rebecca's mouth, circling her teeth. Rebecca's hands are frantically fondling her breasts, the nipples being pulled furiously, the woman moaning in the pleasure of the obvious pain.

I try to shake my head, to get Rebecca's attention, but she is lost in her own ecstasy. And in my eye line is the snake tattoo, writhing in its own sublime susurrations. My mind is screaming for this to stop, but every single sinew in my body is filling with the tingle of oncoming orgasm. Rebecca is riding me more frantically, her hips bunny fucking my length now, her vagina muscles squeezed tight around my swelling, hardening shaft. I start to pant quickly through the one free nostril I have, still tongue tickling the woman's cunt, her flowing juices meandering down my chin.

Rebecca's hands are squeezing the woman's breasts faster, as she bucks me faster, my whole body shaking, the glow of orgasm throbbing in my groin as my cock expands, my hips thrust and I come deep inside Rebecca's dripping vagina. She screams, pinching the woman's nipples hard at the same second I bite into her clitoris, making her moan in exquisite agony as well. I thrust again, and again, spilling my whole load inside Rebecca, before my body slumps from tense, back onto the bench, spent.

The woman climbs off my face, freeing my mouth and I take a long deep breath, ready to shout on Rebecca, but the woman speaks first.

'Beautiful John, just beautiful. I don't think I've ever been tongue fucked so intensely. And Rebecca, my nipples are on fire, they are still sending aftershocks all the way down to my clit.'

Rebecca stiffens in concern, still sitting astride me. 'What makes you think that's our names.' she says, flustered and off guard.

'Tattoo.' I say, not using names, as I look up at Rebecca. 'She's got the same tattoo as you.'

Murder Path

'This isn't a place to talk, this is a place to fuck. Let's go somewhere a little quieter and I'll tell you how I know your names. You don't need to worry. I am a friend.' the woman says as she faces Rebecca, her snake tattoo fully visible. She starts to undo the silk scarves binding me to the bench as Rebecca slowly raises herself off me. Rebecca removes the scarves from my legs and I push my torso up with an effort, energy sapped from orgasm, and stand as well.

'There's some private snuggle rooms off the back of the main room, let's go there and get to know each other.' the woman says, her mesh covered eyes looking disconcertingly evil as she sways up alongside Rebecca and takes her hand, leading her on. Rebecca follows obligingly, grabs my reins and pulls me behind.

My synapses are still firing, but not with the pheromones of sexual activity, those ones are abating. They are firing with tastes and textures. The taste of the woman's juices, the texture of her skin. Of the tincture in her voice. I watch her shapely body as she leads us into the main room, through the iniquitous menagerie, and to a door with the words 'Snuggle Room' on it. We go inside and I close it behind us, not believing what my mind is trying to tell me.

'Who are you?' Rebecca demands, her brief panic overcome, her Madame now back in full flow.

'Someone who knows what is happening to you, because it is happening to me as well.' the woman responds, hunkering down onto a deep pile of multi coloured cushions covering the floor.

'And what do you think is happening to us? What makes you think we aren't just a couple out for a fun night of debauched sex?' Rebecca counters, slinking down onto the cushions beside her. I stay standing with my back firmly against the door.

'That tattoo for a start.' she starts, pointing to Rebecca's still exposed stomach and privates. 'It's the same as mine. Exactly the same. The scars on your skin from your time in the Fielding Institute. John, the just healed weals on your penis where Dr Ennis wanked you off wearing a Vampire glove, and the stigmata on your palms. You may very well be out for debauched sex, but you are also John and Rebecca. What is happening to you is the Fallen Angels. Since last week, when Madame Evangeline appeared on TV, they have been happening to me as well. And since then, I have been looking for you.'

'How did you know we would be here tonight, if we are who you think we are?' Rebecca asks, still not admitting anything. Why would Madame Evangeline appearing on TV draw her into this and why would that cause her to look for us. What's challenging my mind at the moment is that her body language is so much like Eve's. She can't be Eve though, because we watched her die. Could she be a twin, like Adam and I.

'I didn't know, I hoped. On the balance of probability you would have been in some sex club tonight, looking for the person who killed McFetrich. Given that the scene in Edinburgh is desolated due to the recent raid, this was the next obvious choice. It's where the Edinburgh crowd have bolted. It's where he might be, looking for his next victim.'

'And why are you looking for us, if we are who you think we are?'

'For answers. A week ago my life was simple. It was shit, but it was simple. I live in a grotty bedsit in the Elephant and Castle in London and have been a prostitute since I had my first period. That was the week after I ran away from the care home I had lived in for all my thirteen years up until that point. I've had this tattoo all my life as far as I can recall. I can't remember ever having it done, it's always been there. Up until last week, I thought I was alone in the world. Up until last week, I thought I would die on my own, either beaten to death by a psycho punter, or choking on my own drunken vomit. Until I saw

Murder Path

her on TV and got a visit the very next day from someone called Adam who had a remarkable tale to tell me.'

'And what did this Adam look like?' I ask, my voice broken and hoarse.

'Just like you John. Just like you.' she reaches up and grabs the back of her head mask and starts pulling it off. 'My name is Eve, and it's not just our names that are the same.' she says, dropping the mask into her lap as she shows her face to both of us. 'We look the same as well. Exactly the same.'

The world turns again as I look in stunned amazement at the third incarnation of Eve. Rebecca's gaze reflects my incredulity as we both look upon Eve's sparkling emerald eyes, her perfect high cheekbones and her porcelain complexion. I slide down the door, my bum thumping on the floor. I reach up and grab the back of my mask and pull it off my head, shaking my hair out as I do.

'I'm John Saul. I think you are right, it's time to talk.' I say as Rebecca takes her mask off as well, still staring at Eve, and introduces herself.

'Nice to be formally introduced, even if we have already fucked. God, you and Adam are exactly the same as well.' Eve says a little coyly, an air of vulnerability surrounding her with the mask off.

'I don't suppose he told you if he and I were twins did he?' I ask, knowing what the answer is going to be.

'No. He told me that was a path you had to travel all on your own.'

'So how long have you been trying to find us, and why?' Rebecca queries, her tone suspicious.

'I got the first train from Kings Cross after Adam talked to me and was in Edinburgh four hours later. I was up there for three days looking for you. I saw you once John. I was in the Scott Monument. It's a great vantage point to view Princess Street and I was hoping I might see you from up there. I did. You rushed from Jenners when the Chinese Hag was exposing Chodak in the gardens. I think you saw me too.'

No, that was Jess I saw. I'm sure of...hold on. Throw a fact into my mind and it will bounce off memories and stir them. Jess was Annie Tait. Ten seconds after I thought it was Jess I saw up on the monument Annie Tait came running into the Gardens with DCI Cruickshank and arrested me. At the time I didn't know Jess was Annie. I do now. So it was this Eve on the gantry of the monument. But I recall her talking to someone. Who was she talking to? Adam?

'I did see you. I thought you were Jess. That is, Jess was Madame Evangeline and Eve, all three at the same time. It's gets difficult to keep track. Now there are physically two of you as well with five different identities.' I say, slightly flummoxed.

'Not quite. At least, that's not what Adam told me. Physically, there were three of us. Jessica died in a car crash. Madame Evangeline, Eve as you know committed suicide, and that leaves me.'

No, that can't be right. Jess and Eve were the same person. They had to be.

'So, you were triplets then, is that what Adam told you?' Rebecca enquires. She must be thinking the same as me, she has to be doubting it.

Eve shakes her head slightly, the question amusing her. 'Not quite, not if you believe the incredible tale Adam told me. If you were to believe him, we aren't triplets, we are clones.'

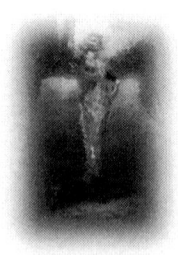

Chapter 23

We all have different ways of coping with the things in our life we can't come to terms with. Mine is building mind rooms. Neat little compartments with precise labels letting me know exactly what it is I am hiding away. They have intricate mind map locks written on the door. They are a certain sequence of memories to be triggered in a specific order if ever the contents of the room try to get out. It boils down to a distraction technique. The day Jacob was born was the very first time the rooms in my mind had ever started to wobble, since the time I built them as a teenager, to lock away the memories of my childhood. That's when the rooms started to become rickety. As we started to understand the full extent of his condition, and it felt to me that his childhood, indeed his life, was as empty as the childhood I had, there were occasional breaches from some of the rooms. I would have flashbacks to the pristine white, windowless space I lived as a child, spending days and weeks alone, on a bed with nothing but my imagination to keep me company. A limited imagination that knew very little of the outside world, apart from needles, tubes, wimples, doctors and Nun's. It was the desolate emptiness I had to hide away, the utter despair of being alone in the world. But when I was in that room, as a child, that's not how I felt. I didn't know what emptiness was, I didn't know what alone was. I just knew that room. It was only when I was moved into a care home and started to interact with people, started to have friends and the positive emotion that comes with those relationships that I started to understand the desolation and despair of being alone and needed to put those memories away.

Every single rickety room burst open when I thought that I had lost Jacob, Jess and Sarah all in the same day. I couldn't sequence the mind maps fast enough. Just as I started to lock one room back up, another would burst open. The desolate emptiness overwhelmed me and my thoughts and my emotions wanted me to kill myself. But my actions didn't, not totally. I gave myself a chance playing Russian Roulette. That chance of possibly dying, possibly staying alive helped to focus the thoughts and the emotions. It is not our thoughts or our emotions that define us. What defines us is the actions we take in reaction to them.

Why did I give myself a chance when my mind was screaming out at me just to kill myself? Is it genetic? Has that bias for action, to experience rather than to observe been bred into me? I wanted to stop myself having sex earlier, but I couldn't, the action overwhelmed the thought. Has it been bred into all of us? Rebecca should be dead. Yet she is sitting on a sofa opposite me, her eyes alive with shared experiences, chatting to Eve as though they have been family forever. Her coping mechanisms are even better than mine. Is that from the mental conditioning that took place at the Institute? And Eve, from the same background as both of us, left alone to fend for herself in the world, without any kind of family. A prostitute at thirteen. In reality, an abused child at thirteen. She seems to have taken on a totally new life in three days without even breaking stride.

We are all from the same genetic family. The same family as Adam and the other Eve's, and I have no doubt the same family as Gabriel. The Fallen Angels. It's a dark and twisted family, but it's a family. None of that explains why. Perhaps this path we have been led down for years is to build the mechanisms for us to cope: to cope with whatever the why is.

Murder Path

'It's been a part of my life away from prostitution, which might sound bizarre. After all, it's sex. But prostitution is how I earn a living, it is money and punters. Going to BDSM munches is about me. It's where I feel in control. I can do what I want, not what the punters want.' Eve tells Rebecca as my ears attune to the conversation once again, returning from my reverie. 'The snake is always a talking point. Do you think we've been branded? Is this the mark of a female Fallen Angel, sin slithering its way out of sex?' she prompts.

'Did Adam mention anything about it?' I query, interrupting their sex talk. Eve is sitting on the sofa opposite, facing Rebecca, the two of them dressed in jeans, Eve in a red t-shirt, Rebecca in a white one. Rebecca lent Eve the clothes. They are both sitting the same way, but mirrored, their legs tucked up under their backside, bodies turned in to each other with one arm draped over the back of the sofa, coffee cup in that hand. While their looks are slightly different, the body language and mannerisms are almost identical.

'No, we never got that intimate. We only talked for an hour and that was mainly about the two of you. He wanted me to find you and join your journey. He said we were all heading for the same destination and it was time to join together, to ensure we get there in one piece.'

'Did he say why now, when you had been blissfully unaware of us so far?' I ask. Rebecca throws me a reproaching look, annoyed at the detective in me coming to the fore.

'Yes, he was very specific about that. I look exactly the same as Madame Evangeline. He knew that I would start to get attention, given that she was all over prime time TV news. He didn't want me to be arrested on suspicion of being her. He didn't want me exposed to religious fanatics that might think I was her. He didn't want me to have to face punters that might get off on the thought of banging a celebrity, even though that might be good for business. What he couldn't do was just say, 'Be aware, you look like someone on the TV.'

Murder Path

What he had to do was give me the background I told you about. Otherwise, I would have just thought he was a nut job.' she answers candidly, her demeanour open and honest.

'Did you still not think he was a nut job? It is an incredible tale he told you. What did he say that made you believe him?' I pursue, deliberately ignoring Rebecca. I need to understand. I need to control. Once again, I feel more than a little blind sided.

'It's not what he said, it's what he showed me. It was a picture of a baby girl, about 18 months old, sitting in a cot, looking up into the camera. Now, it could have been any baby, not necessarily me, but it was the room that made me believe him. It was pure white, sterile, no toys, no furniture save for the cot and a single painting on the wall. A Cezanne. 'The Bathers', a group of naked men and women enjoying the sun at the side of a lake. I remember that room vividly from my childhood, and the blue robed Nuns that would come in and feed and change me. That's how I knew there was substance to his story.'

Rickety rooms rattle. Is she pressing buttons to make them open, or is she being honest. If she is pressing buttons, then she is very good at it because I feel an absolute affinity with her and an emotional empathy on a par with my feelings for Rebecca: and only after knowing her for an hour. Is that family? Or is that being skilfully played? What possible benefit could she get from playing us? If anything, it feels like she is being played as well. She hasn't asked us a single question, only answered every suspicious one I have thrown at her openly and honestly.

'It sounds like you've been on the same journey as us, and know just about the same as we do. You seriously need to ask yourself if you want to be involved with us though. I am an escaped mental patient, we are both fugitives from the law and there is a potential

Murder Path

psychopath trying to frame us for murder, if not kill us.' Rebecca intervenes and continues the conversation as I go quiet again.

'I have nowhere else to go and like it or not, I am involved. I want to know the same thing as the two of you do. I want to know why? Why has my life been a lie? Why have you been hidden from me for so long?

Why are The Fallen Angels doing this? There has to be some kind of reasoning behind this madness. There has to be some greater purpose to warrant the death of the innocent, Michael, Sarah and Jacob.' Eve finishes, her last words emotionally charged, wringing with frustration.

Rebecca looks over to me, a burning question in her eyes. Thought and emotion are telling me not to let her know the one thing she seems oblivious about. But only because trust has been pummelled out of them. But is it only because of that? Who was she talking to when I saw her at the Scott Monument? Why was she with Darrie tonight, the one person in the place who has a connection to me? Why hasn't she asked us any questions at all? Wouldn't you be just the slightest bit curious? So if she were playing me, how would I play her back? Would I even dare go down that route? My bias for action wants to tell her, it wants to take control. It is the one thing she doesn't seem to know. I nod imperceptibly.

'Jacob is not dead Eve. He is very much alive and sleeping in the next room. That's another reason why you have to think seriously about whether staying with us is a good idea.' Rebecca imparts.

It is done. She knows. For better or worse, now she knows. I just hope I'm not playing Russian Roulette with Jacob's life.

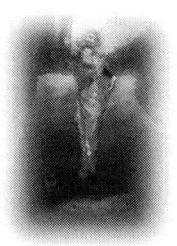

Chapter 24

A blur of light invades the darkness behind my eyelids, enacting a teasing dance as my waking eyes try to focus on it, try to pin it down. It is evasive, enjoying the chase, a watercolour sheen on the greyness of my being, an image my mind captures and stores away, for a future time, when I will paint it. The light warms, not only my eyes, but my body, my mind registering sun, my mind thinking: warm sun, that's way past day break.

My eyes open suddenly as I raise my torso from the bed quickly, reaching over to the side table to grab my watch. I can see the sun outside and from its position, would guess its nine thirty. I check the watch. Nine forty three. Shit, they will have started the morning briefing at HQ by now.

I throw the quilt back and jump out of bed naked, then trot across the room and out into the hallway. The apartment is quiet, all the other bedroom doors closed. I tap on Rebecca's door, opening it as I do. She is lying spread-eagled on her back, in the buff and asleep, her quilt crumpled on the floor. I step in and give her bare backside a quick slap, startling her.

'Come on sleepy head, it's after nine thirty. I need to check in on the morning briefing. Could you pop in on Jacob, see how he is doing for me please?'

'Bastard. Yes!' she grunts, kicking her legs randomly, trying to hit me.

Murder Path

I smile, pulling her door closed, then tiptoe along to the study and enter, heading straight for the monitors. I power them on as I slip into the chair in front of them. The leather is cold on my bare backside, setting goose bumps on my skin.

The HQ screen starts to come on and I see a full Incident room. They have a new white board at the front as well. Strange and Cruickshank are up front together, that's interesting. I hear Strange talking as the audio kicks in.

'So to recap, in order to contain and capture Saul and Angus, within the hour roadblocks will be placed on all roads in and out of Morpeth. Every vehicle coming out or going in will be checked. In addition, more than sixty uniformed officers will start house to house checks across the whole of the town. We will focus on rented and holiday accommodation first, then move on to the rest. A team will also be checking all of the industrial and office buildings in the town. DCI Cruickshank and DI Trentor will be accompanying me down to Morpeth to assist in the search.' Strange finishes, asking for any questions.

What have I missed? What has happened? Why are they moving to roadblocks this quickly?

'When are we going to the press about the two murders Sir? Before the blockade of the town?' Trentor asks. Two murders. Who is the second one? When did that happen?

'There is a conference arranged for lunchtime where we will be informing the press of the murders of McFetrich and Ettrick. We will also be informing them that Saul and Angus are the prime suspects.'

Ettrick has been murdered as well and they think we did it. Shit. I can understand why they want a cordon around the town. A little sooner than I had expected. Still, we've got an hour, and we've got contingency plans. Need to get moving though. I jump from the seat and sprint over to the door, one ear still listening to the audio.

'Rebecca. We've got problems. You need to get in here now.' I shout, turning back to the displays.

'Why are we sure they are in Morpeth Sir?' DI Purves asks.

'Rebecca Angus was as the Fielding Institute in Morpeth yesterday. We know that she took files from there relating to the Seymour family. We have CCTV footage of the vehicle she was driving leaving the hospital grounds but no CCTV footage of it leaving Morpeth. So it must still be in the town somewhere.'

'What's happening John.' Rebecca asks, stepping naked into the door space and leaning against the frame as she rubs her sleep filled eyes.

'Another murder. Ettrick. They must have evidence incriminating us otherwise they wouldn't have received the authorisation for an operation of this size. They know we are in Morpeth and they know you were at the Institute yesterday. We need to start packing and get moving. Is Eve awake?'

'No idea, I've just crawled out of bed. I'll go check Jacob first, then give her a shout.' Rebecca responds, an air of urgency entering her sleepy body as she heads off down the corridor.

'So if she was in Morpeth yesterday, does that not conflict with her being seen with Ettrick?'

What's he talking about. How could Rebecca have been with Ettrick? She was with me?

'The timeline stands up Barry. A good many witnesses saw someone looking like Rebecca Angus, but calling herself Madame Evangeline having drinks with Ettrick the night before last. The Medical Examiner puts Ettrick's time of death at around one thirty a.m. That gives more

Murder Path

than enough time for her to be in Morpeth at twelve yesterday. At this point in time, we have forensic evidence and eye witness statements saying it was Rebecca Angus with Ettrick directly before he was murdered.'

'John, have you put him in the living room, he's not in the bedroom?' I hear Rebecca call anxiously as darkness starts to chew on the pit of my stomach. I spin into the hallway, seeing her approach the living room door. I know I didn't put him in there. I know that it wasn't Rebecca with Ettrick, because she was with me. Which means it must have been a woman who looks remarkably like her, probably in disguise. A woman like Eve.

'He's not in there Rebecca.' I say, striding up to Eve's bedroom door and flinging it open. She follows me, standing at my shoulder as we both look at the perfectly made empty bed.

Eve is gone, and she has taken Jacob.

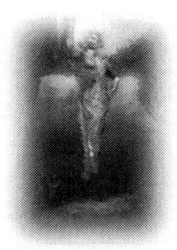

Chapter 25

'That is the main order of the morning ladies and gentleman. This is now a joint operation between the two forces, so open sharing of information and we help each other fully. I don't want any parochialism and glory hunting. We've got enough to keep us busy without in fighting. Do I make myself clear?' Cruickshank shouted out to the assembled detectives in the Incident room. A murmuring of reluctant acknowledgements surfaced around the room. Cruickshank continued. 'Good. We also need to ensure we are on top of everything else local to the case, so let's do a quick round of updates and see if we have any more intel to assist us. Trentor, is there anything from Coleen Naismith yet? She has to be in a position to interview now?'

'Ma'am, good news. She is being interviewed as we speak. The psychiatric liaison officer is with her now. I'm hopeful that we will have something from her in the next half hour.' Trentor relayed with obvious enthusiastic relish.

'It will only be good news if she has something useful to tell us Trentor. Keep your powder dry until then and as soon as you hear anything, then let me know. Did we find anything else out about McFetrich's movements?' Cruickshank reproached, hooking onto the negative in the update. Strange shot Trentor an encouraging smile as he saw the enthusiasm drain from the detective's demeanour.

Murder Path

'Nothing yet Ma'am. His car was caught on CCTV heading out of Newcastle, but we haven't found where he got off. We are still looking. We still haven't been able to locate Sheila Warren. She hasn't been seen since we bailed her after the raid. We are treating her as a missing person now and have her picture out on all the boards.' Trentor relayed flatly and factually.

'In other words, you found nothing useful and we also potentially have another victim. Keep on with the CCTV search. At least that might give us an idea about where he was killed. Right, Gregory. We now know the 'Unknown man' is called Gabriel thanks to DCI Strange. We also know that the latest two murdered murderers had a connection with something called Unas. Research suggests this could be a funerary cult following religious teachings documented in something called 'Pyramid Texts'. One of those texts is a 'Cannibal Hymn'. Given our Pastor Bentley is known to be a cannibal, we need to question him again. DCI Strange will lead the interview directly after this with you in attendance. Watch and learn Gregory.' Cruickshank stated, glaring at the moustached detective, who nodded amiably and took a long swig of his coffee.

'Right, any more for any more before we crack on?' Cruickshank asked, sternly staring at each detective in turn.

Purves raised her hand. 'Yes Ma'am. We've had a couple of bits of info back from Edinburgh Uni in the last hour. The animal DNA they found in the samples from Jessica Seymour and Madame Evangeline are from Ophiophagus Hannah, or the King Cobra. It is snake DNA. They seemed to be very excited about that and said they would call back later on today when they fully understand the implications of that type of genetic manipulation. There words, not mine.' Purves added, looking bemusedly up at Cruickshank before continuing. 'Also Professor Auld from Newcastle Uni remembered the name of the person who looked like Saul. He was called Robert Caldwell. We are looking into that name now. Nothing coming up on PNC so we are checking with other agencies. I'll keep you up to date with progress Ma'am.'

'Excellent work Purves. We have a name and useful forensic evidence. If we collectively keep that kind of hit rate up, we might start to make some headway. Right everyone. We cannot for one second take our eye of the ball on this case. There are far too many moving parts for us to get complacent. All of you need to be on your 'A' plus game. All of you need to deliver insight that will move this investigation to a conclusion. Dismissed.' Cruickshank finished, the collected detectives dispersing dejectedly, and turned to Strange, who was shaking his head disconsolately.

'I am not saying a thing Gaynor, other than people are noticing your bias.' Strange pre-empted when he saw the look of thunder flash over Cruickshank's features at his head shaking.

'You don't need to say anything Strange, your demeanour tells me exactly what you think about how I dealt with that. You are sailing close to a strike two, regardless of the fact we are now a joint task force. Just be warned. What's your thoughts on the intel back from the University?'

'I wouldn't hold out much hope on the name. We've seen how the Angels can get into computer systems and add, change or delete anything they want to. Don't get me wrong, we need to chase it up, let's just not hold our breath. Snake DNA. Now that is interesting. The blood that was poured over Michael Angus at Featherstone Hall was from snakes. Jessica and Madame Evangeline had a snake tattooed on their abdomen. Adam and Eve. The Garden of Eden. The serpent of temptation. The emissary of sin. I don't know how it helps us right now, but it is certainly starting to colour the picture of The Fallen Angels and what they may believe in.' Strange reflected, ignoring Cruickshank's indignant dig.

Murder Path

'I agree. There's nothing there at the moment that changes our course of action.' Cruickshank answered with a cursory nod of acknowledgement before being distracted by DI Trentor walking excitedly back into the Incident room. 'Don't tell me Trentor, you've forgotten something?' Cruickshank asked, admonishment in her tone.

'No Ma'am. We've just heard back from the psychiatric liaison officer. Coleen Naismith now has full recollection of what happened in the cave, and who did what.' Trentor started as he arrived beside Cruickshank and Strange.

'And!' Cruikshank demanded as he paused for breath.

'Desiderata Bentley had Madame Evangeline bound to the metal bench in the cave and was dismembering and sexually abusing her. Pastor Bentley was watching. Saul, Angus and Fenny Bentley arrived and tried to stop her. Fenny managed to lock his father up in a cage, but then Desiderata tried to strangle him. Angus stabbed Desiderata in the back to stop her. Fenny knew nothing about what his father and sister were doing. According to Naismith, he said he didn't want to live with that knowledge and threw himself on the knife sticking out of Desiderata's chest. Fenny killed himself. Another man entered the room at that point, calling himself Adam. A man who looked exactly like John Saul. She also mentioned that Adam talked to Saul about someone called 'The Man Who Makes Murderers', in reference to someone in the photographs.' Trentor blurted out in one long breath, his face flushing red both from excited anticipation and the lack of oxygen.

Strange was about to speak, but Cruickshank shushed him and responded. 'Trentor, that is brilliant news. That's the kind of lead that we need on this case. Now that she has talked to the psychiatric team, get yourself down there, we need an official statement. Start to probe a bit if she's up to it. See if she recalls anything more specific about this Adam and Madame Evangeline. Well done.' Cruickshank praised, forcing a broad smile awkwardly onto her face as she reached out a hand and shook Trentor's, who looked down at his own shaking limb in obvious surprise.

'Thank you Ma'am. I'll get down to the hospital straight away.' Trentor replied, his face unsure of how to react to the positive feedback as he turned and left the room.

'Okay.' Cruickshank started. 'We now have an eye witness who can conclusively state Angus and Saul did not murder the Bentley's. Angus may have killed Desiderata, but in trying to stop her killing Fenny. Crown Prosecution Service would see that as self defence and not give us the authority to press any charges. We can conclusively state that Saul has a twin, or perhaps a clone. Whichever, there are two of him, which backs up everything he was telling us not only about the Fallen Angels investigation, but also the Featherstone Hall investigation. We've also got another reference to this 'man who makes murderers' from another source. It looks like you could be right Jerry.' Cruickshank offered openly, without a hint of sarcasm or bitterness, only excitement an admiration singing from her tone.

'It doesn't change our approach though. The facts still tell us John and Rebecca were involved in the McFetrich and Ettrick murders. As we discussed last night, regardless if they were responsible or being played, we need to bring them in. We need to bring them in because I have an unnerving feeling they may be very close to killing, I think that's how far they are being pushed. What this does do is give us ammunition to use with Pastor Bentley. I think we might be able to break him now. We might be able to get him to tell us who Gabriel is. I think we have enough leverage to do that.' Strange answered, concern dripping from every single word.

Murder Path

'Gregory should have him in interview room four now, so let's get on with it.' Cruickshank stated simply and stomped off to the entrance of the Incident room.

Strange followed nonchalantly behind, cogitation emblazoned on his face as he hugged his files into his chest. Cruickshank didn't wait for him and headed straight past the Interview room to the control room. Strange stopped outside door four, composed himself, popped his earpiece in, and entered the room. He said nothing as he sat in a hard grey plastic seat next to Gregory, not looking at Pastor Bentley who was watching his every movement in a similar chair at the opposite side of the table. He sighed heavily as he placed the brown Manila folder on the innocuous grey table in front of him, looking at it, not Pastor Bentley. He sat back in his seat, crossed his arms, shook his head disparagingly, tutted loudly, then looked directly into Pastor Bentley's eyes, his gaze radiating disappointment.

'For the benefit of the tape. DCI Jeremiah Strange has entered the Interview room.' Strange stated, then asked simply, 'Do you feel safe Edward?'

Bentley's defiant glare twitched slightly, a fleeting glimpse of confusion entering his gaze. 'Safe? From you?' he queried.

'From anyone. I mean, you are in a pretty secure cell in a locked down isolation facility in the middle of a police station with hundreds of officers here to keep you in, and anyone else out. Does that make you feel safe?' Strange reiterated.

'Safe isn't a feeling I pay much attention to. I am here, that is all there is to it.' Bentley answered.

'I'm sure your son felt safe when he was locked up in here. Safely away from you and his sister. It must have been devastating for him to find out what the two of you had been up to. It must have destroyed him to find out that he had been unwittingly complicit in

Murder Path

leading every one of those women to you: to their deaths. But he wasn't safe here. We couldn't protect him. We couldn't stop the Fallen Angels getting in here and spiriting him away from right under our noses. I don't think we can keep you safe either.' Strange relayed without emotion.

Bentley rocked back in his seat and let out a sardonic guffaw. 'Safe from the Fallen Angels? They put me in here, why would they want to get me back out?'

'Oh, not from the Fallen Angels. From someone much worse. From Gabriel.'

Bentley's seat shot forward as his body straightened up, the laughter dissipating in an instant, to be replaced by a silent, cold glare.

'I'd like to think we can protect the four of you from him, but I don't think we can. You see, he has already killed two of your cult in the last two days. I say killed. I am being disingenuous there. He has tortured, mutilated and flayed two of your cult to death in the last two days. He must be unhappy with you for some reason?' Strange continued, calm and controlled.

'Cult, what do you mean, cult?' Bentley rumbled.

'Oh we know who Gabriel is. He's the man who makes murderers. Archbishop O'Driscoll has told us about him. Collen Naismith, who has now told us everything that happened in the cave under your house, also remembers Adam and Madame Evangeline talking about him. We know that he taught you how to murder. We know that he wanted you to radicalise your faith. We suspect that he is unhappy you have setup a religion of your own. The cult of Unas.'

Bentley stayed silent for a moment and a look of panic strayed into his eyes, before he spoke. 'I do not fear death. If it is my time, it is my time. My god will judge my worth.'

Murder Path

'It's not death you need to fear, it is dying. To say that he killed McFetrich and Ettrick would be a gross understatement. It fills me with mortal dread to think of the suffering they must have gone through before they died. To have your skin flayed from your body, every single bone broken, and your internal organs removed while still alive. Well, if that doesn't set the fear of God into you, nothing will. I don't know if we can keep you safe from that. We will try, but I don't know how successful we will be.' Strange added, not an ounce of malice in the words.

Bentley looked at Strange with a calculating expression in his eyes, no other emotion present in his still features. 'Whatever it is you think I can tell you, as you quite rightly point out, you can't save me from him, so why would I tell you anything?'

'Well, that's the thing. At least we can try to stop him. You can't. Perhaps you could tell us something that might help us find and capture him, before he comes for you: and he will come for you. What have you got to lose? If you don't tell us, you could spend days in hellish torment dying. If you do tell us, we might be able to avert that. It's your choice. I'll leave you to think it over. Just let me know when you have decided.' Strange finished nonchalantly as he stood up and headed for the door. Just as he placed his hand on the handle, Bentley spoke.

'There were six of us in the cult. Ennis, McFetrich and Ettrick. They are dead, you have me and so that leaves only two. You will never find him if you go looking, but if you find the next one of them before he does, you might have a chance.'

'The next one? There's a sequence?' Strange queried.

'Oh yes, there is always an order to his chaos. You should always watch those closest to you DCI Strange, always. The next one is George Darrie.'

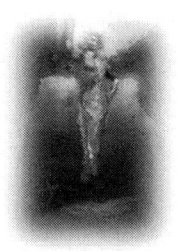

Chapter 26

My cheek explodes into a maelstrom of pain, the impact of the furious fist hitting it reverberating around my shaken skull, making me stagger, making me fall backwards onto the bed.

'You fucking cunt! You lowlife bottom sucking piece of sewage?' Rebecca spits furiously at me as she raises a foot and kicks me right in the bollocks. Electric stings singe up my veins, all the way to my aching skull, bursting the agony into my brain, causing me to double over and close my legs involuntarily: instinctive protection.

'What the fucking hell possessed you! And they thought I was mad! You've fucking killed him, you murdering bastard!'

Her words fall with pummelling fists, each one hammering home into my torso, knocking the air out of my lungs, bending my ribs under the force of her furore.

'Who the fuck do you think you are? God! You had no right. You had no right to play his life like that!' she screams as she pummels, my whole body tensing under the impact, bathed in searing pain. The words falter, and stutter, tears interweaving with the fury as the punches ease and she collapses into a gibbering heap on my chest, raking her nails deep into the skin on my arms.

'You've just got him back. Why have you killed him again?' Rebecca cries into my throbbing ribs.

Murder Path

'I haven't killed him Becca. You said it yourself. What if this is about creating the pure child of an Angel? Who do you think that child is? It is Jacob. This has always been about Jacob. I haven't killed him Becca, I've just played him. I've moved our king into check.' I slur in abject agony.

'Have you heard yourself John? Kings, check, fucking playing him. He's a boy. A beautiful, gentle, ill little boy. He's not a fucking toy. What gives you the right to use our son like that? What gives you the right to play god with his life.'

'It wasn't me who started to play him Becca, it was Adam and Eve, all the way back there in a crate in Featherstone Hall. Even before that. Even at the point of his inception. Just as they have been playing us all our lives. At some point, we had to start making moves.'

'But you had the choice not to continue playing Jacob. We had him back, and we could have just kept him safe!'

'How Becca. How could we keep him safe? For the second time in two days we have had to run. The police think we are murderers. We have a murderer after us and we have the fucking Fallen Angels ready to drop us into another whole heap of shit at any minute. No one is going to harm Jacob. For whatever reason, he is important. Not just to the Angels but possibly to Gabriel as well.' I reply in frustrated pain, my whole body aching as Rebecca lies on top of me sobbing quietly. Suddenly the sobbing stops and she sits bolt upright beside me and wipes the tears from her puffy eyes with hands still shaking furiously.

'You are a bastard John and you should have told me. I thought we were a team. Together, we might have thought of a plan. That's too late now. Jacob is in someone else's hands. What I need to understand now is, what the fuck else have you done, what's next, and have you been playing me too?' she asks, looking down on me accusingly, rabbit punching my arm to rid herself of the last vestiges of vexation. There it is again, flipping from emotional chaos to practicality in the sparkle of a tear. She's right though, I am a bastard. Why didn't I tell her what I had in mind? Do I still not trust her, is that it? Or is it a control thing? No time to reflect on that now, she just needs to know.

'I'm not playing you Rebecca, please believe that. Yes, I am a bastard. Yes, I should have talked to you. But I didn't. I can't change that. I can change what I do moving forward. I will change what I do moving forward. As for what else I have done. Well. We are being led down a path. Adam has been steering us, with leaflets left about Chillingham Hall as an example. Gabriel has been steering us, by implicating us in the murders, by suggesting that we will find out more by delving into the world of BDSM. Our path is being plotted from two sides. What I have been doing is ensuring that when we get to the end of the path, we have a fighting chance of getting out alive.' I answer, pushing my torso up on the bed into a sitting position beside Rebecca. She has stopped punching me but I can tell there is still an underlying insecurity, as much as she has switched to practical. One hand is circling the scar tissue on her other wrist.

'I see that. I realise we aren't here by chance. But what have you done?'

'Nothing dramatic. Ian Bear didn't go missing. I left him in the apartment for Strange to find. I left a message inside for him. We needed an ally inside the police. He was the only person I felt I could trust. Letting you use an open internet connection was deliberate as well. I wanted the police to see what we could see, so that they knew we are looking for the same things. I also expected them to throw a cordon around Morpeth, so signposted the fact we were here. It would have been easy to have changed your disguise and use a different car to throw them off the trail, but we need them. We know Eve is here. If she is here then Gabriel is here as well. I have a feeling Adam won't be too far away either.'

Murder Path

'When did you suspect that Eve was lying? I didn't see it, I only saw someone as confused as us.'

'Three things. When I saw her up on Scott Monument, she was talking, but there was no one with her. I think she was talking into an earpiece. That and the fact she didn't ask any questions. All of this happens to a person in such a short space of time and yet she doesn't have any questions? Even then I wasn't sure and half of me still though she was genuine. In fact, I think her background probably is. But hearing what we have just heard, I've no doubt that she is with Gabriel and probably killed McFetrich and Ettrick. I've no doubt that Gabriel is teaching her to be a murderer.'

'And you still thought it was okay to let her take Jacob?' Rebecca throws in, full of barbs and recrimination.

'It was a calculated play. Gabriel is after us because Adam put us into his line of sight. Think about it. All of the Fallen Angels involved in the reveals killed themselves. Who did Gabriel have to go after to find out why they were trying to expose him? The two people who walked away from it. The two people one of his prodigy's claimed killed his children. Us. We are the bait. We are being played. But I don't think Gabriel knows why yet either. If he did, we would be dead by now and he would have Jacob anyway.'

'So what do we do next? We don't know where Gabriel is. We don't know where Adam is. Do we just sit and await our fate?'

'That's where the third thing that makes me suspicious about her comes in.' I lean over to Rebecca and stroke her elbow, gripping the loose bit of skin there between my thumb and finger. 'Do you know that this piece of skin is called?'

'It has a name?' she responds with incredulity ringing through the words, as she reaches around and cups my hand affectionately.

Murder Path

'Surprisingly it does. It's called a Wenis. Wenis is another name for our dead pharaoh Unas. Do you know who told me that was a Wenis?'

'I have no idea.'

'George Darrie. The same George Darrie that we saw last night. The same George Darrie that was with Eve when we met her. I think she was there to target the next person in the Unas cult and I think that person is Darrie.'

'Okay, so what do we do next?'

'At this point in time, Gabriel and Eve are hopefully preoccupied with Jacob. We get to Darrie before they do. We interrogate him to find out everything he knows about Gabriel.'

'Stop, stop, one step back. We interrogate him? Interrogation suggests capture. Capture suggests hunting. Are you seriously suggesting we go on the hunt for a potential serial killer for the second time in two days?'

'I am suggesting that, yes. I'm also suggesting that we do everything we possibly can to make him talk. Even violent persuasion. But we don't need to go hunting him. I know where he lives.'

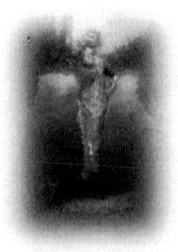

Chapter 27

The babbling stream chattered a whispering meander through the dense coppice, cold tanned leaves already falling from the tall verdant trees, adding a covering of copper to the effusion of woodland greenery sprouting from the ground. Broken branches, withered and dry, littered the foot worn pathway through the trees, which headed off in the direction of a white painted house just visible through the shimmering leaves.

Dry branches snapped underfoot as Saul stealthily moved between the trees. He was dressed in a black Armed Response Officers uniform, with a mask over his face, only the white rims of his eyes breaking the solidity of the colour. Rebecca was a stride behind him, dressed the same, carrying a small black backpack. They slowed down on approaching the edge of the wood, using the trees as cover until they were a few feet from the large expanse of lawn surrounding the white house.

Saul hunkered down behind a tree, Rebecca repeating the same stance right beside him, both of them scanning the perimeter of the grounds to the large white house in front.

'The whole of this back border opens directly into the woods. There isn't a separating fence, so if we do have to run, head this way and back to the car the way we came in. If we get separated and you get to the car first, just go. Don't wait on me.' Saul instructed as he reached over to the backpack and took out three slim metal canisters.

Murder Path

He threw one five metres to his left and one five metres to his right, dropping the third at his feet.

'Smoke flares which are Infra Red activated. You've got a key fob with the button to active them on your utility belt. If you need to activate the flares, count to ten when you pass by, and then set them off. There's only one road up to the property with fields either side, and a single entrance. I've set a trip wire on the gate. If it trips, the same key fob will vibrate. If the police come, they will enter from the front and then jump in the fields to circle around the back. So head out of the conservatory and directly across the middle of the grass. Remember the plan. Understand?' Saul questioned, looking over to Rebecca sternly.

'Affirmative Sir. Would you like a broom to stick up that stiff arse of yours?' Rebecca responded sarcastically.

'We aren't in a position to joke Rebecca. This is the world I know about, so you have to take my lead. Darrie is potentially a killer. He may be overweight and unfit, but don't underestimate what he could be capable of. We can't assume the police don't know about Darrie either, so we have to keep a watchful eye out for them. Okay. Are you ready?' Saul reproached.

Her face wore worried. 'It's just bravado John. I'm nervous, but I'm ready.' Rebecca answered. Saul leant over and kissed her full on the lips, wrapping his arms around her shoulders and pulling her in tight.

'Me too.' he answered as he broke the embrace and looked back out over the lawn once more. He quickly rummaged around in the backpack once more and pulled out a pair of binoculars, and raised them to his eyes, scanning the windows of the house.

'I can't see any movement at the back windows. The conservatory looks like it has red blinds which are shut. That's good. If we can't see in, he can't see out. There's two bushes on the way up to the conservatory doors. We head to the first, pause, recce, then head to the second, pause, recce, then up to the doors. Okay?' Saul asked, tenderness entering the tirade of orders.

'Affirmative Sir.' Rebecca answered, smiling nervously this time, her voice echoing the smile.

'Go on three. One, two, three!' Saul hissed in a loud whisper, and the two of them sprinted out from the overhanging branches and headed directly to the first bush, crouching down behind it. Saul scanned the windows of the building through the binoculars as Rebecca surveyed the perimeter. 'Clear.' they whispered in tandem, immediately sprinting off to the next bush, ducking down as they reached it. Rebecca looked around the perimeter once more, Saul observing the windows. 'Clear.' she whispered. Saul didn't respond. The binoculars were trained on the conservatory doors.

'John, what is it?' Rebecca asked, her voice full of concern.

'I don't think that's red blinds in the conservatory. I think that's blood. They may have beaten us to him. Keep your wits about you. They could still be in there.' Saul responded as he put the binoculars into the backpack, his anxious gaze not leaving the conservatory.

Rebecca shot out a hand and grabbed his knee tightly for reassurance, her heartbeat so heavy it rode down her arm and pulsed through her tightly gripping fingers straight into Saul's leg. He turned from the conservatory and saw her concern, his features filling with confidence as he reached out a hand and cupped her quivering chin. 'If we see anybody, just kick them in the privates like you did to me earlier, and you'll be just fine. Anyone who sees your foot heading towards them should worry.' he cajoled, with a calming candour.

'Now, on three, up to the doors. One, two, three.' Saul whispered firmly. They both shot up together and sprinted the last ten metres to the conservatory. Saul slid to the left of the door, Rebecca to the right, crouching down in front of the brick base, below the level of the windows.

Saul raised his head and tried to peer through the window, but his view was blurred by rivulets of blood spatter slowly meandering down the inside of it. He shuffled across to the French doors and tried to see through the small panes of glass, but they were covered in dripping trails of blood as well. He put his ear up to the glass and listened intently. Silence. He raised a hand and slowly turned the brass door handle. It turned freely, clicking open. With deliberate precision, he opened the door, a millimetre at a time, focused entirely on listening for the slightest noise from the room. Still silence. Rebecca watched Saul nervously from the opposite side of the opening door as he cautiously slid his head into the widening gap and looked inside.

Inside was a bloodbath, the inside of the windows, right the way up to the apex of the conservatory were covered in multiple criss-crossing trails of spatter, slowly oozing down to the sills. Below the sills, the trails continued onto the brickwork and over the rattan seats at the edges of the room, and on the periphery of the terracotta tiles covering the floor. The trails stopped abruptly and a circle of floor tiles around four metres in diameter were clear of any spatter. In the centre of the circle however, was a bulbous mound of glistening bodily innards sitting on top of a spread-eagled body. At the top of the mound the start of the large intestine, chewed and bitten, snaked down the steaming entrails and started to weave a tapestry of words around the body. They sidled over outstretched flesh flayed arms that had row upon row of feathers stapled directly into the exposed broken bones. They rounded a faceless head, every piece of skin stripped from it, the skull poking through, with gobbets of muscle and sinew still attached, lipless teeth wearing a macabre rictus grin. Eyes dangled down the cheeks, ripped from their sockets, the thinly stretched shining strands of optic nerve the only thing stopping them from dropping to the floor.

Murder Path

Saul started to rise slowly, his body sliding through the conservatory door, his face contorted in horror as his gaze devoured the grotesque scene in front of him. 'Jesus H Christ. Prepare your mind for carnage Becca. They got here before us. Darrie has been mutilated. Follow me in slowly, step where I step.' Saul instructed, his voice wavering with disgust as he took a stride over the spatter at the edge of the room and stepped onto the blood free tiles. Rebecca took position behind him, for the first time seeing the floor of the Conservatory.

'Fuck John. What have they done?' she whelped in terror, her emerald eyes widening with morbid curiosity, her mouth agape. She mirrored Saul's footfalls and stepped into the middle of the room, standing beside him.

'Even Fallen Angels Have Wings'. Saul read, his eyes following the trail of intestines around the body, taking in the mutilation at the same time. 'It's the same as what they did to McFetrich and Ettrick. Every bone in his body broken, the flesh ripped from the muscle, the innards exposed, the intestines bitten and chewed and a message screaming louder than a klaxon that the Angels were responsible. Somewhere on that body will be traces of you and me. This clear circular area suggests they had plastic or some covering down while dissecting him to keep any of their forensics contained, so they could easily remove any traces of them. The house is deathly quiet, so I don't think they are still here, but be on your guard. The trail of flayed skin heading out into the main house will undoubtedly lead to where Darrie kept his trophies. We won't find anything out from him now, but we might find something there. Let's go and check.' Saul suggested, still staring down at the body, beguiled by the barbarity.

'Shush.' Rebecca interjected, grabbing Saul's arm instinctively, 'What's that noise?' Saul stood still, silently listening. A low, guttural rasp entered his ears. His eyes widened in abject incredulity as they focused on the source of the sound and saw bubbles of bile and blood dribble from Darrie's opening teeth.

Murder Path

'For the love of God, he's still alive!' Saul exclaimed, dropping down quickly to his side, agitatedly looking for somewhere to put a hand on the ravaged body, to offer some comfort.

'Darrie. Can you hear me? It's John. John Saul.' Saul asked as he placed a hand on a sliver of skin still intact on Darrie's shoulder. Darrie moaned in agony, the bulbous mound of entrails and blubber on top of him moving slightly. Saul removed his hand immediately.

'She said you would come.' The words came through stuttering teeth in a slurred watery whisper, gurgling in his throat, bloody sputum flowing between the teeth with every agonising syllable.

'Eve?' Saul queried.

'Yes, Eve. His latest pretty puppet. She wants me to tell you something.' Darrie slurred, his ravaged skull turning slightly, the dangling eyeballs rocking sickeningly.

'Don't you want to tell me something George? We've been friends for years. My wife and son visited you here for fucks sake, and you're a bloody murderer.' Saul hissed through mortified lips.

'Don't ask me to apologise John, I won't. I am what I am, I have always told you that. She wants me to give you a name.' Darrie gargled, his tombstone teeth blowing blood bubbles.

'I thought you were talking about your sexuality, not your fucking murderous tendencies. Tell me the name? Is it the sixth Unas member?' Saul seethed angrily.

'I said she wanted to give you a name. Did you know you only need five organs intact to keep a person alive? One of those organs, the most important one of those organs, is the heart. If you want the name John, you will have to rip open my heart and take the silver phial she injected into it out. The name is inside.'

Murder Path

'That would kill you. You may be one sick, twisted fuck of a monster, but I'm not going to murder you George. You are alive, and you are going to pay for your crimes. Just tell me the fucking name?' Saul retorted incredulously.

'Understand one thing John. I am dead. There is only a shadow of life caressing these broken bones. I will never tell you the name. You have a simple choice. Kill me and find out, or don't, and you will never find your son.' Darrie's throat rattled out the words in a viscose stutter.

'Not going to happen...' Saul started, shock searing into his features, stopping the words dead in his throat as Rebecca pushed the mound of steaming blubber off Darrie's chest, the flesh and entrails sliding to the floor by his side. He jerked back on his haunches.

'What are you doing Becca?' he stupidly asked in a high pitched panic as he watched her reach between Darrie's broken ribs —one of them missing- and wrapped a hand around his imperceptibly beating heart.

'Putting him out of his misery. Putting you out of your misery. Saving our son.' Rebecca answered calmly as she twisted her hand and rived Darrie's heart out of his ribcage. His body jerked, what was left of his spine arching his chest up slightly, before it fell back in a heap, a low guttural whisper of air escaping his lips as the last breath seeped from his lungs, carrying the shadow of life from his body. Rebecca tore the bleeding organ apart in her bare hands, blood pouring out of the ripped valves. She rummaged her finger around inside the red flesh and grabbed the end of a small bloody tube, dropping the decimated heart disdainfully back onto Darrie's chest.

Saul looked at her hands aghast, complete consternation radiating from him, his body visibly shaking as he watched mesmerised while she unscrewed the small phial and took out a sliver of paper. Just as she did, the keyfob on her utility belt started to vibrate. They both ignored it, eyes transfixed on the paper as Rebecca unfurled it, letter after letter becoming visible, until the whole name was exposed.

'Robert Caldwell.' Rebecca recited, her voice filled with confused dismay.

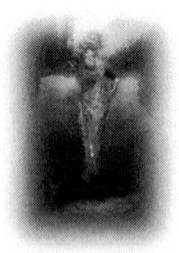

Chapter 28

A thunderous boom echoed around the conservatory, rattling the glass in the white wooden frames, slightly accelerating the drips of the spatter trails on their decent down the windows. Saul stood at one side of the slightly open French doors with Rebecca standing opposite him at the other side. Saul looked through the frosted glass of the doors from the conservatory into the main building, to the blurred outline of the front door to the house, the source of the noise. His ears were acutely listening out for sounds in the garden outside. A second boom shook the house, and through the frosted glass Saul could see the front door burst open and black shadowy shapes pour through it, an authoritative voice screaming 'Go, Go, Go!' over the diminishing boom.

Saul looked over to Rebecca with an unnerving calmness, holding his hand up as a signal for her not to move. He moved his head closer to the open French doors, ears concentrating on the garden as the shadows in the hallway moved closer to the frosted glass doors into the conservatory. He heard the shuffle of running feet on the grass outside and dropped his hand, signalling Rebecca to move.

Rebecca pushed open the French doors and staggered out, bending double, grabbing her chest as she retched, throwing up bile onto the lawn at her feet. Saul stepped out after her, surreptitiously scanning the perimeter, seeing the approaching ARO's slow down in confusion at the sight of two colleagues coming out of the French doors.

Murder Path

'Guys.' Saul shouted, 'Conservatory is clear of perpetrators, but there's a grotesque dead body in there. It's a bit too much for Five. Secure the doors and I'll take her to the perimeter to get some air and calm her down.' Saul instructed commandingly as he reached down and circled his arm around Rebecca's back, leading her quickly across the lawn.

The two closest ARO's nodded in acknowledgement and approached the French doors with expressions mixed with concern, confusion and curiosity, instinctively slowing down as they got closer. They peered around the edges of the doors, both turning their heads away quickly as they saw the slaughtered body inside. 'Jesus. I can understand why she barfed.' one said to the other.

The frosted glass doors at the far side of the conservatory burst open and gun barrels preceded the arrival of two focused ARO's on the room's threshold. 'Body in the conservatory Sir.' One of them screamed. Strange was striding down the hallway behind them, walkie-talkie in hand, his face a mask of agitated concentration.

'Why are the perimeter doors open? Your orders were to secure them, not enter!' Strange shouted as he reached the entrance to the conservatory and stood between the two ARO's looking down in disgust at the mutilated body on the floor.

'We didn't Sir, Five and Six came out, Five was barfing after seeing that and Six is keeping an eye on her.'

'What are you talking about? This is Five and Six.' Strange stated in frustration, pointing to the two ARO's either side of him, his gaze looking between the two ARO's standing in the French doors, looking towards two black garbed figures sprinting into the woods.

'For fucks sake, that's the bloody perpetrators. Get after them!' Strange screamed, raising the walkie-talkie to his mouth. 'Every ARO on the back perimeter, engage in pursuit of two perpetrators wearing

Murder Path

ARO uniform currently running into the woods. Go, go, go!' Strange watched as the two ARO's in the French doors peeled around and sprinted across the lawn, followed in turn by six other officers falling in behind them. He skirted the edge of Darrie's dead body, giving it a fleeting horrified glance, and stepped out into the garden, just as three loud reverberating explosions echoed in the still morning sunshine and a wall of thick acrid smoke engulfed the edge of the woods, billowing into the gardens.

'Fuck. They were ready for us!' Strange blasphemed to himself, before raising the walkie-talkie to his mouth, watching the ARO's ahead slow down as the smoke started to surround them. 'Focus guys, remember your training. Keep your eyes on the ground, walk at pace straight ahead. Be aware of other potential hazards. They have used smoke, so there may be trip wires. Listen for sounds. Do not shoot, repeat, do not shoot. They are dressed the same as you and they are distracting you. You do not want to shoot a colleague. Keep your ears open, keep in touch with your colleagues constantly.' Strange instructed quickly, running a frustrated hand through his silver afro.

'Very fresh meat.' Cruickshank started as she stepped out of the conservatory onto the grass next to Strange, mesmerised by the steam vaporising above Darrie. 'Did you see who they were?'

'I didn't. The two ARO's at the door might have, but they are in pursuit now. They had uniform on and looked to be travelling light. I don't see any obvious blood trails out here onto the grass. There's a pool of bile on the grass over there from the one that pretended to be sick, so we will get DNA evidence from that. I think it was John and Rebecca, but I don't think they did that to Darrie.' Strange offered, watching the thinning smoke ahead and trying to see his officers as he listened intently to the crackling of the walkie-talkie.

Murder Path

'Really? You don't think we disturbed them in the middle of the act and they bolted. Granted, they took precautions to escape, but it definitely looks to me like we caught them in the act.' Cruickshank retorted sternly, staring at Strange with a bemused ire.

'Look around the body Gaynor. The floor is clear of blood. Someone mutilated Darrie with a sheet around him and removed it. That same someone would have been covered in the splatter that's dripping down the windows. The two people running weren't covered in blood, have left no blood trail and didn't have anywhere to be carrying a bloody sheet of the size required to cover the floor in there. I think they were doing the same as we are: trying to get to Darrie before Gabriel did. We both failed miserably.' Strange replied, his words full of irritation, his expression vexed.

'Or they could have hid the sheet and the spattered clothes in the house somewhere.' Cruickshank tersely responded as she turned and headed back into the conservatory. 'I'll go and check that. At least one of use should be an objective Detective!' she sarcastically added.

'Guys, anything?' Strange queried impatiently into the walkie-talkie. A chorus of 'Negative Sir.' sang back, along with one 'There's a road at the far side of the woods Sir. I did hear a car but when I reached the road, it was gone. Nothing else Sir.'

'Shit.' Strange mumbled to himself, before speaking into the walkie-talkie again. 'Okay guys, head back to the house slowly and search the woods between the roads and the garden. Look for anything out of the ordinary. Thanks guys and be careful, there could still be traps. Frank, Simon, did you happen to see the two of them, where they both male, female, a mix?'

'Man and woman Sir.' Replied two voices in unison.

'Thanks.' Strange finished, then turned and entered the conservatory, taking in Darrie's body in front of him. He shook his head disconsolately, pained disappointment oozing from every nuance of his face. 'I thought you were my friend George. What kind of fucking monster were you?' he whispered to himself, rhetorically, before stepping around the body and heading into the main house.

ARO's were lingering in the hallway, some heading back outside the front door and scanning the perimeter. Strange followed the trail of flayed skin as it snaked across the oak floor boards in the hallway and then headed up the stairs to his left. He followed it up. At the top of the stairs it turned directly to the left and through an open door, voices coming from the room. Strange entered, his brown brogues clacking off the black marble tiles on the floor. He looked at his multiple reflections staring disconsolately back at him from the four mirrored walls, and watched them weave through the myriad of sexual apparatus set out around the room as he walked past them. They all disappeared with him, as he entered an open panel in the mirror on the far wall of the room.

The room beyond was brilliant white. The floor, walls and ceiling painted the same, the edges hard to distinguish so bright was the colour. Pinhead lights sparkled through diamante crystals embedded in every surface, their glow ululating, making the whole room mesmerizingly sway. Cruickshank was walking around the edge of the wall, behind white marble pillars set out in a circle. She was staring dumbfounded at the large glass bowls sitting on top of the pillars, watching the decapitated female heads gently floating in the liquid inside, their eyes, wide open, staring lifelessly out toward the middle of the room, where DI Munro was standing.

'Sir.' Munro started, addressing Strange. 'I recognise most of these women. I recognise their faces and the names on the plaques. From missing persons cases. Some of them from the Ennis case. Their hearts where in his jars.' he finished, morbidly transfixed by the soulless stares directed at him.

Murder Path

'We think Darrie was part of a murder club. The cult of Unas. Look on the stand over there. It's an instrument case, for a snare drum I would guess. Have a peek under the handle, you'll find the word Unas embossed in gold lettering.' Strange suggested as he started to walk around the inside of the ring of heads, following opposite Cruickshank. He looked over the top of one of the bowls, directly into Cruickshank's irritated eyes, which were glaring back at him. 'Sorry.' he mouthed. The irritation flew from her eyes and the suggestion of an appreciative smile fleetingly danced on her lips, before she was distracted, and looked down at the last bowl in the row.

'It's empty?' Cruickshank started, walking around to the front of the bowl and looking at the plaque on the pedestal, her stern small frame sagging, her shoulders hunching as she took in the name and date. Strange came up behind her, his arms reaching up and his hands embracing her shoulders with affectionate firmness. She didn't flinch away this time, but rather raised a hand of her own, and squeezed his tightly. He looked down her eye line and read the plaque too, dejection entering his gaze.

'Sheila Warren, died yesterday. Jesus, they have just bloody killed her. Where is the head then?' Strange asked.

'Sir, I think I've found it.' Munro answered.

Strange and Cruickshank turned quickly, Munro standing behind the instrument stand, the lid of the drum case in his hand. His eyes lowered, their eyes following his gaze, as all three of them looked into the open case. Cushioned softly in crushed velvet, her blonde hair lovingly styled around her tight skinned, beautifully made up face, lips a deep rouge, cheeks dappled with blusher, blue eye shadow accentuating the cobalt of her empty eyes, lay the severed head of Sheila Warren.

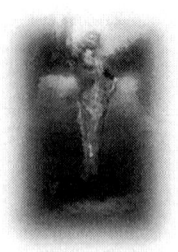

Chapter 29

What is it about us, as humans that heightens the propensity to hurt, to inflict pain, to torture and eventually to kill? Is it our animal instinct? Or is it our intelligence? Most animals kill to eat and to survive. That feels like instinct. The cat that traps the mouse, and teases it, toys with it, maims it so that it can't run away and then eventually leaves it lying there, as a present for you, twitching in the throes of death doesn't feel like instinct. That feels like intelligence without morality. Watch a hundred different cats and they will all treat a mouse in the same way. Why? What is it in their DNA that makes them do that? What makes us treat life in that way? What is it that makes people like Darrie capable of killing the women he did? What is it that makes Eve able to butcher Darrie the way she did? What is it that made Rebecca able to rip his heart out?

I pull the Mini that I am driving into a secluded lane off the main road from Mitford into Morpeth and head down to the isolated farmhouse we have rented, pulling up inside the open large garage beside it. We have travelled the two miles back from Darrie's house in silence, recovering from the exertion of outrunning the police, but also in differing modes of contemplation as to what we witnessed and did.

I step out of the car, letting the cool, clean countryside air fill my still aching lungs, hoping it will get rid of the overwhelming odour of death that still lingers in my veins. I walk up to a fence bordering a narrow strip of trees, a golf course visible beyond, and beyond that, the edge of the west side of Morpeth. Two roads head into town from here, one either side of the golf course and I can see about a mile up ahead on the roads the flashing lights of stationary police cars, where the blockades are located.

I hear the passenger door of the Mini quietly shut and feel the presence of Rebecca as she comes up behind me, wraps an arm around my waist and snuggles into my side, her eyes taking in the view in front. My body involuntarily tenses under her touch.

'I know you think I am a monster right at this moment John, for ripping his heart out. I can see that in your eyes and feel it in your body. I understand that, I really do, because I feel the same about myself. In my mind, there are three possible reasons why I killed him. One, because he was a brutal, barbaric monster that deserved death and every bit of pain Eve had inflicted on him. Two, because no one should have to suffer the torture he had endured, and he needed to be put out of his misery. Three, he had the information to potentially save Jacob in his heart, and I will literally stop at nothing and do anything to save our precious little boy. Which do you think it was?' Rebecca asks with a hollow sadness echoing from each word as she looks out over the golf course.

Perhaps our contemplations weren't that different after all. I thought exactly the same things, but with one additional, overriding impulse. Justice. I wanted Darrie to pay for his crimes. I wanted closure for all of the families of his victims. I wanted to know that our morality had prevailed. But what kind of morality is it that would save a broken, dying man, just because I think that would allow other people to be at peace. From my own experience, that never works. Knowing who the killer of your loved one is, knowing that they are locked away from society never, ever takes away the pain of the loss. I know why Rebecca did it, I know why she feels like a monster. Thirty seconds later, and it would have been me ripping his heart out.

Murder Path

I turn to her, the emotion of knowing what I am capable of spilling from my eyes as salty, stinging tears, and I hug her tightly, my head snuggling into her shoulder, my lips next to her ear.

'All three Rebecca. It was all three. And I felt exactly the same. I was ready to kill him as well. But none of those was the overriding feeling in your mind. There's the fourth one you felt. Yes, you wanted to stop his pain, to stop his suffering, then you wanted to save Jacob and lastly you wanted to kill him for what he had done. But firstly, you wanted to kill him so that I didn't have to.' I whisper in broken, agonised sobs.

I feel her body start to wrack as the emotion overwhelms her too, the quiet sniffles of suffering escaping from her quivering lips. She squeezes into me even tighter, digging her hands into my back.

'You aren't a murderer John, and I'm not going to let them make you one. You aren't like Darrie, or any of the others and certainly not like Adam.' she whispers gently.

'Neither are you. You have been totally selfless, you have killed to save. To save Fenny Bentley, to save me. You aren't a murderer. You may have killed, but you aren't a murderer. Whereas it looks like Adam, or Robert Caldwell, to give him his birth name, is exactly that.' I pull gently away from her tight embrace and look down at her blotchy, tear stained face, her sparkling emerald eyes, bloodshot and puffy, looking back up at me in saddened agony. I bend down and kiss her willing lips, letting my tongue explore her mouth, searching out the gnawed stump of her tongue, feeling its warmth and wetness, understanding the pain she would endure to save the ones she loves. Her beauty and selflessness radiates from every single injury on her body. I reluctantly break the kiss and embrace.

'So this note suggests that Adam is the sixth member of the Unas cult. Eve and Gabriel were desperate for us to know that. I can't visualise in my head a scenario where that doesn't mean Adam has killed a lot

Murder Path

of women. How could he keep up the pretence of being a murderer and an active part of that cult if he didn't? Is that a sacrifice that he made in order to infiltrate them and find out about Gabriel? Or is it just something that he wanted to do?' I muse, as we both turn and head back towards the house. I quickly pull the garage door closed on the way.

'Either way, we have his name and an address. Which Gabriel and Eve have as well. It feels like they are setting us up.' Rebecca answers, wiping the tears from her eyes with a bloodstained black sleeve, it leaving a red smear on her cheek. I rub the smudge off with my finger as we enter the front door of the farmhouse, and head off across the hallway to the study, where the monitors are set up.

'They are definitely setting us up. The question is, why? Do they know Adam is Robert Caldwell, or is it the last opportunity to get us where they want us? There is no way we can't go. This feels like the end game for us. To find out about ourselves, to travel the path back to Adam and the Angels and to expose Gabriel. We just need to figure out how the hell we manage to stay alive at the end of the game and come out of it with Jacob.' I finish, perhaps too flippantly, because flippant isn't how I feel inside. Furious is how I feel inside.

I sit down at the monitors as Rebecca pulls up a seat beside me, and reach to switch them on. Just as I do, I feel a vibration in my left arm just above the wrist. I turn to Rebecca, perplexed as she is lifting her right arm as well and pressing her thumb into a similar place. Six thrumming bursts, and then it stops.

'Did you feel that as well?' I ask.

'Six vibrations? Yes. That is the tracking implant that the Angels put into us. What the hell does that mean?' Rebecca ponders, looking at me quizzically.

Murder Path

'I have no idea. I just hope that implant is nothing more sinister than a tracker. Could they be trying to contact us? If they are, how the hell are we supposed to react? It's not like we've got a hotline or anything.' I reply in frustration.

'Let's just keep an eye on it, and if it happens again, we should perhaps consider ripping them out, like I did with the one in my other arm?' Rebecca suggests, more than seriously.

I nod in agreement and then look toward the screens that have all powered up. I open up a web browser on one of them and punch in the address we have for Robert Caldwell into Google Maps. An ariel view of Morpeth comes up, with a pin right in the middle of the house, right in the middle of town, looking out over the river, just off the main street.

'That's in a built up area and there are going to be a lot of police around. Escape routes could be tricky. Let's see. You've got three alleyways back onto the high street. You've got a footbridge fifty metres to the left over the river with three exits at the opposite side and a footbridge two hundred metres to the right with two exits. I suppose that's eight ways out. We've always got the option of jumping in the river as well. We just have to figure out how we could potentially secure those routes and setup any necessary distractions. We've also got to consider the possibility of using the police to help us, unwittingly of course.' I suggest, ruminating openly.

'What have you got in mind? I can see your plotting.' Rebecca asks, still rubbing her wrist where the implant vibrated, nervously glancing down at it occasionally.

'Jerry is in town now. Perhaps it's time to have a quiet word and bring him up to speed with everything we know and find out what else they found out at Darrie's place.' I suggest.

Murder Path

'And how are you going to do that? Call him? Do you think he'd even listen? They are going to find our real DNA all over the Darrie crime scene any minute now, with mine all over his ripped up heart. In half an hour they are holding a press conference to tell the world we are fugitives at large. He thinks we are murderers.' Rebecca says scathingly, her tone incredulous.

'Very probably, yes. But he is in Morpeth, and after that press conference, there is only one place that he is going to go. One place I can guarantee he will be visiting. I need to go and meet him there.' I answer calmly, the conversation I need to have forming in my mind.

'Are you fucking loco? Walking into the middle of town and directly up to the Police officer accountable for catching us? Not a good idea John, not a good idea at all. And how the hell are you going to know where he is?' Rebecca challenges in exasperation.

'It's where we would always meet on a Sunday, when Sarah and I took Jacob for a walk. We even had a regular bench we would sit at, with a bag of stale bread to feed the ducks. In the park by the river. He will go there because in the note I left him inside Ian Bear, I suggested that he did. I asked him to bring the bread.'

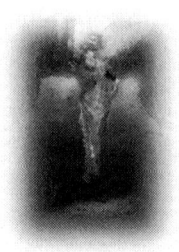

Chapter 30

Bridge Street, the main thoroughfare in the bustling market town of Morpeth was crowded not only with midday shoppers, but the streets were lined with a cavalcade of television and radio station satellite vans, national and local press vehicles with a smattering of police cars in between. Reporters were still jumping out of the vehicles and heading off down the street towards Oldgate, where the old clock tower stood imposingly in the middle of the road. They veered off to the left before reaching the tower, into the Town Hall building on the corner with Newmarket. The late arrivals tried to jostle ineffectually through the already large vociferous crowd that was gathered in the foyer to the hall. That crowd had already spilled over from the packed, noisy main hall beyond. At the front of the hall sat a single table with two chairs tucked in behind it, the surface of it covered in microphones. Behind the table stood a large banner with the Northumbria Police logo and telephone numbers emblazoned upon it and a plasma TV screen.

The old clock tower outside the hall chimed twelve and on cue, Jeremiah Strange and Gaynor Cruickshank emerged from a side door just to the right of the table. They made their way to the two seats, Cruickshank nodding sternly to the quieting crowd as she sat down staunchly, Strange smiling amiably at the reporters he recognised before nonchalantly settling in beside her.

Strange coughed, and the murmuring conversations in the hall were curtailed, quietness descending. 'Ladies and gentleman, thank you

Murder Path

for your attendance at this briefing today. I am Detective Chief Inspector Jeremiah Strange and my colleague here is Detective Chief Inspector Gaynor Cruickshank. Police Scotland and Northumbria Police are now engaged in a joint force operation as a result of the recent case in Northumberland at Featherstone Hall and the activities of the Fallen Angels case in Edinburgh last week. We have very strong evidence to suggest that those cases are linked. We also have compelling evidence to suggest that the people we are looking for may very well be hiding out in the Morpeth area. You will have noticed coming into the Town that we have roadblocks and police searches are taking place. We also have officers going door to door through the town. My colleague, DCI Cruickshank will bring you up to date with the most recent developments in the case. Please, if you could hold any questions until after that as the updates are extremely important.' Strange finished, nodding affectionately over to Cruickshank.

'Thank you DCI Strange. It saddens me to tell you this, but over the past three days, three more murderers have been exposed in circumstances similar to the Fallen Angels reveals in Edinburgh. While the circumstances are similar, they are not exactly the same. In these three cases, the serial killers we found have been murdered. Connor McFetrich, the politician for Leith in Edinburgh was found dead two days ago at his country home. We found evidence at his home of his involvement in the murder of multiple women. Douglas Ettrick, a prominent businessman from Edinburgh was found dead yesterday at his penthouse apartment in Dean Village, Edinburgh. Evidence was found in the apartment indicating his involvement in the deaths of multiple women. George Darrie, a Medical Officer working for Northumbria police was found murdered this morning at his home in Mitford, just outside Morpeth. We also found evidence associating him with the deaths of multiple women. The evidence we found at the three crime scenes also links back to the victims of Gordon Ennis who was exposed as a serial killer as part of the

Murder Path

Featherstone Hall investigation. That is one of the reasons for merging the investigation.' Cruickshank relayed factually, reading rote from the notes in front of her. She paused for a breath, taking a drink of water, the astonished gasps from the audience turning into hushed, quick conversations. A few of the reporters darted to the back of the room, into the foyer, mobile phones in hand to ring in the news quickly.

'The second, and more important reason for merging the investigations is due to the evidence we have gathered that suggests the involvement of three people in all of the recent events. Our three prime suspects are,' Cruickshank started, the TV behind her bursting into life, three pictures adorning the screen. A tumulus susurration of gasps waved around the room, interspersed with the incessant clicking of camera's going off, as Cruickshank continued. 'Detective Inspector John Saul, the escaped mental patient Rebecca Angus and a man known to us only as Gabriel. We have very strong evidence to suggest they are in the Morpeth area and feel it will only be a matter of time before we have all three in custody. We do not believe there is any direct danger to the public at this point, however we would urge the public not to approach any of them. If you do feel you have seen them, either in Morpeth or the surrounding areas in the last twenty four hours, please ring the number on the banner behind you straight away. Our officers are waiting for your calls. At this point in time, that is all the information we are able to share with you. We will answer sensible questions now, so please ensure they are related to the case and the information we have given you.' Cruikshank finished, a furore of noise breaking from the agitated, eager crowd.

Strange pointed to a journalist on the front row, and the voluminous questions ebbed, allowing him to speak.

'Jones, Daily Mail. Given a number of police employees seem to be involved in these cases, John Saul, George Darrie, Annie Tait, Richard Le Fenwick, are you concerned that the force itself has been compromised and may be in some way complicit in these events?' the bespectacled, brown quiffed reporter asked.

'It saddens me to see colleagues that I have worked with closely over the years associated with the atrocities we have witnessed in the last few weeks. I do feel that we have been manipulated by a number of people during that time, but I can assure you, the two authorities themselves are not complicit in these events whatsoever. We are, and will continue to work tirelessly until the three suspects are apprehended and the full facts of this case are exposed.' Strange answered firmly, pointing to a thirty something woman with a short auburn bob sitting in the middle of the crowd, her Parker pen waving furiously in the air as the hubbub raised in crescendo again. 'Sophie, your question please.' Strange finished, smiling at the reporter.

'Thank you DCI Strange. Sophie Middleton, The Journal. We are hearing reports that you have been consulting scientists at Edinburgh and Newcastle University about the possibility of the Fallen Angels being involved in some kind of gene manipulation. Could you confirm those reports?' Middleton asked.

Cruickshank responded before Strange had a chance. 'As with any investigation, we will examine every piece of forensic evidence. If we need to engage with subject matter experts, we will do that. We have engaged with biomedical scientists from both universities and they are assisting us with forensic examinations. As this is an ongoing investigation, I am not able to go into the details of those examinations at present.' she answered, the waving of hands and shouting of questions blaring out before her last word was even out of her mouth. 'Gentleman on the left, end of the third row, your question please.' Cruickshank shouted above the din.

'Baz Golightly, The Sun. Is it true that Ettrick and McFetrich were frequent visitors to the BDSM clubs in Edinburgh and were arrested in a raid on a club last week, but then subsequently released? Are the police covering up the sordid sexual exploits of these rich and famous people? Is that why the Angels are trying to expose them, because you aren't doing your job?' Golightly asked, sneering the questions. He was a paunchy, sweating man, with a greasy comb over strand of hair attempting to cover his almost bald head.

'I pointed out earlier that we would answer sensible questions, not ludicrous accusations. Thank you for your time ladies and gentlemen, we have an active investigation to continue. We will hold another press conference at twelve noon tomorrow where we hope to have further information.' Cruickshank answered abruptly, throwing Golightly a scathing glare as she steadfastly stood up and marched towards the side door, ignoring the verbal cacophony of questions raining through the air. Strange nodded appreciatively to the audience and followed her out into adjoining room, where Munro was waiting for them. The room was setup as a mini Incident room, with mobile whiteboards against the walls, already filled with pictures and evidence scrawl. A dozen seats were set out in three rows of four facing the boards.

'Bloody Sun reporters.' Cruickshank cursed as Strange closed the door on the incessant din. 'You ask for sensible questions and all they are ever after is sensation. Munro, any updates from the house to house or roadblock searches. Tell me we have been able to get CCTV footage of the car leaving Darrie's residence.'

Munro lethargically leant against the back wall of the room, notepad lolling in his hand as he answered. 'Not a chance on CCTV Ma'am. There are no cameras down that road. We asked around the neighbouring houses but no one had seen anything untoward at Darrie's house. We do have positive news on the car that Rebecca Angus was driving when she left the Fielding Institute. We found that parked outside apartments in Mains Place, which looks out over the Wansbeck River. One of the apartments is a holiday let. It looks empty. We've been able to contact the owner and she is meeting us

Murder Path

there in half an hour. It was rented out this week to someone called Abigail Braithwaite, but the owner didn't see her as the booking was all done over the internet. Forensics are already on their way to check the car out.'

'It sounds like they have probably abandoned it and moved on elsewhere, but we might find something that points us to where they have gone. Thanks Mick.' Strange offered encouragingly, pre-empting the snide jibe that Cruickshank's features looked about to impart. 'Were you able to find anything up at the Institute?'

'Good news there as well Sir. I was racking my brains to understand where Angus got the files from and went back to search Ennis's office. I noticed scuff marks on the carpet in front of a chest of drawers. On moving them, I found a retinal scanning device embedded in the wall. The wall was false and there was a hidden alcove behind it. For the most part it contained empty filing cabinets, which must have been where Angus got the files from. But it also contained a musical instrument case with the word Unas embossed on it. Confirms that Ennis was part of the cult Sir.' Munro offered smugly.

Just a Munro finished, the back door to the room opened from the alleyway beyond and Harris, a tall, thin man wearing spectacles and blue PPE overalls entered, slightly out of breath.

'Are you alright Ian?' Strange queried, as he walked over to Harris and placed a concerned hand on his shaking arm.

'Sorry Sir, yes, just a little in shock and I've just ran from the Forensic Van parked down by the river. I've just had the lab on the phone. They have started processing the forensics found around and on Darrie's body.' Harris replied in stuttering breaths.

'And?' Cruickshank demanded, stomping up alongside Strange, glaring up at the Forensic officer sternly. Strange shot Cruickshank an admonishing glance, before returning his gentle gaze back towards Harris.

'And they have identified three different sets of DNA. Twelve different occurrences of John Saul's DNA, from skin, hair and sweat. Twenty different occurrences of Rebecca Angus's DNA, from the same sources, but also including a sliver of fingernail found in Darrie's ripped heart.' Harris paused, catching his breath.

'And the third set?' Cruickshank prompted impatiently.

'The third set were from sexual fluids found in the folds of Darrie's foreskin, which was the only bit of skin left on his whole body. The DNA is almost an exact match to Jessica Seymour's and Madame Evangeline's. It looks as though there is a third clone.'

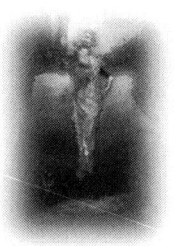

Chapter 31

Strange sat quietly on the empty park bench, feeding the incessantly quacking ducks circling his feet with broken up pieces of bread from the bag in his hands. The park was busy, the dazzling warmth of the afternoon sun having drawn families out to enjoy the open space, with its paddling pool, swings, slides and roundabouts. The screech of excited children playing tag, hide and seek and ball games vied with the quacking ducks for vocal superiority, the children slightly ahead. Strange looked down over the meandering River Wansbeck, watching the boats leisurely row by, their occupants enjoying the tranquillity of the water.

An old, grey haired man, glasses perched on his nose, wearing beige slacks, white polo shirt, a brown zig zag tank top and Jesus sandals on sockless feet ambled up the path from the river, wheezy breathing as he came to the bench on the incline and sat at the opposite end from Strange. The ducks cautiously backed away from him, but not that far they weren't in grabbing distance of the dropped bread. The old man smiled toward Strange.

'It's a long time since I've fed the ducks in this park. Tends to be something you do with littlun's rather than as a grown man.' The old man observed pointedly, in a whispered, gravelly voice.

Strange smiled back, throwing some more bread onto the ground. 'Just waiting for the kids to arrive, taking the opportunity to relive memories.' he answered, not elaborating further.

Murder Path

'When you get to my age, the memories are all that you've got. I remember playing in this park as a kid. There used to be a long wooden rocking horse where that see-saw is now. We would come here every Sunday, from the care home, and I would see the same family, with their dad, playing on it religiously. There were three daughters and a son. They often dressed in home made clothes. Once they all had purple cowboy check material matching outfits, the girls all in dresses, the boy in a shirt the same, wearing shorts, all lined up in a row, riding the rocking horse. Their dad was a man I'd see around Morpeth, putting up the market stalls, working in the bookies, doing odd-jobs here and there. They always seemed to be such a happy family. I envied them when I was younger. Looking back, years later, I wondered where their mum was, and realised that perhaps they weren't the normal family I thought they were. I think mum and dad were probably divorced, and that Sunday afternoon was his time with the kids. It made me realise that the thing I had been searching for all my life –to be part of a normal family-, didn't really exist. More importantly, it made me realise that normal is not what makes you happy. Being a part of a family and having their love, no matter what the social make up of that family, is what is important. Most of my life, I didn't think I had a family. Recently I've found out I am part of the most bizarre family in the world. It tells me I have its love, but so far it hasn't showed me that. So far, all it has tried to do is kill me.' the old man reminisced, looking longingly out over the gently flowing river.

Strange's expression changed through the telling of the tale, from disinterested, to inquisitive and then to focused, looking at every nook and cranny on the old man's face, taking in every furrow in his wrinkled complexion. 'John?' he queried, incredulously.

'Just keep feeding the ducks Jerry and look directly ahead of you, to the upper right window of the last house before the swimming baths on the opposite side of the river. You will see the window is open. You will see the black barrel of a rifle sticking out of it. Rebecca has it

Murder Path

sighted directly at your heart. If you try and apprehend me, she will shoot. All I want to do is talk Jerry. All I want to do is let you know what we know. Keep feeding the ducks.' Saul answered, his voice still whispered and gravelly.

'I didn't quite know how you were going to get here. I assumed some kind of disguise, but that is extremely convincing. Truthfully, I am not wired and there are no officers under my control in the park. Just to be clear, that doesn't mean you won't see officers wandering through the park, given what's happening in the town. They will be on the lookout for you, but right at the minute, I won't be alerting them to your presence. As far as anyone is concerned, I am taking a five minute breather after the press conference, before I walk on up the river to Mains Place and check out an apartment we suspect you were frequenting.' Strange answered calmly, throwing some more bread down for the quacking birds.

'Pleased you've found it. There's something in there that will explain how I know everything you do about this case. I'll not spoil the surprise. But I do know everything you do about this case up until you left Edinburgh this morning, including the conversation you had with Bentley that pointed you towards Darrie. That's why we were ready for you earlier. We were trying to get to him before Gabriel as well. We didn't make it.' Saul responded, his eyes dancing around the park, scrutinizing the faces of the people walking by.

'And what do you know about Gabriel. We haven't got much more than a first name and the pictures of him with the four murderers.' Strange queried.

'We know his surname, but that won't get you any further at the moment. We know that he used to be part of the Fallen Angels, but became far too extreme, even for them. We suspect I am related to him. We know that he turned people into murderers. He made the four murderers the Angels exposed and also the dead men that have been turning up recently. We know he has a female accomplice. We know that female accomplice is a third clone, Jessica and Madame Evangeline being the other two. We have met her, and she tried to convince us she was an innocent party in this, just as we are. She isn't. We suspect she killed McFetrich, Ettrick and Darrie. We suspect they were killed because of the cult they set up on their own. We know that he is trying to find out what the Angels are up to as well. We know that he will try and kill Rebecca and me. We know he has Jacob.' Saul reeled off in a whispered refrain, not even pausing for breath.

Strange sat silent for a moment, digesting the information, throwing a few more morsels of bread out for the ducks, before answering. 'Jacob. Explain to me how he is alive? I was with you when Featherstone Hall exploded. He was inside that crate in the hall.'

'He wasn't. He was in an apartment on the Quayside in Newcastle with Dr Ben Hanlon/Adam all along. What we saw was a video feed from there on the screens in the Hall. What we found in terms of DNA evidence was two pints of Jacob's blood Dr Hanlon/Adam had put inside the crate.' Saul answered, still scanning the afternoon revellers faces.

'I suspect he isn't with Gabriel by accident. I can't imagine you letting that happen.' Strange enquired, his face thoughtful.

'Correct. We had to test the validity of our new Eve. Arguably he is in mortal danger. After all, his is with a man who makes murderers and who is himself a murderer. But we think this is all about Jacob. We think Jacob is the bait that will bring this all to a head. Nothing is going to happen to him until Gabriel understands what the Angels are doing and why Jacob is so important. Right at the minute, we think he is searching for exactly the same thing you are, exactly the same thing we are: why?' Saul responded, for the first time briefly looking over at Strange, noting the DCI's furrowed, reflective brow.

Murder Path

'Why do you think Jacob is so important John? You must have a theory, you are very good at theories.' Strange asked quietly.

'You already know that the Seymour family have been selectively inbreeding for decades. I don't think you found out that historically, there is a link in the family back to a puritan minister called Cotton Mather. He believed that fossilised remains found back in the 17th century were of a Nephilim, the offspring of Fallen Angels and humans. We believe that he set the wheels in motion to purify a bloodline, by selective breeding, and latterly genetic engineering, so that the Fallen Angels could create a person with the characteristics of a Nephilim, the child of an Angel. We think that is what they believe. What you don't know is that Jacob is not Sarah's son. Sarah only carried him. Jacob is Rebecca's son. The Angels keep telling us we are special, that Jacob is special. That is the theory we are working on. But it's just a theory.' Saul imparted, looking down to the watch on his wrist, then back up to scan the surrounding park.

'It sounds incredible. I'd say farfetched even, if I hadn't seen the forensic evidence for myself.' Strange ruminated, flicking the last bits of bread out to the still ravenous ducks.

Saul's old, furrowed lips curled sardonically. 'More incredible than believing a man can be crucified, buried, then rise from the dead and turn into a holy ghost. The facts are easy. We have been selectively bred and genetically modified. It's the belief and the unwavering conviction in their faith that is hard to grasp. But then that is faith for you.'

'So what's next John. At what point does the world you are descending into consume you. At what point do you become killers too, if you haven't already. We found a part of Rebecca's fingernail in Darrie's ripped open heart.' Strange queried, scrunching up the plastic bag that had the bread in and putting it into his inside pocket, taking something else out at the same time, hiding it in his hands.

Murder Path

'We continue until we find out why. That is the path we must walk down. For Jacob's sake, we need to understand what they have done to make us. If that path leads us to murder, well, so be it. Perhaps with your help, we might not get totally consumed.' Saul answered.

'And how can I help?' Strange asked.

'You already are. You are here, you have a cordon around the town, and you are ready to spring into action when we need you. You aren't here by chance Jerry. You are here because we wanted you here. You are going to the apartment in a moment because we want you to go there. What is inside the apartment is there because we want you to find it. We also know who the sixth member of the Unas cult is. Keep an eye on PNC later today, you might see some interesting information miraculously appear on there about him.' Saul answered, turning side on and looking directly toward Strange. 'If we don't become murderers today, there is a very real chance we will be murdered. I want you to know that you have been an invaluable friend to me, to Sarah and to Jacob. I will never be able to repay the kindness that you showed us, especially the time you spent here, on this bench, sitting feeding the ducks with Jacob.'

Strange turned in as well, his eyes glistening with the dew of sorrow as he took in Saul's honest, sincere, saddened gaze. He opened his hands, Ian Bear springing from a crushed ball to a full teddy in a second. Strange reached over and handed him to Saul. Saul took the bear willingly, Strange holding his hand empathetically for a split second. 'The next time you see Jacob, give him his bear back and let him know, that if he keeps Ian Bear close, Uncle Jerry will be there for him too.'

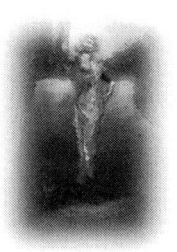

Chapter 32

Eve's slender, naked left leg sprang out from her midriff, where she had curled it up, at right angles from her standing, bare right leg. With the force of her whole body behind it, the foot slammed into Caldwell's stomach. He stumbled backwards, knees buckling as they banged into a whipping bench, his body toppling back over, his hands scrambling for grip on the leather top, trying to stop himself hitting the floor. He rolled to the right, just as Eve smacked a fist into the bench where his head had been a second earlier. He then rolled again and sprung up on his knees, and jumped beyond an upturned inversion rack, spinning around and angling the body bench toward Eve, using it as a barrier between them. Eve's firm, naked body danced agitatedly on tip-toes, her firm breasts jiggling under the incessant, adrenaline fuelled movement.

'Nice to see you get a rise out of the violence.' Eve smirked, looking at Caldwell's naked, toned torso, then down to his lengthening semi erection.

'I didn't quite think that was what you meant when you said let's play.' Caldwell countered, still catching his breath from the stomach kick.

'Are you complaining? I'm here because I thought you liked dominant women.' Eve teased as she flitted lightly from side to side, jabbing her shoulder in intermittently to intimidate Caldwell. She started to circle a stretching rack to one side of him, then swiftly jumped on top of it, crouching down, her legs akimbo, with the luscious pinkness of her open vagina lips staring enticingly toward him.

'Not complaining at all.' Caldwell responded in a rumbling tone, his gaze devouring her glistening lady garden, 'Just wondering who told you I like dominant women.' he finished.

'Ah, that would be telling. Let's just say a mutual friend. If you want to know more than that, you'll have to beat me. If you want to beat me, you'll have to catch me. If you want to catch me, you'll have to stop me beating you.' On the last word, she leapt from the bench into the air, angling her feet toward the edge of the body bench on the inversion rack, landing full on it, causing the opposite end in Caldwell's hands to shoot up on the pivot and catch him in the chest, throwing him backwards, where he landed on his backside on the black marble floor, scrabbling back immediately to the mirrored wall behind him. Eve landed gracefully, perfectly balanced on the floor, sidestepping the inversion rack as she cautiously approached Caldwell, her dazzling emerald eyes not leaving his calculating gaze: which couldn't resist ogling the curves and contours of her natural beauty.

'Perhaps I don't want you to stop beating me. Perhaps I deserve it.' Caldwell answered, his chest visibly heaving under the exertion and excitement, his penis now fully erect and tickling his belly button.

'Oh you deserve it. For every single depravity you have performed on unwilling, unwitting women, you absolutely deserve it.' Eve seethed, her body swaying hypnotically, drawing his gaze into her ululating curves. For a moment his whole being was lost in the rhythm of her mesmerising skin, but then his mind registered the underlying animosity in her sibilant words. Eve's left foot had been gently rising while her body writhed, and was at knee height, angled toward Caldwell's genitals, his bollocks fully exposed, her intended target.

Murder Path

Her foot dropped, Caldwell's eyes now focused on it, and just as it passed his raised, open knees, he clamped them shut tightly around her calf, then thrust his body to the left, pulling Eve off balance in the process. Her right side thudded into the floor, her head jolting on landing and banging into the floor as well, dazing her momentarily. Long enough for Caldwell to grab a manacle from a rack beside him and snap it onto her flailing wrist, fastening the other end to a nearby wrought iron pillory, which was bolted to the floor. Eve scrambled to her knees and lashed out her free arm, directing it straight at Caldwell's head, the fingers talon elongated, nails primed to scratch. Caldwell pulled his head back, but not quite in time, the nails raking across his left cheek.

Eve spun around and stood, dragging the manacle up the frame of the pillory, getting ready for a retaliatory strike, looking towards Caldwell's face to see what damage her razor nails had inflicted. Caldwell stood slowly, just out of her reach, his head bowed down, taking in her sweating, heaving body from foot, all the way up to her defiant face, where the defiant expression turned confused as she saw the impact of her nails. There wasn't any blood. There were rips in the skin, flaps of it hanging loosely on his cheek, but no blood.

'Gabriel has taught you well. You are a strong dominant woman who knows how to use her body and mind to gain control. The verbal foreplay earlier was particularly enlightening. He has evolved his techniques. But there is one thing, perhaps, that he neglected to tell you.' Caldwell started, looking directly into Eve's resolute glare, which was at odds with the obvious confusion she was trying to hide in her eyes. He started to pick away at the loose bits of skin on his cheek, revealing real skin below the prosthetic over layer.

'And what would that one thing be?' Eve asked sternly, a realisation forming on her face, entering her tensed and expectant body, making it even more alert, making her step back a few paces, in line with the pillory rather than in front of it.

Murder Path

Caldwell wriggled his fingers inside the hole in the prosthetic skin on his cheek and forced them inside, ripping it along the line of his nose, right the way to his other cheek. He pulled the bottom half of the flap firstly off his chin, then secondly up over his eyes and forehead, revealing the wry, brooding smile and intensely searing eyes of Adam. 'Probably the most important thing he should have told you, if he suspected for one minute it was me you were trying to play. Gabriel and I grew up together. I taught him everything about mental and physical manipulation that he knows. From the creative ways I have seen him show his disciples how to murder, he has definitely evolved them, but the basics will always remain the same. I'm a man, expose your genitalia at me and I will be mesmerised by it. Sashay your body towards me, with seductive, fuck me eyes, and I am bound to be ensnared in your hypnotic, nymphotic dance. On any other man, who wasn't expecting it, it would have worked, and they would now be trussed up, being tortured and maimed by your exquisite, sensual, murderous hands. Now the opposite is going to happen, which is a shame, because I adore your body and your mind, you are exactly the same as your sisters.'

'Hardly sisters. Genetic freaks of your family's deranged experimentation. A misogynists mannequins, to be used and abused, played and paraded, ceremoniously sacrificed for a tin pot sham of a hollow, empty religion. They were weak to be taken in by a murdering misogynistic monster like you.' Eve seethed through gritted teeth, slowly edging her way around the frame of the pillory, positioning it between herself and Adam.

Adam laughed, reaching out to the whip rack beside him and grabbing a cat of nine tails, flicking it, a loud crack echoing around the spacious dungeon. 'Poor, deranged little Eve, believing Gabriel and his God complex. You are part of this family. He is part of this family. We are all part of this family's *deranged* experimentation. We are all part of a greater journey. Let me enlighten you.'

Murder Path

Adam raised the whip and with a ferocious glint in his eye, flicked it around the frame of the pillory, expertly sending the tails sailing toward her neck. Eve tried to step back and duck at the same time, but Adam's flick had pre-empted the movement and the tails circled her neck in an instant, constricting it sharply as he tugged on the handle in his hand firmly, pulling Eve's head directly into the cross bar of the pillory, stunning her. With the other free hand, he quickly raised the cross bar and forced her neck into the head hole, slamming the bar shut.

'Bastard' Eve screamed, flailing her free arm, trying to thump his ribs. He stepped back a fraction, her furious fist flying through thin air.

'Did Gabriel ever tell you why the torture and the sex together are so important? Did he explain why the torture heightens the sexual act? You are trapped now, your mind knows that I am going to inflict pain on your body, your cunt is dripping, your nipples are erect and tingling and the fear and panic that are exploding in your stomach are riding on a wave of sexual excitement that are all vying to open up every one of the synapses in all three of your nervous systems. When that happens, when your body is being exposed to the two most intense emotions that a human can endure, orgasm and pain, then you are open. Open to receive the spirit of whatever God you happen to believe in. Open to the rapture.' Adam relays, then raises a fist and punches Eve squarely in the nose, breaking it instantly, the room filling with her excruciating, echoing scream.

'Tell me, how does that excite you? I can see the areolas of your nipples tightening and turning purple and that tells me the sexual endorphins are kicking in even more.' Adam asked, slowly circling around the pillory, around behind her, his own excitement obvious in the throbbing of his bulbous penis. 'It is the animal in us and the instinct baked into our very DNA.'

Murder Path

Eve raised her head, the skin on the brow of her nose ripped, the bone underneath visible. Blood poured from the wound, joining two other tributaries from her nostrils, the river flowing down over her open lips, onto an outstretched tongue licking it in. 'Oh, I am feeling just sensational. My whole body is tingling in heightened euphoria, and you are quite right, my breasts are throbbing, my juices are bubbling and my little clit is sizzling. I know exactly what the relationship is between the two. What you need to understand is that I have learned to control the animal. Gabriel has learned to control the animal. Have you, given there is a dead, dismembered woman sitting behind that wall? Or are you still succumbing to it?' Eve responded provocatively, tilting her head to try and see Adam, who was now standing directly behind her.

'You think she died because I couldn't control myself? She died so that I could find Gabriel. She died so I could infiltrate the Cult of Unas and find out what warped path Gabriel had set them on. She died, so that you would end up here.' Adam answered, picking up a spanking paddle from one of the nearby equipment racks and slapping it off his hand, the resulting sound full of intimidation.

'Finding Gabriel or me didn't require the death of a single innocent person. Like the low life men you have become associated with, it was all about personal desire, personal gratification, personal misogyny, in the self-fulfilling belief that you serve a higher purpose.' Eve retorted, her body tensing excitedly, anticipating the slap that was coming.

Adam smirked, nodding his head quietly, then began to raise the paddle, stopping in mid air as out the corner of his eye, in the mirrors, he saw the reflection of a gun barrel snaking through the open door to the dungeon.

A gun barrel followed by a booming order. 'Lay one more finger on her, and I'll blow your fucking brains out.'

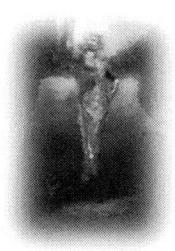

Chapter 33

The languid, lapping river grew forceful and intense where it weaved its way between the moss covered stepping stones that traversed its width. Strange stepped onto the first one at the right of the river, just as Cruickshank stepped onto the first one on the left. In tandem, they stepped from stone to stone until they stood facing each other, the roar of the constricted water flowing between the stones bubbling up to their ears.

'Well?' Cruickshank queried, looking up to Strange's reflective gaze with a worried sternness.

'He was there. He wanted to talk and bring us up to speed with what they know.' Strange answered, his eyes not leaving Cruickshank's.

'Well, I could hear a mumbled conversation through your mic, but overriding that was the bloody quacking ducks. But I guess that's why he asked you to take the bread, and if the ducks weren't quacking, he wouldn't have talked to you?' she said, a glimmer of concern entering her stern countenance. 'How was he?'

Strange's lips started to quiver, a welling emotion overcoming him as the reality of Saul's situation shivered through his body. 'Honestly, he is getting ready to die. He is forcing this to a conclusion and he is prepared for an outcome where he is killed if that is what it takes. We are here because he wants us here. We are here because at

Murder Path

some point this evening, he will want our help. He has left something in the apartment for us.'

Cruickshank reached out her hands and took hold of his across the water that divided them, squeezing them tightly for a moment before letting go, the sternness suddenly returning. 'I trust you Jerry. But I will state this once again, I do not trust Saul. I feel for you, not for him, so let's get beyond the emotion quickly, and pick through the facts you have gleaned from him. That was the overriding reason for meeting him, so let us now focus on that. And hopefully it goes without saying, not a word to anyone about what we have just done. Come on, lets go and see what scraps of evidence he's deigned to furnish us with.' she finished sarcastically, spinning around on the last words and heading back across the stones.

Strange followed, speaking, 'Trust me, not a word, and thank you for trusting me. I realise what a risk you are taking.'

'It's as you said Strange, we can be the patsies being played, which we both have been over the past few weeks, or we can start to play too. Has he found out anything about Gabriel?' Cruickshank asked as she stepped off the stones and back onto the bank, heading up a path towards the apartments.

'Well, he knows who the sixth member of the cult is and he is expecting Gabriel and Eve to be paying them a visit imminently. We have to keep an eye out on PNC for some info relating to him.' Strange offered as they approached a silver people carrier surrounded by police cordon tape, two forensics officers in PPE overalls inside examining it.

'How on earth is anything new going to turn up on PNC? I hope his access has been revoked!' Cruickshank admonished sternly as she nodded towards the officers, passed them by and headed for an open door, then walked into the apartment, Strange following.

Murder Path

'Hadn't even crossed our minds Gaynor.' Strange retorted sarcastically, rolling his eyes incredulously.

Trentor was in the hallway talking to Harris, and looked up with a slight grimace of concern when he saw Cruickshank striding in.

'Have we found anything Trentor?' Cruickshank demanded, heading directly past him to the open study door behind him, seeing the profusion of white PPE overalls moving about inside.

'Yes Ma'am, I've just been talking to Harris about it. There's a monitor set up in there that has a live feed from our Incident room up in Edinburgh on it.' Trentor imparted, scurrying after Cruickshank and pointing toward the study table where a forensic officer was dusting the surface for fingerprints.

Cruickshank looked at the screen, tilting her head as she studied the angles of the visible room furnishings, deep in thought. Strange joined her, looking over her shoulder, tilting his head the same way. 'The camera must be above the main entrance to the room.' he suggested. 'What's above the door?' he said out loud, while he bent into Cruickshank's ear and whispered quickly, 'This could be what he's left us, a pointer as to how he knows what we know.'

Cruickshank nodded gently. 'Trentor, there's a plaque above that door with the station motto on. Give the duty sergeant a call and get someone to check it out. Somehow it must be connected to the internet. That might tell us something.' she ordered. She caught a reflection of the walls behind her in the monitor, seeing hierarchical boxes. She turned and walked toward the family tree on the whiteboards.

'Ian, are tech forensics nearby to check out the computer? Where's Mick by the way?' Strange asked Harris, who had just entered the room.

Murder Path

'Young Reynolds is on his way Sir, he'll be here in about half an hour. Munro got a call and headed off up to the Institute. Something about an image on the CCTV up there.'

'Excellent, Steven was the one who cracked the video feeds at Featherstone Hall, this could be the same type of thing. Thanks Ian.' Strange answered as he turned toward the whiteboards as well, standing by Cruickshank.

'You can see the parents of the Eve clones, and of Rebecca Angus, and a dozen or so other people who must be Fallen Angels, but there is no Saul. No Adam and no Gabriel. Why is that? Trentor, are you running the names on this board?' Cruickshank enquired.

'Yes Ma'am. They have all been fed back to HQ and the team are running them through the systems now. I've told them to call the second they get any matches.

Strange's phone rang, the chilled out opening notes of Shaggy's 'Mr Boombastic' breaking the sombre professionalism of the near silent study. Cruickshank shot him an annoyed stare, her lips puckering sternly. Strange just shrugged nonchalantly, took the phone from his pocket, checked the number and hit 'Answer'.

'Mick, what's happening up at the Institute?' Strange asked, looking through the names of the lineage on the boards.

'Sir, you should get yourself up here. We've been checking through the CCTV footage from the grounds of the wider hospitals back beyond yesterday to see if Saul or Angus had been here previously. We've found a car leaving three nights ago, early hours of the morning, and although the image is blurry, it looks very much like Eve driving with Gabriel in the passenger seat.' Munro relayed, Strange's features changing from inquisitively listening, to agitatedly excited in a breath as he stabbed the speaker button on the phone and tapped Cruickshank on the shoulder, motioning for her to listen.

Murder Path

'Have you got a registration, make and model?' Strange questioned.

'All three Sir. I've already done a PNC check. Car is registered to a hire company. We're just waiting to hear back from them on who rented it. CCTV shows it coming from the direction of the old asylum, so I've sent a couple of officers over to have a look around.'

'Great work Mick. We'll head up there right away and help out with the search. See you in a couple of minutes.' Strange answered, ending the call.

'That was the night McFetrich was killed. He was down in Newcastle during the day on business. Could he have been killed in the Asylum? Come on, let's get up there and check it out.' Cruickshank pondered, striding for the door mid sentence, brushing brusquely past Trentor, not even glancing in his direction.

Strange followed slightly more sedately, but still with a boisterous excitement in his step. He reached out a hand and squeezed Trentor's arm reassuringly as he passed, smiling at the detective. 'Good work Barry. Call us straight away if you get anything back on those names.' then followed Cruickshank toward her Fiesta, which was parked between two police vans on the road into the cul-de-sac.

Cruickshank slid demurely into the driver's seat, straightening her skirt out methodically as she waited impatiently for Strange to get in. As soon as he closed the door she pulled out of the space quickly, and did a tight, erratic five point turn, revving the engine noisily, before the car faced the right direction, and she sped down the lane to the main road.

'Three things Strange, before you say 'I told you so.' Firstly, it doesn't prove that Saul and Angus weren't involved. Secondly, these images are blurry, and just look like Eve and Gabriel. Thirdly, they have been scrupulously careful up until now, why would they make such a

Murder Path

simple mistake? Could this be a play?' Cruickshank offered as they turned out onto the main street.

'Turn next right, then next left and head off up Cottingwood Lane, toward St George's Park.' Strange instructed. 'The last thing you said, could this be a play, was the first thing on my mind. The first thing you said, about 'I told you so', was the last thing on my mind. You'll get to know that about me Gaynor. I hold no grudges or beef. We all get things wrong, and we learn and move on. My next thought was, who the hell is making the play. Now, we've seen images injected into CCTV on this case before. We just have to be mindful of that. But let's check it out before jumping to conclusions.'

'Agreed. What you will get to know about me Jeremiah, is that I do hold grudges, and don't tolerate mistakes.' Cruickshank retorted as she steered the car up Cottingwood Lane, the road rising on a steep incline, the rows of houses either side thinning out, to be replaced by open green fields. Up ahead, the tall steel walls of the barrier around the Fielding Institute filled the middle of the verdant landscape, slightly obscuring the red brick old asylum behind it.

'Oh, I already know that.' Strange teased jovially, as he scanned the car park opposite the Institute, looking for Munro. 'Over there, just in front of the old building entrance.' Strange instructed, pointing toward the figure of Munro leaning against the redbrick wall, puffing on a cigarette in his stained tan raincoat.

Cruickshank pulled the car up in front of Munro and the two of them climbed out. 'Stand up smart man, and at least look like you are interested.' Cruickshank admonished immediately on rounding the bonnet of the car as she approached Munro. 'Well, have they found anything?'

Munro stuttered straight, flinging his cigarette onto the floor and stamping on it before answering, slightly nervously. 'Yes Ma'am. We have. Follow me. Be careful as we go through the corridors, there's lots of loose floor tiles and debris in there.' Munro answered, then led them into the main entrance, where boards had been ripped off the door frame to allow access.

They walked into a dark, gloomy corridor, shafts of late afternoon sunlight squeezing through the gaps of the boards blocking up the ground floor windows, dust dancing enigmatically in the tapestry of interspersed brightness. An eerie silence danced with the dust, just the distant echoes of a brooding, creaking building invading, until the clacking footfalls of Cruickshank's firm stride started to bounce off the old cracked floor tiles.

'Up the stairs to the left, to the top floor. It's even darker in the stairwell, so watch your step.' Munro instructed and they ascended the thickening shadows upwards.

'Ordinarily, I'd tell you to lay off my staff and remind you that it's up to me to give them a bollocking, but I think your brusque, efficient mentality is having a positive effect on Mick. I've never seen him stub a fag out that quick.' Strange whispered into Cruickshank's ear as he walked closely behind her.

'Horses for courses Strange. Not everyone needs a cuddle. Some of us just need a good verbal slap.' she whispered back, a smug smirk forming in the darkness.

'It's just up ahead, and be prepared for a change of scenery.' Munro advised as they reached the top of the stairs, and turned right into another dilapidated corridor, a closed, thick oak door up ahead. Munro approached it, grabbed the handle, and opened it outwards, the pure brilliance of the white floor and wall tiles in the corridor beyond invading and inverting the darkness around them.

'Well, someone's definitely been busy sprucing up the old place.' Strange voiced, surprise in his face as he walked into the wall of whiteness, heading toward another open oak door at the far end of the corridor. They walked into the tall ceilinged, wide oak floored room, looking around the empty white walls, taking in the clean, glazed window opposite, before their attention was taken by the thick metal chain hanging from the ceiling, a large hook dangling from the end of it.

Cruickshank started to circle the edge of the room, looking at the walls, scanning the floorboards, taking in the cornice on the ceiling as she slowly paced the perimeter. Strange crouched down in the centre of the room, looking at the splintered floor boards below the hook, running a finger over the holes on the wood.

'McFetrich was impaled through the genitals on some sort of hook and had nails through his hands. This could be where that happened.' Strange offered, flicking a piece of loose wood from one of the holes.

Munro's phone rang and he answered it, stepping to the door to take the call.

'You could be right.' Cruickshank replied as she passed the window and looked out over the main road three storeys below. 'The walls have been scrubbed. You can see the abrasions in the paintwork. Same with the floor.'

'Sir!' Munro shouted eagerly, turning back into the room. 'We've had a sighting of the car Eve was driving. Number plate recognition picked it up entering a car park about an hour ago. The car park was down in Morpeth, just off the main street. There's no record of it leaving.'

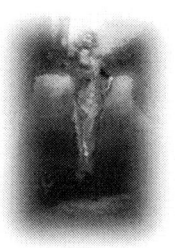

Chapter 34

Rapture is how he described it. Orgasm and agony. Joy, bliss and ecstasy is what the word conjures up in my mind. His sentiment is the same as Ennis's, when he nailed me to a chair in the asylum and wanked me off with a vampire glove. It was hell, but I couldn't stop getting aroused. I couldn't stop feeling the ecstasy, no matter how hard I tried. Then there is the other context of rapture, where believers will be caught up and carried into the clouds to meet their maker, with the second coming of Christ. Is that their belief, is that the mantra the Fallen Angels preach? Is that why they do this, to open up the mind, ready for the rapture?

I edge into the dungeon, the Nagant pistol held firmly and steadily in the hands of my outstretched arms, pointing directly at Adam's head. I am still in my old man disguise, the Jesus sandals I am wearing making sucking sounds on the black marble floor tiles, which are littered with discarded clothes. Rebecca, in her old lady garb, is directly beside me, her features a contortion of confusion and desolate disappointment.

'What the fuck are you doing Doc?' she asks incredulously while stooping down and picking up a cream blouse from the floor and heading off towards Eve. She reaches the pillory and starts to dab the pouring blood off her face.

'Nothing that she didn't want me to. Nothing that she didn't enjoy.' Adam answers, standing tall, bare skinned and brazen, his erection

Murder Path

throbbing, slapping paddle in hand, looking between me and Rebecca with a tinge of humour in his green eyes. It is disconcerting seeing yourself standing so openly like that, looking at a body and a face that is exactly the same as your own. I keep the gun levelled and walk slowly towards him, kicking a pair of jeans on the floor in his direction.

'Get dressed, this isn't time for fucking foreplay. You've got some hellish explaining to do.' I rumble, anger bubbling up inside.

'You do realise, if I hadn't put her in the pillory, she would have killed me.' Adam states calmly, while he bends down and slides on the jeans.

'Only after torturing your worthless body intolerably. Nothing less than you deserve for the atrocities you have performed on women and on your own family. Do you know what a monster this man is?' Eve interjects. Rebecca finishes cleaning the blood off her face, then gathers her skirt and underwear and starts to clothe her.

'I'm starting to. Is that why you led us here?' I ask Eve, sidling up against a cage between myself and Adam, watching every twitch his body makes.

'Yes. There's only one reason I'm in this pillory, and that's because I let him put me here. You need to see who the real monsters are John.'

'From where I'm standing, I'm surrounded by them. I've seen first hand what you did to Darrie. I've seen the pictures of Ettrick and McFetrich. Don't even begin to pretend you are any kind of Angel.' I retort, my voice grumbling with an undercurrent of anger.

'I think you'll find its Adam who pretends he's an Angel. I killed killers. Nothing more. I would kill every one of them again. I never pretended to be anything other than that. Get him to show you what he has done.' she answers demandingly. Rebecca finishes clothing her bottom half, not able to put her top on due to the pillory. She steps back to my side.

'Show us then Doc. Take off this one last mask and show us who you really are. Because this isn't the enigmatic Ben Hanlon I knew, or the thoughtful, professional Rob Adams that looked after Jacob, or the slightly pompous yet friendly Harry Massah that helped us find Bentley.' Rebecca demands, staring at Adam defiantly.

Adam says nothing, simply nods and slowly walks to the far mirrored wall. He pushes a hand against one of the mirror tiles, the low hum of an electric motor kicking in as the wall slides back, revealing a room beyond. Adam steps back and reaches out a hand, waving for us to enter. I reach to the nearest stand and grab a pair of handcuffs, throwing them over to Adam. He catches them, smirks and then fastens them on his wrists.

'What you need to understand is that each and every one of us is looking for the same thing. Every individual, every religion, every cult, every faith, every belief. You also need to understand that religion is a human construct, a control mechanism that preys on an individual's instinctive fears, that makes us do extraordinary things in its God's name, in our pursuit of immortality. When you walk into this room that is what you will see.' Adam relays as he steps off the black marble tiles and onto brown sandstone slabs, covered in hieroglyphics.

'What you will see in there is barbarity and the sick, twisted depravity of a psychopathic mind.' Eve interjects vehemently from the pillory as Rebecca and I follow Adam into the room.

Every surface is sandstone slabs, every one of those slabs filled with hieroglyphics. A long sandstone bench runs down the left on the room. On top of it wide, circular glass tubes. Inside each tube is the limbless and headless torso of a woman, floating in a thick, viscose

Murder Path

liquid. Some torso's have holes in the chest, where the heart cavity is located. All have a hole in their stomach. Still pointing the gun at Adam's head, with a morbid terror eating away at my stomach, I approach the tubes and read the names on the small plaques in front of them, following the line to the one at the end. It reads 'Sheila Warren', and as well as the torso, her dismembered legs and arms are also floating in the tube.

'I tend to agree with Eve. What the fuck is religious about this. This is just a psychopath's abattoir, a trophy cabinet of the deranged. What the hell is that for?' Rebecca asks, her voice dripping is disgust as she looks to the wall opposite the grotesque torsos. There is a large circular stone leaning at a thirty degree angle against the wall, carved into it, hollows in the shape of human limbs, torso and head, the hollows combined in the shape of a body, the arms outstretched and the legs wide apart. Between the leg hollows a slice of the stone has been removed, on the ground beneath it a small plinth. I look over to the tubes filled with torso's, at the dismembered limbs, remembering the instrument cases, and the collections at the other killers homes. I stare at Adam in fascinated disgust.

'You put body parts into that contraption? Different body parts from different women? What is it, a mix and match my perfect dead partner device? Why the hell is there a gap between the legs?' I ask with a maelstrom of despair screaming in my stomach, already knowing the answer.

'Pharaohs were living Gods John. They believed in the afterlife where they would rule for an eternity. Every single pyramid verse in Unas's pyramid is replicated in this room. Verses that his funerary cult over the centuries have kept alive. Verses that his funerary cult recite when they give their life force, through the channels of the dead, to keep his spirit eternal, so that they will one day join him and feast at the table of immortality. That is what the cult of Unas believe. That

Murder Path

is their faith. That is their religion.' Adam relays calmly, walking up to the funerary wheel.

'That's the excuse they use to fuck dismembered human remains you mean, and you were part of it, part of a cult that could do that to women. Monster doesn't even come close to describing what you are.' Rebecca rages, picking up, as I did, on what he meant by 'giving their life force through the channels of the dead'.

'I did what I needed to do, in order to find Gabriel and protect the Fallen Angels.' Adam responds calmly.

'So who are the Fallen Angels and what do they believe. How do they aspire to immortality? We know that you've been selectively breeding for centuries. We know that you've recently been genetically modifying and cloning us. We know that somehow, Jacob seems to be the key. But why Adam? What does rapture mean for the Angels?' I ask, every sinew in my body wanting to rip his emotionless face to bits.

'We believe in achieving mental and physical purity John. We believe that will open up our body and minds to receive the rapture. Our rapture is immortality too. The ability for our spirit to pass from body to body and remember what it has lived before. To recall every single experience that has shaped it. Cotton Mather set off down that path centuries ago simply believing that if we made the blood line pure, back to that of the first children of this earth, then it would open up the mind. But we found the mind couldn't cope, and madness would inevitably take over. So we started to experiment with the body and mind, to make them stronger. There isn't a single thing you can't remember about your life John. Right the way back to when you were a single cell and that single cell split, igniting your consciousness. You are the first of us that have been able to do that. Rebecca, you are a mental masterpiece. Your ability to absorb and cope with every single thing we have thrown at you is just astounding. I took me less than two weeks to bring you back from insanity up at the Asylum, and we threw everything we could think of to make you insane. Directly, Jacob is your son. Indirectly, he is the result of four hundred years of belief. A belief that in him, we have the first Fallen Angel ready to receive the rapture, ready to receive and cope with the eternity of his spirit. We don't fear death John, because in Jacob, we have created a body that can transcend it.' Adam recites, his voice tinged with a lilt of fervour.

That's all we are to him, an experiment. A means to an end. Still a pawn in their creation game. I don't know what I had expected. Some kind of consuming, loving family: a place to eventually feel at home. Nothing about me is me. Nothing about Rebecca is Rebecca. We have been moulded and manipulated for a fucking crazy, tin pot bloody religion. Our little boy is the way he is because of how they have messed with our lives: no, played God with our lives.

'That might be a noble aspiration, if not for the death, destruction, torture, agony and horror you have inflicted on all of these women, on us, on everyone you have used, in the name of your religion, all along wearing a mask of sadistic pleasure. You are no better than any of the men you exposed, no better than any of the murders Gabriel made. In fact, just as I said, you are worse than a monster, because there isn't an ounce of compassion in any single thing that you have done. I can understand why Gabriel went extreme, if this is what you asked him to believe.' Rebecca seethes, her fists clenching and her whole body shaking with fury.

I take one hand off the gun and reach down into my pocket, tapping the screen on my phone. Just as I do, I feel my arm vibrate again, six sharp blasts from the place where the tracker is implanted. 'Why is the tracker vibrating Adam?'

Murder Path

For the first time in all of his warped revelations, his face changes, filling with furrows of concern. 'How many vibrations!' he demands agitatedly, feeling his own arm.

'Six blasts. It's the second time today. What is it?' I ask, watching the panic rise through his features.

'Six blasts is a catastrophic emergency. A call for all Angels to return to base, to be briefed. A call that only I can instigate, and I haven't instigated it?' he answers, his words filled with a panicked urgency.

From the other room, Eve laughs, the noise echoing around the dungeon ominously.

'I told you earlier Adam, you didn't need to murder anyone to find Gabriel. All you had to do was go home. Now he has Jacob, all the remaining Fallen Angels, and now he knows exactly what your plans are.'

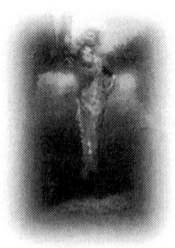

Chapter 35

Cruickshank's Fiesta swerved around the tight corner at the junction of Main Street and New Market, heading down the road at speed, three police cars, their lights flashing and sirens blaring, following her. She turned the car quickly into the large, full car park to the right, opposite the Swimming Baths, and jumped out of the car, her eyes scanning the parked vehicles around her.

Strange was at her side a second later, the two of them walking up the first row of the car park, eyes darting from side to side. 'Over there.' Strange shouted, pointing to a red Land Rover Evoque in the back row.

Cruickshank broke into a controlled trot, darting between the cars until she was beside the vehicle, Strange arriving a second later. The three other police cars were now parked up and a gaggle of officers had jumped out and were approaching the car as well.

'Right gentlemen.' Strange started as the officers arrived. 'We have reason to believe that our suspects, Gabriel and Eve, were using this car. It parked up here about an hour ago so what I would like you to do is fan out from here and visit every shop, restaurant, building, house and flat in the immediate vicinity and see if you can find them. They are extremely dangerous, so do not try and be heroes. If you see them, call for backup immediately. Now, go!' he instructed firmly. The officers paired up, turned, and headed off in a drilled, organised arc away from the car park.

Murder Path

'Impressive co-ordination Strange. The troops certainly have more about them than the detectives in your team.' she dug, scathingly, before raising an elbow and banging it straight into the driver's window of the Evoque, smashing it instantly, setting off the alarm.

'Well, we can do methodical efficiency just like the best of them, when it's required. The trick is knowing when it's required.' Strange baited back as he opened the passenger door and started searching around in the storage compartments in the car. Cruickshank did likewise from the driver's side, avoiding the broken glass on the seat.

'Any beeps yet?' she queried enigmatically as she looked up at Strange.

'Nothing yet.' he responded, just as Mr Boombastic started ringing from his jacket pocket. He took the phone out and tapped the answer button. 'Jeremiah Strange.' he introduced.

Cruickshank looked over at him expectantly, his features intently listening.

'When did it come up? Five minutes ago. Repeat that please. Robert Caldwell, house name is 'Gihon', on Waterside Road. Got it. Thanks.' Strange relayed, hanging up the call. He looked over to Cruickshank's inquisitively expectant gaze. 'A hit has just come up on PNC for Robert Caldwell. An address, as you heard. It's just around the corner from here. If that's what John has put onto PNC, then Adam is the sixth member of the cult.' Strange finished with a tinge of trepidation in his tone.

'And here we are in a car driven by the woman we expect to try and kill him. How convenient. As we said, who is trying to play us Jerry? Regardless, let's get around there sharpish.' Cruickshank answered cynically, then stood up out of the car.

Murder Path

Strange did the same, grabbing a walkie-talkie from his pocket and speaking into it as the two of them set off towards the river. 'ARO team one, make your way down to Waterside Road immediately, wait next to the Chantry Footbridge and await my instructions. Door to door Officers, set up a fifty yard perimeter around a building called 'Gihon' on Waterside Road. Don't let anyone in or out.' he ordered as they reached to bottom of the car park and headed left down the road next to the river.

'Worse case here, we have another murderer murdered, John and Rebecca are dead and Eve and Gabriel have flown the coop. Best case, John has somehow managed to capture them in the act and has them restrained rather than killed.' Strange mused as they trotted together along the side of the river, Cruickshank scanning the windows of the buildings lining the road to their left.

'Best doesn't come into this, we are working on degrees of worse now.' Cruickshank answered dryly, observing a handful of uniformed officers sprinting onto the road in front of them, forming a cordon. They both ran past them, Strange shouting out orders. 'Remember, no one in and if anyone tries to get out, detain them.' They slowed slightly on approach to a large sandstone building up ahead, noting the name sign on the wall. Strange grabbed Cruickshank's arm gently and angled her to the side of the road, behind a bush in front of the last house before 'Gihon'.

'ARO's. We are at the building now. It's about fifty yards from where you are. Head down Chantry Place, then past the old boathouse and it's the next building. Four around the back, two each side and six at the front. We are just past the front of the building in front of the next house along. Stay in position until you here from me. Go.' Strange ordered, then looked down the road, expectantly. A few seconds later, the sound of hobnail boots echoed off the black tarmac, a stream of ARO's angling down the road, some heading

Murder Path

directly towards them, others peeling off around the back of the building.

'Right, let's get in there.' Strange said, stepping out from behind the bush, Cruickshank following, both approaching the six ARO's coming the other way. They convened outside the entrance.

'Right gents. We expect our suspects to be in there, but we don't know where or doing what, so caution is the byword. It's a big building with three stories. I want one left and right first floor, the same second and third floors. Sound off if you find anything at all. You have permission to shoot, but no kill shots, just injure, unless your life is in danger. Is that clear?' Strange ordered efficiently, looking anxiously into their masked faces, which all nodded. 'Right, ram that door in now!'

Two of the ARO's peeled off and the first hoisted a battering ram off the second ones back, lined it up between them in one stealthy movement, ran straight at the door, thumping the ram with force into the blue painted wood. The door burst open, splinters of wood flying off the frame, the loud bang shaking the timber. All six ARO's streamed into the building, the first two splitting to the left and right on the ground floor, immediately dipping into open rooms. The other four bounded up the stairwell in the middle of the hallway directly ahead of the busted in door.

Cruickshank and Strange stepped through the damaged frame, Cruickshank stepping to the left, staying close to the wall as she slowly started to survey the hallway, watching the ARO up ahead dart in and out of rooms, shouting 'Clear' as he did. Echoes of 'Clear' rang out from the upper floors.

Strange walked past Cruickshank and into the first room on the left, a dining room, noting the laid out table with half eaten meals and empty wine glasses. 'Someone was entertaining. Just two people. There's a stiletto kicked off under the table and lipstick on one of the wine glasses, so one of them was definitely a woman.' he relayed, stepping back out into the hallway, his attention caught by a second stiletto at the far end of the hallway, beside a door slightly ajar, the ARO just about to open it. 'Stop!' Strange shouted toward him, sprinting down the passage. Cruickshank strode sternly behind him and reached down to pick the shoe up.

Strange looked into the ARO's masked face. 'Right, there's at least two people in here. One woman. Probably behind that door, so go careful.' he relayed as the other ARO's jogged down the hallway from the upper floors and the right of the ground floor. 'All clear', they sounded off as they arrived.

The first ARO nodded, then poked the barrel of his rifle around the open door, pulling it open to reveal a stairway downwards, light emanating from the foot of the stairwell. He entered through the door and stealthily stepped down to the bottom of the stairs, furtively, yet precisely angling his gun through the opening into the room beyond. He looked back up the stairs, signalling an 'OK' with his fingers. Strange and Cruickshank descended quickly and followed the ARO into a large BDSM dungeon, the walls and ceiling mirrored, the floor tiled in black marble and covered in the accoutrements and instruments of sexual torture.

'More clothes.' Strange stated as they walked over the room, stepping over a pair of underpants strewn on the floor. Cruickshank walked past him, following the ARO to an open panel in the far wall. The ARO thrust his rifle into the opening and arced it around the perimeter of the room, shouting 'Clear' in a hoarse, gagging voice, before he turned back out of the space, thrusting a hand over his mouth. Cruickshank shook her head at him dismally, walking past him into the sandstone room.

Strange cocked an ear, catching a slight squeaking above the noise they were making. His gaze focused on the source, a pair of manacles dangling on the crossbar of a metal pillory that were moving slightly. He approached the pillory, looking at the head hoop, seeing the sheen of blood on its edge, his gaze drawn to the floor and a small pool of glistening redness. He bent down, dipping a finger into the viscose substance. 'Still warm.' he whispered to himself, lifting a finger to his mouth and tasting the liquid. 'Blood.' he said, before standing and walking toward the sandstone room to join Cruickshank.

'There's warm blood out here and a swinging manacle. Whoever they are, they haven't been gone long, minutes at the most. To be honest, I don't know...' Strange started, words stopped in his throat as he entered the sandstone room and saw the hieroglyphics, the tubes and the floating torsos within them.

'What don't you know Strange? Which degree of worse this could possibly be. We have another room full of dead women. We have no Saul, no Angus, no Eve and no Gabriel. More innocent people killed and their murderers having us running around like bloody amateurs.' Cruickshank seethed, standing in front of a tube containing the dismembered remains of Sheila Warren.

Strange looked around the room incredulously, his jaw dropped in disbelief. 'I don't know how they got out. I don't know how they got past us. Someone was in that pillory not a minute ago, so if they didn't go past us, how on earth did they manage to get out of this room.'

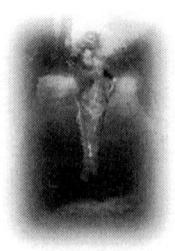

Chapter 36

When I looked into Jacob's eyes, before he was able to dilate his pupils, I just saw emptiness. The emptiness of forever. I didn't see any indication that he could sense things, feel things or even understand things. I just saw emptiness, for an eternity. It's an immortality, of sorts. Now I know he feels, and he senses, and he understands, and he fears. He fears the pain of a condition that has been genetically bred into him by a religion that doesn't seem to feel or sense or understand and definitely doesn't fear. A religion that feels empty to me, bereft of the one thing that gets you through the emptiness, the one thing that would make forever bearable. Love. Where is that, in a single thing they have done? Where is that in any religion? Understanding why they have done this to us doesn't help my emptiness. It doesn't take away the ache of an empty childhood, a loveless upbringing with no heart to call home. I still don't know who I am, even though I now know what I am.

The tunnel is dark, devoid of any ambient light, the way ahead illuminated by the torch on the barrel of Adam's rifle. Water drips incessantly from the rough hewn roof millimetres above my head, into a stream that runs along the tunnel floor. For my sins, I let Adam loose. He is possibly the only person that can take on Gabriel. He is definitely the only person who should take on Gabriel. Eve walks behind him, her hands now cuffed behind her back, a gag in her mouth, her blouse now over her top. Rebecca is after that, her eyes not leaving either of them. It's hard to see her face in the darkness,

Murder Path

but I feel her emptiness as well, currently being filled with anger and animosity toward Adam and Eve. I take up the rear, my Nagant ready in my hand for the slightest hint of either of them trying anything untoward.

The darting beam ahead illuminates some steps carved out of the stone. Adam slows, raising a hand for us to do the same. He turns around to face us.

'In an emergency, we all convene in the main hall, around the long dining table. That's where they will be. I have no idea where Gabriel will be. We have to keep eyes and ears open and focus. This isn't a play now John. This is life and death. I know you hate me and that is fine. But you need to follow my lead if we are to find Jacob. These steps lead up into the old kitchen of the Castle. The main hall is through the door on the left.' Adam relays, perceptive about the hate at least.

He heads up the narrow slippery stairs and reaches an old, rotting wooden door with rusting metal hinges and a large key in an antiquated lock. He turns the key easily, without it even making a small rusty squeak. That suggests it has been used recently. He pulls the door open, to reveal a blank sandstone wall. He then reaches to his left and pulls a metal lever, the wall moving, the stone grating as it trundles to the right. Adam steps surreptitiously into the kitchen, listening keenly for sounds of life. He signals us to follow, and we all enter a high ceilinged, recently used modern kitchen. The nearby surfaces are filled with chopping boards, pans, pots and crockery, freshly prepared food in abundance.

Adam turns to Eve, and looks at her in obvious frustration. 'Was he bringing them here for a supper?' Eve shrugs her shoulders, staring at him with a gagged, lopsided grin. He sneers at her lividly, then turns and walks quickly toward the large double doors into the hall, placing his ear against them.

Murder Path

Rebecca sidles up to me and slides her hand into mine, squeezing it tight, fear etched into the old face she is wearing. I reciprocate, then bend down and whisper into her ear. 'Stay close. As much as he said it isn't, this still feels like a play. I'm just not sure who's.' We walk over to Adam. I see confusion in his eyes.

'What's wrong?' I ask.

'There's not a sound coming from the room. There should be twelve people in there. There's no way he could have incapacitated them all, they are much to savvy for that. Only one way to find out.' he answers, his features concerned as he slowly opens the door.

The hall is vast, with high vaulted ceilings, large stained glass windows in between wood panelled walls. Flags and banners hang from the walls, motionless in the still, silent air. Only the slight crackle from an open fire in a huge inglenook at the far end of the room breaking the disquiet. Above the inglenook is a large tapestry of The Last Supper. In the middle of the room, a long old oak table fills the floor, its chairs haphazard, each filled with a person and each person slumped over the table. Adam stealthily steps toward the table, rifle out in front of him, eyes scanning every alcove in the room. I follow a few steps behind, Rebecca staying at the kitchen door, holding on to Eve. There are pewter goblets lying on the floor, red wine spilt from them. More are tipped on the table, the wine soaked into and staining a white tablecloth covered in an abundance of uneaten food. I head for the nearest person, a middle age man with black, slightly greying hair, his green eyes open and lifelessly staring in agony up at the ceiling. I know he is dead, but I still check for a pulse. None. His body is cold, the flesh starting to tighten. He has been dead for at least a few hours. I set off clockwise around the table, checking each body, Adam doing likewise the other way, my gut an aching emptiness as one after one, I feel no pulse, only the cold cloak of death. I reach the last person just as Adam stands up from checking her negative vital signs. He looks at me in a visible rage.

Murder Path

'If you ever wondered what Gabriel is capable of, then now you know. He has killed a faith and killed a family. All because he could. Do you doubt that he wouldn't do the same to you, or Rebecca, or even Jacob.' Adam finishes, striding over the short distance back to where Eve is standing, her façade reflecting astonished horror. He grabs her short hair, pulling her head right into his face with one hand, spittle forming in the corners of his lips, as his other hand grabs her throat.

'Did you know about this? Did you know he was going to kill my family? Your family?' he snarls into her terrified face while squeezing her windpipe.

She shakes her head, mumbling 'No' through her gag. Rebecca jumps in and tries to pull his hand off her throat, as I step up behind him and do the same, not even budging his bulging, tense bicep.

'Adam, stop. We've just lost twelve of us. We are the only ones left. We are the only family you have. We shouldn't be trying to kill each other. We should be trying to help each other. Right now we've got a common enemy, and that isn't any of us. That's Gabriel. And right now, Gabriel has Jacob.' Rebecca hisses into his ear, pummelling his constricting hand with hers. Adam's gaze darts furiously between the bulging emerald eyes of Eve, and the beseeching tears of Rebecca as I ineffectually thump his ribs, his body not even baulking under the pummelling. He screams in frustrated fury, a gut wrenching roar, and releases Eve, who falls to the floor, coughing, choking on her gag. Adam steps to one side and kicks the kitchen door. I kneel down at the same time as Rebecca, both of us reaching for Eve's gag, and pull it from her mouth. She breathes in deep and hard, welcoming the elixir of air into her lungs.

Rebecca looks down upon Eve imploringly, her mental strength shining through the peril of our predicament, her empathy obvious. 'You told us a lot of lies last night, but also a lot of truths. You are

Murder Path

being played, just as we are. You said one thing in particular that I would ask you to seriously think on now. You said there had to be some greater purpose to warrant the death of the innocent, Michael, Sarah and at the time Jacob. Michael and Sarah bled for us. They were innocent angels and they bled for us. Please don't let Jacob, our last little angel, bleed. You've heard Adam's purpose for Jacob, and it's not that great, in fact, it's just religious bunk, but then neither is killing him just because Gabriel feels like it. Help us save our son. Where does Gabriel have him?'

Eve splutters as she tries to talk, her throat still raw and sore from Adam choking it. 'They are no different, are they, Adam and Gabriel. When you bring it back to basics, they are psychopathic killers pretending to play God. I am so sorry I took Jacob. I thought Gabriel was trying to rid the world of the evil the Angels had created. All he really did was make me into a murderer too. He has him in the chapel.'

I help Eve to her feet, Rebecca doing the same, and we walk towards Adam, who is circling in an acrimonious apoplexy, the veins prominent and pumping on his exposed torso.

'Welcome to the world of being played. Welcome to the world of being out of control. You need to calm down Adam, otherwise you will be of no use to anyone. This is only about one thing now, regardless of what you were trying to play. It's about getting Jacob out alive, and not because of your warped understanding of what he is, but because he is an innocent little boy who has had no choice in any of this. Each and every one of us has had plenty of choices and chances to walk away, and yet here we all are. If that means each and every one of us dies trying, then that's the way it will be. So you have a choice Adam, die trying to save Jacob, or die trying to kill Gabriel.'

Murder Path

Adam looks at me in a fiery rage, his body physically shaking from the chaos coursing through his veins. His eyes don't leave mine, and I see his mind ticking in them, doing what I do when I lose control, trying to shore up the rickety rooms and compartmentalise everything. It's the one thing I still don't know. What are we to each other? Brothers or clones? What are we to Gabriel? His shaking starts to subside, calmness descending on him again, a complete composure enveloping him in the whisper of a second.

'Follow me, the Chapel is this way.' he instructs simply, not articulating his choice, then turns and heads for a large oak door in the far end of the hall, next to the open fire. He flips the rifle off his shoulder and directs it toward the door. We follow him, supporting Eve.

Adam eases the door open circumspectly, casting a quick glance down the corridor beyond. It is empty and quiet and he signals for us to proceed. Silence engulfs us as we surreptitiously stalk down the corridor, everyone's eyes delving into every brooding shadow. We reach the end, Adam pointing to an ornate, stained glass door. He approaches it with stealth, placing his ear against the oak slats below the glass, listening keenly. There is no sound, so he slowly turns the metal ring handle, the slightest of squeaks coming from the metal bar latch lifting, then pushes to door gently. It glides silently open, surprisingly, not a sound from the old hinges. He pokes the rifle through the widening gap, into every corner, and stands as he sidles his body through, fully into the room.

'No sign of Gabriel. Come in, but be cautious.' he whispers. We oblige, and enter the sumptuously decorated chapel.

My eyes are instantly drawn to the altar about twenty metres ahead and Jacob's prone body lying full length on his back on top of it. I run across the room towards him, Rebecca by my side. As I get closer, I notice tubes coming from his legs, six in each, flowing down onto the

Murder Path

floor both sides of the altar. Rickety rooms break again, and a memory of my childhood, in the white room, floods in. They are the same tubes I had attached to my legs. I reach into my pocket as I near him, and pull out Ian Bear, bending his body until I hear a click. My mind is firing, my senses acute, listening around for Gabriel, being overwhelmed by seeing Jacob, just wanting to grab him and run from the room, but conscious that we could be shot down any second. For a moment though, all I want to do is hug my baby boy. We reach him, Rebecca a second before me and she is in kissing his cheek, tears streaming down hers. I wrap an arm around her back, and snuggle into them both, kissing Jacob as well, as I secrete Ian Bear into the fold of his neck.

'Sorry son.' I whisper through quivering lips, 'Uncle Jerry says hello. He found Ian Bear for you. He told me to let you know to keep Ian close, and wherever Ian is, Uncle Jerry won't be far behind.'

Rebecca turns her head up to me, surprise in her teary eyes. I nod imperceptibly. Then I see her eyes look past me, the surprise turning to panic, just as I hear a loud swishing noise. She grabs me and pulls me backwards, onto the floor, as a large, square glass container descends from the ceiling, trapping us within it. I jump to my feet, Rebecca doing likewise, and simultaneously we bang on the glass, Rebecca looking toward Jacob, while I look everywhere else, trying to see Gabriel.

What I see is Adam, dragging Eve to the other side of the altar, opposite us. What I see is Adam looking over to us, calmly efficient, his rifle flung over his shoulder. What is see is another square glass container drop from the ceiling around them as well. I look around the room quickly once more, knowing it is pointless, knowing that I won't see Gabriel.

Murder Path

Adam looks across at us, a wry smile rising on his face as he bends his head, his neck cracking, and says, 'Welcome to the end game John. Perhaps I should formally introduce myself. I am Gabriel.'

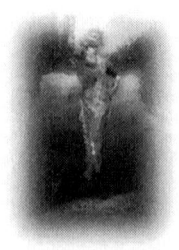

Chapter 37

Strange strode up the cellar stairs two at a time, then sprinted along the hallway of 'Gihon' and out into the road, circling around the building to his left, the early evening sun casting a red tinge to the clouds crouching low over Morpeth.

'Did anyone at all come out? Even if they didn't look like any of our suspects. Anyone at all?' Strange shouted as he ran past the ARO's at the side of the building, looking frantically into every surrounding doorway. The ARO's shook their heads as Strange ran past them and around the back of the building, repeating the same mantra, all six ARO's responding negatively. Strange slowed down as he came down the right side of the building, the ARO's already shaking their heads negatively from hearing his shouted request carrying on the slight breeze. He walked disconsolately back to the front of 'Gihon', where Cruickshank was standing out front, her arms crossed vexed across her chest and a black brogue tapping of the tarmac impatiently.

'Now that you've finished running around like a headless chicken, do you think we could get on with some real detective work?' Cruickshank admonished harshly, before seeing the tears in the corners of Strange's eyes. Her features softened slightly and she approached Strange, uncomfortably lifting a hand and placing it on his forearm reassuringly.

'I just needed to check, Gaynor, for my own peace of mind. You are right, this is the worst degree of worse. What we can do now is get on to the council and see if there are any known tunnels in this area. Alongside that we will get uniform out immediately to continue the house to house. They were here two minutes ago, they can't be far away now. We also need to bring the roadblocks in and tighten the cordon around the town.' Strange replied, appreciative of her softened stance.

'Sounds like a plan. I'll call in and ask about the tunnels and sort the roadblocks out, you go and brief the ground troops.' Cruickshank instructed, immediately taking the walkie-talkie from her pocket and talking into it. Strange nodded and headed off to the line of officers manning the perimeter.

'Gentlemen, listen up.' he shouted on approach. 'The house is empty, but there was someone in there not long ago, which means they must still be in the immediate vicinity. I want the odd half of the cordon to immediately start house to house within this radius while the even half maintain the perimeter. Shields, you are number one.' Strange finished, tapping Shields on the shoulder as he passed through the cordon, his attention caught by Harris running along the road toward him.

'Sir.' Harris shouted breathlessly as he slowed his sprint down, his PPE overalls scrunching noisily. He stopped in front of Strange, doubling over, dropped his bag on the road, and placed his hands on his knees while sucking in a huge lungful of air.

'You are going to have to watch this physical exertion Ian, it's going to kill you. What is it?' Strange questioned, reaching out an arm to support his breathless colleague.

Harris straightened up, taking in another deep breath, then spoke. 'I've just lifted a fingerprint off the wheel on the Evoque and entered in into PNC. We got a match straight away. It is Jessica Seymour's.'

Murder Path

'Hold on, hold on. That can't be right. We had confirmation that the DNA found in the car crash was Jessica Seymour's. We also had confirmation that the DNA found on Darrie's body was from a third Eve clone, not Jessica Seymour's.' Strange ruminated. 'There's a pillory in the cellar in 'Gihon'. Can you go and see if there's any prints on it. There is also a pool of blood. Get that DNA tested as quickly as you can, and tell the lab that needs to be minutes, not bloody hours.'

'Right away Sir.' Harris responded, then picked his bag up and slightly less strenuously, headed towards 'Gihon.'

Cruickshank approached Strange, watching quizzically as Harris trotted past. 'What did Harris have?'

'He found a print in the Evoque. It is Jessica Seymour's. Our evidence tells us it can't be hers, but that's what he's found. I've asked him to see if he can find anything on the pillory. We now have a CCTV image of her and a fingerprint. That's not getting sloppy, that's trying to tell us something.' Strange pondered, looking down at Cruickshank's intently listening face.

'She's pointed us towards Adam's place. She's making us aware that she is involved. Is she trying to help Saul and Angus? Is that what she is trying to tell us?' Cruickshank offered.

'Well if she is, thank fuck for that, because at the minute, they need all the help they can get. Still no signal.' Strange finished, his expression concerned.

'Be patient.' Cruickshank started, just as Strange's phone rang, Mr Boombastick adding levity to the sombre mood. Strange rifled around his pocket and pulled the phone out, hitting answer and putting it on speaker at the same time.

'Jeremiah Strange.' he introduced.

Murder Path

'Ah, DCI Strange, it's Professor Janice Auld here. We talked yesterday about Robert Caldwell and you asked me to call if I had any further information.'

'Hello Jan, how are you? Yes I did. I've also got DCI Cruickshank here with me. What have you found out?' Strange enquired.

'Hi DCI Cruickshank. I'm doing well, still buzzing about what you brought to us. For some reason, we couldn't find anything on our computer records for Robert Caldwell, so we've been digging into the paper archives and have found the student records for him. Interesting reading. He was a straight 'A', A level student and had an unconditional offer to get into the University. He studied Biomedicine here for two years and was always top of his class. His notes show that he had a particular interest in cell biology and was involved in some ground breaking research exploring the possibility of storing external information into the nuclear DNA at the heart of a cell. The other thing his records show is that he was a very highly strung student, extremely temperamental, very isolated and not at all sociable. He had quite a few altercations with the ethics committee on where he wanted to take his research, eventually leaving when they wouldn't back him with his DNA experiments. We don't have any records about where he went afterwards.' Professor Auld relayed.

'Do you think he could have been involved in what you have seen in the Seymour family?' Cruickshank asked.

'No, I don't think so, he would have been too young. However, if he is part of the same family lineage as the people who were involved, then it would explain why he was so good at it. I think he wouldn't have any misgivings about trying any genetic experiment, no matter what the morality or ethics involved.' Auld finished.

'Was there anything in the files about his family? Mother, father or siblings?' Strange questioned.

Murder Path

'Not that I saw. There's no one here who remembers him that well to ask either.' Auld answered.

'Thanks Jan. That has been very useful. As always, if you think of anything else, just call.' Strange wrapped up, then ended the call.

'So John's potential twin was ever so slightly mentally unbalanced and a genetic whizz kid. We also know that he is a murderer. John said this was all about Jacob. What kind of weird and warped experiments has Adam been trying out on him?' Strange queried rhetorically, his features creased with the pain of the thought.

'While the worst is we don't have them, that's not the worst it could be. At least we know they aren't dead, yet. So we still have time. Not a lot I don't think, but some. I should have trusted your judgement earlier about John as well. I can see now that he is trying to find out why and I can see that wherever possible, he is trying to help us.' Cruickshank offered, with the slightest hint of humility breathing from her words.

Strange raised a silver eyebrow in surprise, a glint of humour entering his pained, furrowed face. 'Gaynor Cruickshank, that wouldn't be your attempt at an apology by any chance, would it.'

'No Jerry, that's me just being honest and stating the facts as I see them.' she responded sternly, her eyes lighting up with the fire of affection for a second as she continued in a whisper, 'I'll apologise properly later.' she finished, then turned abruptly and headed back towards 'Gihon'.

Strange looked longingly after her for a second, whispering to himself. 'I think this old codger might need to hang up his brazen braces, because that's the woman who I want to be my home.' Strange stepped after her, back towards 'Gihon', and caught up with her striding steps beside the front door, just as Harris came out.

Murder Path

'Ian, have you got something helpful for us!' Strange queried on seeing the Forensic Examiner.

'I did manage to get a number of prints from the pillory. I can confirm that there was another one there for Jessica Seymour. I also found prints from John Saul, Rebecca Angus and a fourth print that we don't have on file. That fourth print was all over the dungeon and all over the tubes with the torsos in as well. I need to get the blood away to the lab, but it's going to be half an hour before it gets there and they have a chance to process it.' Harris relayed.

'Well, as soon as they have anything, let us know. I think it will just be for confirmation. A second fingerprint in the same place with the other three seals it for me. I think Jessica Seymour has been the clone involved all the way through this, and she has used the other two as distractions. I'm not quite sure at the minute who she has been trying to distract, but I think that's been her play. Now, is that fourth print Adam's or Gabriel's?' Strange offered, ushering Harris past, slapping his back as he went.

'I think its Adam's. What if she found out what Adam was up to, being part of the cult of Unas and involved in killing all of those women. Was that her play, to try and uncover him, without letting him know she knew? Trying to get Saul and Angus to help expose him?' Cruickshank mused.

'It's a theory Gaynor, but a little light on facts.' he teased, before continuing seriously. 'They all know now that Adam was involved in killing those women. I just hope that has put them all on the same side in this, and that they can help each other, because right now, they are somewhere around here with two murderers, Adam and Gabriel. Anything from the Council on Tunnels yet?' Strange finished.

'Nothing yet, I asked them to call me when they did. I'll give them a chase up, otherwise we'll just be standing here like prize puddings.'

Murder Path

Cruickshank answered, taking her phone out of her pocket and redialling the last number.

'Hello, DCI Cruickshank again. Have you found any plans yet? Oh you have. Were you planning on ringing me back, I did say it was urgent.' she admonished, rolling her eyes towards Strange in frustration.

Strange reached into his pocket and pulled his phone out, clicking on the mapping application. He looked down at it with disappointed expectation, then scanned his perimeter, taking in the Chantry Bridge to his left, the houses and pubs on the far river's edge, and the crenellations of the castle behind them. His phone beeped, a red dot appearing on the map.

'So 'Gihon' was an old distillery, and there's smugglers tunnels underneath, running under the river, towards the castle.' Cruickshank relayed with agitated urgency.

'John's just activated the tracker.' Strange interrupted and showed her his phone, the red dot on the map now pulsing and bleeping continually. 'He has found Jacob, and they are in the Castle.'

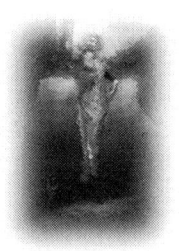

Chapter 38

'When you boil us all down to our basic components, we are nothing but a string of zeros and ones. On or off. There or not there. Then you build a collection of those ones and zeros up. More than three billion of them, to create a single strand of DNA that lives in a single cell. Then that single cell splits and creates us. Every bit of what we become starts with zeros and ones. On or off. There or not there. Chaos becomes simple when you understand that. Did you know that we have already developed the technology that allows us to store more than seven hundred terabytes worth of data in one gram of living DNA? That's something like fifteen thousand High Definition movies, or seventy billion books, all in a single gram of DNA that can live in your body. That's more books than you would ever be able to read in a million lifetimes. Just imagine what we could do, if we were able to store our memories there.'

Adam, or Gabriel, whoever the hell he is, is standing at the glass opposite us, spouting forth calmly and eloquently as I look in confused fury over to him. Rebecca is beside me, pawing the glass, looking down upon angelic Jacob.

'Less of the mental bullshit, who the fuck are you?' I demand, banging my fist into the toughened glass.

'Do I have your attention Mr Saul?' he says, in a clipped, precise home-counties accent, the same one he used when I heard him on the phone for the very first time in Featherstone Hall. I stop banging.

Murder Path

I look at his calm, controlled demeanour and realise that at this moment, there is very little I can do.

'You have my attention.' I answer.

'Excellent John. Now, what I need you to understand is that at the moment, Jacob is safe. What I need you to understand is that there are explosives in the altar beneath Jacob, and if you do not do exactly as I ask you, then I will blow us all up. Do I make myself clear.' he asks calmly.

'Crystal.' I rumble, staring in anger at his patronising face.

'Good. Now behind you is an inversion bench. Rebecca, I would like you to strap John up in that please, the tighter the better. Just so you don't feel left out, Eve is going to strap me into a similar bench in here. Eve, I'm going to unfasten your handcuffs. Now I know you will probably want to kill me for how I have played you, but you need to understand something too. One of the triggers for the explosives under Jacob is a tiny transmitter injected into my arm. As long as the transmitter can feel my pulse, then the trigger won't set off. The second my pulse stops, it explodes. So, kill me, and we all die. Do I make myself clear?' Adam asks, while bending down and releasing Eve's handcuffs.

In an instant, Eve's hand shoots up, the fist balling, a swift uppercut unleashed that follows her body as she springs from the floor and the fist connects directly with Adam's chin. He staggers backwards into the glass behind him as Eve follows through with the other forming fist and thrusts it, with the weight and momentum of her body behind it, straight into Adam's stomach, winding him.

'Oh, I'm not going to kill you. Torture you until all your body parts are broken, yes, but not kill you.' Eve hisses furiously, her body shaking with rage and coursing with adrenaline.

Murder Path

Adam simply laughs through a deep breath as he stands, not even trying to defend himself. 'That is exactly what I want you to do Eve. Break me, until there are only five things in my body keeping me alive. Now, I would suggest you strap me into the rack rather than waste your energy on what will be a one sided fight.' he relays and walks over to the rack as Eve looks at him, then over to us in confusion.

He wants to be restrained. He wants to be broken. He wants me to do the same? There are tubes in here, like the ones I had in my legs as a child. Rickety rooms are falling apart once again. I look at Rebecca, fear feasting on my stomach, and back my body into the inversion rack. She starts to strap my legs in, whispering across to me as she does. 'What's he doing John? He's trapped himself inside a glass case, is being restrained in a chair and wants to be tortured. It doesn't make sense.'

'He'll tell us in a moment, he won't be able to help himself. But you need to prepare your mind. He's going to ask you to torture me, to break me. Get yourself ready for that.' I answer, her silent features vehemently disagreeing with me.

'You asked me who the hell I was John.' Adam starts speaking, as Eve viciously ties the restraints on his legs. 'I know what you really want to know is who the hell are you, and what is our relationship. Much like you, I spent my childhood alone, in a pristine white room, on a pristine white bed, with pristine white sheets. Occasionally the Nun's would bring me food, and say prayers over me. Every day they would take me off to a clinical operating theatre, shining silver, where a doctor would stick needles and tubes into my bones, sometimes feeding things in and sometimes taking things out. Do you know, I was probably in the next room to you, only a foot thick wall keeping us apart. But just as you didn't know I was there, I didn't know you were there. But I had a friend who played with me and helped me to while away the lonely hours. Gabriel. He was an imaginary friend to

Murder Path

start with, just a construct to have a conversation and to play games with. I got his name from the only picture in the room, of the Angel Gabriel. As the years passed, and the treatments became more painful, he became more than imaginary, he became part of me, and the person I became when I was in that theatre. He became an inquisitive soul, wanting to know what they were doing, wanting to get involved, keen to understand why he felt pain. You might say that I was suffering from dissociative identity disorder. I didn't know what that was at the time, but certainly Gabriel became a real personality inside me. It's not really surprising, given who our father was. Right, Eve and Rebecca, there are six tubes on the floor, each with a needle at the end. You need to force them into our legs, right the way into the bones. Just look for the injection scars as a guide to where they go.'

So we are related and lived our childhoods a foot apart. He dumped his agony into a second personality, I locked mine away into rickety rooms. Rickety rooms which are fully open now, the memories of lying in that theatre, on that bench, feeling the excruciating pain of the needles sliding into my bones burning my mind and overwhelming me. My body shakes as I see Rebecca raise the first tube, and with every part of the control I have left, that the memories haven't overwhelmed, I try and hide the fear from her, I try to encourage her. She rolls up the beige leg of the slacks I'm wearing, exposing the flesh below: exposing the scarred flesh. She places the needle of the tube over the scar furthest down my shin and looks up at me in imploring agony, shaking her head uncontrollably, her eyes wide in terror.

'Put it in.' I sing softly to her tortured emerald eyes, not breaking her gaze, drinking her in. She doesn't break our gaze either, an apologetic whimper escaping her lips as she forces the needle in. Electrical impulses fire every synapse, my back arcing, my limbs shaking, the very breath in my lungs forced out of my wracking body,

Murder Path

a muffled grunt escaping with it as I try and subdue the scream my mind wants to wreak.

'Impressive John.' I hear Adam's words sail into my ears, his voice ever so slightly pained, as I tilt my head and see Eve thrusting the needles into his legs. 'I remember screaming for what seemed like weeks the first time that happened to me as a child. Only five more to go.'

'You said, our father. There is nothing in the files we found at the Institute that says who we are. Are we twins, or are we clones? Who was he?' I ask, my head turned towards him, his to me, as we look at each other over the still, quiet form of Jacob.

'I'm surprised you haven't worked that out yet John, what with you being an excellent detective, fastidious in the detail. There's one detail that has been in your face constantly since the first time you met Dr Ennis at The Fielding Institute. You were never going to find it on file either. Even secret religious organisations like the Fallen Angels have their darkest secrets, that they want to keep hidden from everyone else. That's us. We are twins John. From the same biological father and the same biological mother. Created from one egg that split into two. Our mother was Clarissa Seymour, the sister who moved to Italy. What can I tell you about our father, to give you a clue? I know. He had two overriding characteristics. A brilliant artist, a psychopathic killer. You guess which trait each of us inherited.' Adam reveals, his voice hardly even changing as Eve thrust the remaining needles into his legs throughout.

While my mind screamed in agony every single time Rebecca pushed one of them into my legs. But that didn't stop my mind blazing away down the trails of realisation, to the significance of paintings, to the Angel with the stretched out arms, stigmata on his palms, painted by the lunatic , Frederick Charlton, my father, that hangs in the reception of The Fielding Institute. But the timelines don't add up.

Murder Path

He died in the early nineteen hundreds and Clarissa wasn't born until the nineteen fifties.

'I can see the penny has dropped John. Yes, Freddy the Mangler was our father. I can also see your confusion. How can we be the offspring of two people separated by half a century? Simple, they froze his sperm, much like yours was frozen to make Jacob. Now the questions you should have asked are, why did they feel it necessary to use the frozen sperm of a dead madman? Why did they feel the need to introduce his DNA back into the bloodline?' Adam teases, his face alive with the power of control, revelling in the revelations.

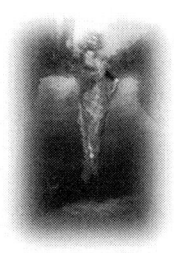

Chapter 39

The incessant, high pitched thrum of the helicopters rotors filled the evening sky, it's flashing lights highlighting the extent of the craft's body in the evening dusk. A spotlight shone down from the front of it, circling the grounds of Morpeth Castle below. The spotlight created shadows trailing the black garbed ARO's that were surrounding the building and the two detectives that were approaching the main entrance.

Strange strode up to the tall, grandiose oak doors that marked the entrance to the castle, holding his phone out in front of him, eagerly obeying the continual bleep on its screen. Cruickshank was at his shoulder, her indomitable gaze not leaving the small screen either. Both of them wore protective vests and trousers. A gaggle of ARO's marched behind them. Strange stopped, then turned to address the officers.

'Right gents. The signal is coming from the far right of the castle. Plans tell us that is the chapel area. The entrance to the chapel is via a corridor off the main hall. There are no other entrances. There are two stained glass windows in the chapel that face out to the rear of the castle. We have a secure perimeter, so no one should be getting out. When we enter, there is a main hallway with three doors either side, which leads up the entrance of the main hall. Secure the rooms behind those six doors, then convene at the hall before we carry on. Just remember, there are killers in there, so you have authority to shoot, if necessary to kill. Everyone understand?' Strange instructed,

Murder Path

receiving affirmative nods from all of the officers. 'Good. On my mark: Go!' Strange finished, a stream of eight ARO's slinking past him stealthily into the castle.

'I'm surprised at myself for saying this, but is a kill order the right thing? You've got Adam and Saul in there and they both look exactly the same. We could be shooting an innocent man.' Cruickshank whispered over to Strange as they waited for the first call backs from the ARO's.

'John's a policeman. He knows the risks, he knows what he has let himself in for, and he wants to save Jacob, no matter what. I can't pretend it's not breaking my heart Gaynor, but I know it's what he would do.' Strange responded, his features painted in the heartbreak.

'Come on then, let's see if we can help him do just that.' Cruickshank replied encouragingly, affectionately squeezing Strange's arm, this time, without a hint of awkwardness.

'Clear.' Came the staccato shouts from the ARO's. Strange and Cruickshank trotted into the hallway, the ARO's congregating around the entrance to the hall, two ready with their hands on the handles, the others crouched, lined up ready to raid the room.

'Go!' Strange shouted. The doors were opened and the ARO's swarmed into the hall, rifles pointing in every conceivable direction quickly and skilfully, the officers dispersing in an elaborately choreographed ballet, covering every part of the hall, honing in on the table in the middle.

'Cold bodies!' came the cry from the first officers to reach the table, an intensity entering all of them as their focus doubled. Strange and Cruickshank strode over to the table, between a line of ARO's, and looked at the desolation around the table.

Murder Path

'Jesus. Twelve bodies. All look to have been dead for a while. No sign of blood, wounds or traumas of any kind. It looks like poisoning, which the spilt wine goblets would corroborate.' Cruickshank relayed factually, her face a mask of horror as she felt for a pulse on the neck of the nearest victim. 'The question is, who the hell are they?'

'Munro!' Strange shouted into his walkie-talkie, his tone full of disquiet. 'Get the forensic team around here immediately and just to be safe, the ambulance and paramedics.' He finished, dropping his hand carrying the walkie-talkie to his side disconsolately.

'Straight away Sir. Sir, we've just had word back from the lab as well. The blood stain from the dungeon was from Jessica Seymour.' Munro relayed.

'Twelve people around a table, a banquet laid out, a huge tapestry of 'The Last Supper' above the fireplace over there. If that's not some kind of religious statement, I don't know what is.' Strange ruminated. 'This is one of two things. Either Gabriel is making a statement of intent and showing his strength, or, if our suspicions about Eve are right, this may be the last meal before the final reveal of the Fallen Angels.'

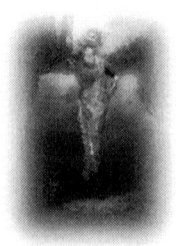

Chapter 40

'Before you answer that John, and I can see you are eager to, I think it's time for some pain. Rebecca, Eve, break every finger on our left hands, one at a time. Don't question it, just do it.'

Rebecca looks at me imploringly, not quite sure what to do. While he has revealed a lot, I still don't know what he is trying to do with Jacob. Even if I had a choice, at the moment, we have to do what he wants us to. I nod at Rebecca and whisper, 'Break them.' She reaches down tentatively and holds my little finger between her closed hand, squeezing it with a look of love and anguish ingrained on her face. She twists and a tsunami of agony engulfs me. 'Quickly!' I mumble through a scream, shaking the other four fingers at her. She sees what I mean, and stealthily breaks them, the augmented pain riding on the wave of the first torture. I look over to Adam, his face a mask of euphoric misery as Eve does the same to his.

'So what do you think John, why did they feel it necessary to use the frozen sperm of a dead madman? Why did they feel the need to introduce his DNA back into the bloodline?' Adam teases through teeth grimacing in pleasure painted agony

'The same reason that we started to be genetically modified and cloned. Because what the Angels thought would happen when the bloodline was pure, that the body would open up to the rapture and receive the spirits of past lives, never happened.' I relay, my mind

Murder Path

starting to piece together the snippets Adam had already said earlier, with all the other evidence and weaving a theory about him.

'Exactly. Imagine how it must have felt for Henry and his siblings, to be the guardians of a four hundred year old belief, to have taken every single step that Cotton Mather prescribed to purify the bloodline, and to discover that it didn't work, that their belief was just another cargo cult, like every other religion. They concluded something must have gone wrong along the way, and looked to back engineer the bloodline, but also looked to science to see if there was something they has missed. They reintroduced evil. In the shape of DNA from a madman for you and me, and the DNA from snakes for our beautiful ladies.'

'And that's where your path started. Being brought up as Adam the Angel, being brought up with the beliefs of The Fallen Angels. Creating the personality of Gabriel, with the traits of Freddy The Mangler, who you made into a mad scientist, who could see the flaws in what they were trying to do, who somehow found a different way, a scientific way to achieve immortality. Being a psychopath though, it was never going to be something you did quietly. You want the world to know what you have achieved. You wanted to discredit every other religion in the world, to expose them for the bunk you believe they are. You wanted to do the same with the Angels and make them appear to be murderers. You made murderers for fun, just because you could, just because you wanted to play God. And you played, teased and tortured Rebecca and me just for the hell of it, just to engineer this big reveal, just to watch us all die to satisfy your psychopathic needs. That's what this is all about. That's why the two of us are linked into Jacob. You believe you have found a scientific way of moving the spirit between bodies?' I respond, looking at the tubes between us, flowing up into Jacob's legs.

'I am impressed John. Nearly, but not quite. Oh, the stuff about being a psychopath and wanting to show every religion in the world

Murder Path

for the horrific, murderous control mechanisms that they are is spot on. As is wanting to create murderers for fun, and toying with you. You've missed the bigger inference completely though. I do those things not just because I am a psychopath. I do them because I am a God, and that is what God's do. Create and destroy, at will, without question or remorse. We are all Gods John, each and every one of us. The only difference is that I realise that, and you don't. It is mankind that strives for immortality. It is mankind that constructs religions. It is mankind that makes murderers. It is mankind who are the gods. When we look to the heavens and try to find the God Particle, the thing that will allow us to transcend death and become immortal, we are looking in the wrong place entirely, we should have been looking at the zeros and ones. Time for more pain. The arm restraints in these inversion racks bend all the way back on a hinge about halfway up the forearms. Bend them and break our arms.' Adam instructs, his eyes alive with a crazed fire.

Rebecca shakes her head, blubbering 'No, no, no.' down at me through snot dribbling down from her running nose, joining tears from her cheeks, all slavering onto her quivering lips.

'Look at Jacob. Think about Jacob.' I plead through gritted teeth, still riding the agony of broken fingers. Still wondering, why the pain? 'Don't procrastinate, just fucking do it!' I scream, shocking Rebecca out of her grief. She twists the restraints, sending me into a maelstrom of oblivion, riding on the piercing of a scream. Consciousness swims around me, threatening to leave under the pains intensity, but then the instant shock starts to subside and lucidity returns. I hear Adam laughing in agony.

'Zeroes and ones John. We are made from DNA. DNA that holds the physical characteristics of our ancestors. DNA that holds the animal instincts of our ancestors. DNA that holds the mental state of our ancestors. That's what the scientist in me knows. This is what the scientist in me believes: DNA also holds their memories. My research

Murder Path

has found a way to unlock those memories in DNA. Just think. A person that has the ability to recall every single memory from every single one of the ancestors in their family tree. Now tell me, does that sound like immortality. We don't have to go searching the stars, we don't have to create nebulous deities. We just have to open up the blockers in our own DNA. Jacob is the first human with those blockers removed.'

I look at Jacob, at his still, quiet body. How can that be? He can't even move, apart from dilating a pupil: on or off.

'I know what you are thinking John. Jacob is ostensibly lifeless. He's not. He's just processing centuries worth of memories. That doesn't happen in an instant. That takes time. It could take decades. But I believe that time will get shorter, in his children, then in their children. The other thing to understand is that he won't have your current memories, only those that were in your DNA up to the point of conception, carried in the sperm that created him. But I have also found a way to get recent memories into him. A variation on the way that we are already able to put data into DNA. That's why we are hooked up to him John, so that he will receive either yours, or my recent memories, whichever one of us happens to die first. So this is your final choice. Kill me, and your son will have my memories. Kill yourself, and he will have yours. How do you like the sound of becoming immortal John?'

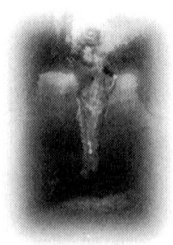

Chapter 41

Skilful feet stride stealthily along the stone floored corridor, the line of ARO's progressing in near silent synchronisation. The first officer holds up a hand, the trail slowing as he does, as he sees the entrance to the Chapel just to his right, the door slightly ajar. Cruickshank and Strange sidestep the line of ARO's up to the front and step in at the side of the open door.

'Voices.' Cruickshank whispers, listening intently, holding a finger up to her lips in a shush.

'How is that a choice? The second you die, the bomb will explode and we will all die.' Saul's voice booms in a contained echo.

'John, Jacob and a bomb!' Strange mouths over to Cruickshank as he raised two fingers, counting on his left hand.

'Not if we reach the rapture before we die. And we will reach the rapture. You may be in agony John, but you are also sexually aroused. The chemicals in your body are mixing, your senses will start to heighten and your cells will start to ignite. The more pain we suffer, the more sexual pleasure we indulge in, the more our DNA will melt, breaking down the blockers that hold our memories. That happens first in the bone marrow, where the needles are secreted in our legs. When we hit the rapture, just at the point of orgasm and death, then the marrow will flow from us into Jacob. When it hits the needles in Jacob, the bomb will diffuse, and one of us, whichever is the first, will be immortal. How quickly do you want to die John?' Adam revealed, a manic tone to his pained voice.

'Adam? Why is he making threats?' Cruickshank queried in confusion. Strange raised a third finger.

'If it saves my son from your deity delusion, then right now. Just kill me Rebecca, kill me now!' Saul screamed.

'Four!' Strange mouthed, raising a fourth finger, panic in his eyes, as he stepped towards the open door.

'Stop Rebecca, don't do it!' Eve interjected forcefully.

'Five!' Cruickshank whispered, throwing out a hand to stop Strange progressing further. 'I'm not having you get killed on me. We don't know where the hell Gabriel is!' Strange raised a fifth finger.

'That's all I needed to know Gabriel.' Eve said calmly.

Strange and Cruickshank looked deep into each other's eyes, realisation dawning on them both simultaneously. 'Adam is Gabriel!' they both whispered synchronously, Strange's features becoming focused and alert. He turned to the ARO's and addressed them quickly, with ruthless efficiency.

'Five people in there. By the sounds of the echo in the voices, behind some kind of screen. There's a bomb as well. It sounds like Adam/Gabriel is in control of that. Nobody sounds in a position to shoot at us. I want an arc of officers just inside the door, guns pointing into the room, but no firing, this is purely intimidation. He needs to know we are here.' Strange relayed quickly. 'On my mark: Go!'

Two by two the ARO's lined up, then stormed into the Chapel, scything off left and right, rifles pointed straight ahead, focusing on the four visible people in the two glass cases. They formed an arc just

Murder Path

inside the chapel door, leaving a space, through which Cruickshank and Strange entered, side by side, taking in the macabre vista in front of them.

'Whatever the hell you are doing, stop, all of you!' Strange ordered firmly, raising a hand in placation, eyes darting between the four people in the glass cases.

Adam's features were half filled with confusion and euphoria in equal measures. His lips started to move, ready to address Strange, but he was distracted as Eve started to pull the tubes from his legs.

'What the fuck are you doing?' Adam spat at her, shaking in his restraints. 'Do I have to remind you that there's a bomb under Jacob. Pull one more of those tubes out and it blows!' he threatened insidiously.

'Go ahead, detonate.' Eve replied calmly, panic entering the eyes of everyone looking over to her. Rebecca ran to the glass and started banging on it, pleading for Eve to stop. Saul started screaming likewise, trembling in his restraints. Strange started to stride toward the glass case, demanding the same. The ARO's backed up, right into the wall of the room. Cruickshank stood stoically observing Eve.

'You think I won't! After everything you have seen me do, you are trying to call my bluff!' Adam sneered in obvious apoplexy, pressing his thumb agonisingly into the button of the trigger in his hand.

'I'm not trying to call your bluff. I'm just waiting for you to understand that yours wasn't the last play in this endgame. I'm just waiting for your crazy, insular mind to realise who is standing in front of you.' Eve relayed with serene composure as she pulled out the last tube and dropped it to the floor, the screams of everyone echoing around the room.

Murder Path

Adam looked furiously up at her, a crazed realisation overwhelming his face. He pressed the trigger, everyone's screams stopping, replaced by silent dread.

Replaced by silence. No explosion, just silence.

All eyes turned to Eve.

'Perhaps it's time to introduce myself Adam. You know me well. I am Jessica Seymour. I am the Eve who has been part of this from the start and I will be the Eve to stop it all. All of your warped, barbaric ideology will be destroyed in the next ten minutes. All of our failings in letting you loose on the world will be redeemed too. I diffused the bomb Adam, and I am going to kill you.' Eve said as she reached over Adam and started to dig her fingers into his chest, breaking the skin with her sharp nails, worming a thumb under the muscle, forcing it through to the bone of his ribs.

Adam looked down at her fingers inveigling their way under the skin, his features twitching, a shimmering of pleasure gleaming from his emerald eyes as Eve started to rip it open.

'So you knew what I was up to? Killing me won't make a difference. You do realise that. While Jacob may not get my recent memories, he still has all of our ancestral memories. He will still be the first of our line to achieve immortality.'

'We suspected. We put plans in place to find out years ago, the very first time Gabriel appeared on the scene. Henry had a suspicion who it was and for a while, let you run free. We all regret that now. We recognise the Fallen Angels have become worse than every single one of the religious atrocities we have revealed, by allowing you to be created and by allowing you to wreak havoc on the world. That ends today. We end today.' Eve replied with a quiet dignity. She reached a hand inside his ripped chest and circled bloody fingers around the bone of a rib and yanked hard, breaking it from its cage. Adam

Murder Path

baulked in his restraints, stifling a scream, riding the wave of excruciating pain.

Strange knocked on the glass case frantically. 'Eve, you don't have to do this. Killing him won't achieve anything, don't sully your hands with his blood.' he pleaded.

'They already are Jeremiah, and the deaths of every single innocent Angel he has killed, or by proxy, made people kill.' Eve responded sanguinely, then turned back to Adam.

'This world should never have known your faith. It should never have needed to fear it. It won't need to fear it anymore.' Eve said, then thrust the broken rib deep into Adam's chest, straight through his heart. His body wracked in its restraints, blood spurting from his chest uncontrollably as his body breathed in the throes of death. He started to gag, the viscose liquid entering his lungs, seeping up his windpipe, filling his throat, spittling from his mouth as with one last gargling breath, life left him, dulling his emerald eyes.

Eve pulled the rib from his heart, holding it tightly in her hand, and turned to face Saul and Rebecca, her body covered in Adam's blood. 'We should have been welcoming you home, into the wings of the Fallen Angels, for bringing the first new child of an Angel into this world. Instead, we nearly killed you all. A belief that can do that to the very family it loves, is not a belief we wanted to be part of this world any longer. All of us, collectively, decided it was time to go: time for our last supper. The faith of the Fallen Angels ends here. Learn from our mistakes, tell Jacob all about those mistakes and bring him up to love the family he has, not the one that may come in our eternal tomorrow.'

Eve turned towards Strange, and walked up to the glass, placing a hand opposite his flat palm. 'We drew them in because we needed them. We needed them to get to Adam. None of this was their doing. It was all us, The Fallen Angels. We will no longer stand in the

Murder Path

shadows of our own God and let these atrocities prevail. We will no longer allow innocent Angels to bleed in the ignominy of our seed. This is where the Fallen Angels end.'

Eve took a step back and raised the bloody rib high into the air, grasping it in both hands. Her face was filled with an anguished sadness, as she looked around beseeching eyes, their agonising cries reaching her ears, flowing with the sorrow of her mourning tears. 'Forgive us.' she whispered, through teeth trembling with grief. Eve brought her arms down fast, the hands heading for her chest, the rib aimed true, ripping through her blouse, piercing her porcelain skin, breaking the ribcage, puncturing her already broken, bleeding heart.

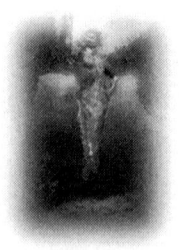

Chapter 42

Zeros and ones. On or off. There or not there. That's what we all start out as. That's probably the only thing that Adam got right. Whether we were created by the cosmos, or made by our maker, it all comes back to either being there, or not there. It's where we started with Jacob. All I saw in his beautiful emerald eyes was nothingness and desolation: the emptiness of forever. That started me on a journey back to my own childhood, my own rickety rooms and my own fear of being alone. But then in amongst a world gone mad all around us, he dilated a pupil, all by himself. There wasn't just a zero any more, there was a one. There wasn't just and off, there was an on. There wasn't just nothing, now there was something. Something to live for.

And now there isn't just zeros and ones. He can now control the length of his dilation and as a family, Rebecca, Jacob and me, we have learned Morse Code together, and we can communicate. He loves the water, we know that because he tells us. We are in the water now, in the clear blue, gently lapping shallows of Lake Garda, a cloudless sapphire blue sky wearing a dazzling golden sun encompassing our horizon. Jacob is floating on the surface, his body ululating with the waves, his pupils dilating madly, as his eyes tap out '...., .-, .--., .--., -.---' spelling 'Happy'. Rebecca smiles radiantly. Her own hair is growing back and the scars on her body are starting to subdue. I am healing too. My arms came out of their casts just yesterday and the fingers are nearly there. Healed enough for me to

Murder Path

paint at least. And lord, how I have painted. Every single conceivable view from the beautiful gardens of Eden out over the lake, to the mountains in the distance. My dark period is over. Now it is all light.

'Time to come out now little angel.' Rebecca whispers, leaning over Jacob so he can see her lips.

'-., ---' , 'No' he replies.

'Oh yes young man, you've been in here more than an hour.' Rebecca chastises, light-heartedly. We float him into the shoreline and lift him out of the water and into his wheelchair. Rebecca grabs a towel from the back of the chair seat and starts drying him down.

We have told him about his family. About the Fallen Angels and where he comes from. He is inquisitive, and wants to understand, so we tell him as much as we can. He absolutely adores his other family as well. Especially because they bring him presents. Jeremiah and Gaynor have visited four times now in the space of a month and stayed for long weekends each time. Most of that time they have spent with Jacob, but we have made time to catch up on how the investigation is wrapping up in the real world, away from our heavenly haven.

Rebecca has had her conviction for murdering Michael overturned. Both of us have had charges for perverting the course of justice dropped. The Crown Prosecution Service concluded there was not enough evidence to charge Rebecca with the murders of Desiderata Bentley or George Darrie. All of the deaths got washed up in the wake of the Fallen Angels. All of the exposed murderers have now been convicted and are awaiting trial. Dozens of families have finally been able to lay their dearly departed to rest. It's a closure, of sorts. It doesn't stop Jerry and I grabbing a bottle of rum and speculating into the wee hours of the morning though. We are detectives. There's never really closure. Our minds will always question and investigate and want to know more. What we are investigating at the

Murder Path

moment is if there are any other branches of our family left out there alone in the world. We have searched all the Ennis files, and ones we found at Henry's home, as well as those we found here in Eden, but so far, we haven't found anyone else. We seem to be the last Angels alive. And because we are the last alive, we inherit all the family assets. Including Eden. When, and that is when, not if, we find others, this will be their sanctuary, as it is for us. A place to rest and recuperate, to experience the beautiful things in life, like floating on the lapping waves and seeing your son's eyes smile, and to know that it is those things, that mean more than anything.

We reach the long patio outside of the villa and lift Jacob onto a laid out blanket, under the midday sun. I tuck Ian Bear into the crick of his neck and run a finger tenderly down his sun tanned arm, to his little hands.

A finger twitches on Jacob's hand. My breathing stops, and I wait on baited breath, my senses becoming heightened. I check his pulse to see if it is dropping, I listen to his breathing to see if it becomes shallow, I smell his breath for burning chocolate, all in a split second, hoping to sense none of them, hoping beyond hope that this is his first natural movement. Hope is not as fragile as it used to be. I am still disappointed, but not desolate now, as the chocolate smell comes, and his breathing shallows and his pulse drops. He starts to fit.

His arms are shaking and I gently stroke my fingers up and down them, relaxing the skin. Rebecca does the same, measured concern in her smiling face as she looks down into Jacob's open eyes.

'Once upon a time, there was an old toymaker called Gepetto....' she starts to tell him his favourite story, one hand now softly stroking his quivering head. I lie down beside him, gently singing into his ear 'Go to sleep little boy, go to sleep. Let the sandman come and fill your

Murder Path

eyes. Go to sleep little boy, go to sleep. Till the morning time and so to rise.' over and over again, in a soothing lilting lullaby.

His legs are quaking uncontrollably now, his whole body in spasm, lifting his back off the blanket, spittle forming in the corners of his mouth. I grab the towel from just above his head and delicately wipe it away, still singing softly into his ear.

'...someday, you will be a real boy...' Rebecca continues as the apex of his fit hits, every limb fully extended and shaking, his head now lolling uncontrollably, while I continue to sing to him, both of us exuding a calm tranquillity, exactly what Jacob needs.

Slowly, the stuttering starts to ebb, and his limbs stop shaking. His torso stops bucking and the lolling of his head eases, then stops, looking toward me, every limb instantly becoming inert as the fit ends.

'Hey son. How you feeling?' I ask, looking deep into his green eyes, anxious to see his pupils dilate. They don't move. I look over to Rebecca, a slight surprise joining the anxiety. This has never happened after a fit, not since he's been able to dilate. She scurries around to join me, tucking tight into my side, glaring into his eye.

'Jacob, are you OK little Angel?' she queries, stroking his cheek.

No movement. My heart sinks, emptiness chewing on my stomach, echoed in Rebecca's frantic gaze. My eyes dart all over his body, looking for a sign of injury from the fit, conscious he may have hurt himself. I can't see any abrasions or bleeding. Then I stop, my chest constricting, my heart suddenly thumping a billion to the dozen. I stare at the little finger on his right hand in utter incredulity.

The little finger on his right hand which is softly tapping an indelible litany.

Murder Path

I nudge Rebecca, and point down to his hand. She looks, and physically shrieks, throwing her arms around me in agitated excitement.

'He's moving John. Jesus, he's moving!' she screams, tears flowing freely down her quivering cheeks.

The other fingers start to move, a gentle susurration waving through them as Jacob stretches his hand and lifts it off the blanket. I look up to his face, and he blinks. And blinks again, his head ever so slowly moving as a tremor enters his lips, shaking them open.

A guttural gasp escapes through them, a grunt from virgin vocal cords. Elation is overwhelming me. I cannot stop the freakish, wide eyed grin that has overtaken my face, nor the boggle eyes as the balls try to burst out of my head in excitement. Rebecca is holding onto me so tight in breathless anticipation, that she is ravaging my skin with her nails.

Jacob blinks again, and then his eyes move, the whole ball, his gaze darting between Rebecca and me. His timorous lips start to curl up at the edges into a subtle smile, as a brightness fills his glistening eyes.

'T...' he spits through dry lips.

'For fucks sake, he's trying to speak!' Rebecca screams.

'They...' he got out, his tongue snaking out and licking his lips.

'Go easy son. You might want to talk, but you may not be able to yet. You've never used those vocal cords before.'

'They put pennies...' he continues.

Rebecca is shaking me furiously, her excitedly mesmerised glare stares at Jacob's enlivening features, before she turns to me. 'He's becoming a real boy John!' she whispers.

Murder Path

All I can do is nod, sobbing uncontrollably.

'They put pennies on my eyes the last time I died, to keep the evil spirits out. It didn't work.'

Visit my website at

www.maxhardy.co.uk

or Facebook at

www.facebook.com/themaxhardy

or Twitter at

www.twitter.com/themaxhardy

e-mail to

max.hardy@live.co.uk

Printed in Great Britain
by Amazon